TRANSIENCE

Stevan Mena

Dark Circle Press • New York

Published by Dark Circle Press

Copyright © 2006 by Stevan Mena

All rights reserved.

ISBN: 978-0-9910005-1-7

All characters in this book are fictitious, any resemblance to persons living or dead is purely coincidental.

www.darkcirclepress.com

Thank you Guy Cohen, I will never forget.

For Diane, Samantha and Victoria

CHAPTER 1

The ghastly smell of the burlap bag that suffocated her for most of the trip lingered on her face and hair. Her own dripping sweat still reeked of its pungent, mildewed odor. It had made her want to vomit. Now the remnants of its awful smell kept her focused as she raced through thick, jagged branches, determined to live. Sharp stones jutting from the uneven ground jabbed and sliced into her bare feet mercilessly. No fear of injury. The alternative was death.

She maneuvered through the endless woods, glancing back just once — he was gaining on her, only a few strides behind. She threw her forearms up to cover her face and dashed right through serrated bushes, the thorny brush ripping up her thin white sundress, tearing at her soft flesh. She imagined she was a rabbit, sprinting from a hungry dog. The analogy kept her from breaking mentally, kept her body moving.

As he dragged her from the car, her captor hadn't noticed her bindings had come loose. She'd been patiently working on them during the drive as rusty, pointed springs jabbed into her skin through the ripped vinyl and yellow foam of the backseat. When the time came and she felt an opportunity, she took it; landing a swift, crushing kick to his groin that doubled him over in surprised shock. She untangled the rope from her hands, tore the bag from her head and disappeared into the dark woods.

Her legs began to burn as she picked up the pace, certain he must be right behind her. Just then something hidden in the tall weeds caught her foot and yanked her down hard. Her face smashed against the dirt, which pushed up her nose and into her mouth. The smell of roots and earth conjured images of dying, repelling her bruised face up off the ground like a reflex. She twisted around to see what had tripped her.

Her right foot was caught beneath a raised tree root. She pulled desperately and felt her calf muscle tear, an awful searing pain. She silenced a scream, squeezing the muddy grass till it squished through her fingers. She could hear heavy boots trampling the wet leaves just a few yards behind.

She pulled again hard — stomping with the heel of her other foot. The thick root released, slicing up her ankle as she threaded it free. She clawed back to her feet, pushing off a nearby birch to propel herself forward, off balance. Pure adrenaline now.

She ran with her head down, sprinting madly. She lost her bearings in a thick of tall trees, stopping to grip one as if it were a muscular hero who'd arrived in the nick of time. Disoriented, confused, every direction looked hopeless, no clear path back to civilization.

Sunlight was just breaking through the trees. Not more than a mile away, sleepy commuters fought traffic on their way to work.

Behind her, his grotesque, out of shape panting closed in. She spotted a patch of thorny bushes, crouched down and held her breath. She locked every muscle — just another shrub, no moving parts. The rabbit was invisible. The thumping footsteps slowed down just a few feet away. She could smell the leather of his boots. The noise of his heavy gasping swung back and forth like a Doppler as he turned in place, scanning.

He made a sound, like a snarling dog, irritated, and ran off. She waited until everything was silent before she breathed again. She slowly stood up, craning her neck to make sure the coast was clear, then dashed in the opposite direction.

There was a steady hum reverberating in the distance just

beyond the tree line. *The road?* She bolted towards it, her rubbery legs staggered as she fought to stay upright. She skidded down a steep incline of mud and dirt, twisting her ankle on a protruding rock that nearly toppled her over. She grabbed a low hanging branch and reached around to balance herself against the trunk, her fingers dipping into oozing sap.

The dirt path curved up ahead. She plotted her next move and flexed to run when something stirred in the shadows. She froze, backing up.

A small squirrel darted up a tree and disappeared. She exhaled and took a step forward, realizing with horror that something bigger had spooked the animal from its hiding spot. The lumbering shape emerged, stepping out onto the path in front of her.

Their eyes met — both surprised to see each other. He smiled a lucky smile, wiggling the fingers of his dirty work gloves with glee. She blinked first, backing up a step. He leaped at her, his arms outstretched, grabbing her torso. She opened her mouth to scream, but all that escaped was a whimper as she narrowly dodged his grasp; her slick, sweaty skin slipping through his fingers. She crawled for her life on all fours like a frightened animal. He grabbed her blood soaked ankle with both hands, falling with all his bodyweight onto her leg.

She drew back her knee to her chest and planted a heel first kick to the top of his head, forcing him to release his grip. He reached out again but she was too fast; he came up empty, his nails scraping along the back of her calf. She scampered to her feet and ran, kicking dirt up into his eyes.

The trail ran downhill, giving her some momentum. She heard a loud, grassy thud, followed by an angry groan that sent shivers up her neck and made her face red hot. She looked back to see his head pop up from under the brush. He had fallen hard, it looked like he might have hurt himself, badly.

A chance.

She scaled a small hill hoping to see the busy highway. But the roaring sound she'd heard was not the road — but a river. Too far and deep to cross, the foamy water rushed fast and loud. She winced in frustration but kept moving, limping on empty to the river's edge.

She crumpled into a heap along the muddy banks, as if her bones suddenly went soft, her fatigued muscles pushed past failure.

She weakly extended her bloody hand into the river, the icy cold water sent a jolt through her system. She shook her head and let out a gurgling, primal moan. She put one hand in front of the other and crawled through the mud, her bruised, bleeding fingers sinking into the wet ground.

As her adrenaline receded, it allowed the pain to flow. Her left arm was especially damaged, probably broken during the fall, and she had to favor her right to keep moving. Within seconds, the pain was too much. Her last ounce of strength evaporated, her elbows bent and she planted face first.

She felt her flesh going numb. She listened to the roar of the water, its hum almost soothing. Just loud enough to drown out the approaching footsteps. She prayed that maybe, if she lay perfectly still, the dog would not see the rabbit, and pass by.

"So, you do like to get dirty."

He jabbed his boot under her ribcage, flipping her onto her back. She spit up, gasping breathlessly. His grimy perspiration dripped into her eyes and mouth as he leaned forward, blocking out the sun above.

He brushed her mud-caked hair from her eyes with his filthy hands. "You were really pretty," he said between gasps of exhaustion.

The past tense of his words lit a fire of defiant rage. She lashed out with every ounce of life left; kicking, clawing and biting. He clamped down on her throat with both hands in a vice-like grip. She felt her head swell, her eyes bulged in their sockets. The dog had the rabbit in its jaws.

She clawed ferociously at his face, her fingernails tearing off at the quick. He straddled her chest, his weight preventing her ribcage from expanding. With her airways completely blocked, she went into a claustrophobic panic, nearly lifting him off the ground with heaving thrusts from her hips. Her legs couldn't get any leverage, slipping in place on the slick wet ground. Her lungs pounded for air as she began to lose consciousness.

She didn't want her last moments to be his horrible face. But as he leaned into his work and squeezed, it was all she could see. It was the first time he'd let her look at him fully, which confirmed he intended it to be the last thing she'd ever see. Instead she defiantly focused on him real hard, staring into his eyes, studying every curve in his face, every detail as her body went cold.

As she went limp, the fight over, he relaxed his grip. She twitched a few times, then fell silently still. During the struggle, her long flowing black hair had tangled around his wrists. He peeled the matted, blood soaked strands from his skin and examined his work. He gazed at her olive flesh, her gentle face.

He took a few deep breaths and cursed himself for letting her get the best of him. Had she made it less than a quarter mile further, she'd have reached the highway. He got lucky.

A twig snapped nearby, standing him up straight. He searched the endless trees for the source of the sound, scanning every direction. He quieted himself, like a hunter in stealth mode, allowing the prey to reveal itself.

He waited a long time, listening, watching, until assured he was indeed alone. Satisfied, he kneeled down beside the body and grabbed a few handfuls of mud from the soft ground. Then some more, and soon he was digging a hole.

But someone *was* watching him.

CHAPTER 2

Victor Sandoval's eyes began to adjust to the intensity of the fluorescent lights overhead. He'd been a guest of the cold grey-walled interrogation room of the Lansing Police Department several times now, and the intimidation factor was beginning to wear off. He was only 19, but having grown up in El Salvador as one of four kids who often had to beg or fight if he wanted to eat, he'd seen his share of shit that makes you old fast — and as a result looked very mature for his age.

He sat calmly as Detective Jack Ridge paced a hole in the floor in front of him. Jack had pushed aside the table between them, leaving him exposed. As Jack passed in and out of the blinding light, Victor noticed how pale and lifeless the detective's skin was. When Jack spoke, his voice was deep and gravel, almost sickly.

Detective John Harrington sat off in the corner behind Jack, his chair reversed, arms draped over the back. Harrington was athletic, very muscular, with protruding veins on his biceps. Went right from high school football to law enforcement. He sipped his cold coffee and winced, waiting for Jack to say something.

They both waited.

Jack bent over the case file strewn out on a nearby table. In the mix was an 8x10 photograph of Angelina Rosa — Hispanic, 18, beautiful — the words *Missing* superimposed at the bottom. He jotted something down in his notes and turned back towards Victor.

"Tell me again. Please," Jack asked.

Victor rolled his eyes and looked to Harrington, hoping he'd intervene on his behalf. But Harrington wouldn't dare. Jack had his reasons for dragging Victor down here again, that's all that mattered. Jack had an intimidating way about him that demanded respect. Maybe because he rarely smiled. And no matter how much time you spent with him, you never really felt like you knew the man. Jack was a leftover from an old breed. A tough guy who refused to admit he was deteriorating by the minute. Everyone in the department noticed. No one said a word about it.

Victor shook his head, frustrated, speaking in a redundant tone as if reciting lines from a play: "She call me in the morning, say she gonna see about a job."

"She didn't give a name, description? The kind of work?"

"I can't remember." Victor used extra emphasis to demonstrate that he really couldn't remember, adding hand gestures and opening his eyes wide to make his point.

"Think."

"Angelina, she do odd job, clean houses. That's all."

"How long were you two dating?"

Victor held the top of his head and groaned as if maybe Jack had Alzheimer's or something. "A year."

"And… that's the last time you heard from her?"

"Her father call me that night, ask if I see her."

"He still thinks you had something to do with it," Harrington said.

"I was working, you know where I was!" Victor stood up. A stern look from Jack put his ass right back in the chair.

"One of your deliveries took over an hour and a half," Harrington added.

"I had a flat tire! How many time you gonna ask me?" Victor put his face in his hands and, for a moment, Jack thought he might sob. Not because he was guilty and they were about to break him.

Because he loved Angelina, and he realized he was probably never going to see her again.

Jack and Harrington conferred in the corner, quietly.

"We're spinning our wheels," Harrington said.

"I know."

"Right. So how much longer we gonna do this?"

"Till he remembers something."

The thick metal door to the interrogation room opened; officer Jennifer Brown entered. Jennifer's brains, fiercely competitive nature, and sports acumen had made her one of the guys, despite her curves. Harrington, when he found out she understood the two point conversion in football, was especially respectful.

She eyeballed Jack. "Captain wants a word."

Harrington pumped his eyebrows as Jack exited the room.

Victor turned to Harrington. "You guys don't know anything at all, do you?" Harrington got up, spinning his chair around with his muscular hand.

"Stay put." He followed Jack out of the room.

Captain Clarence Lafave — 52, short cropped hair slicked back with gel — stood in the hallway, arms folded across his chest.

"Why are you questioning Sandoval again? I never cleared this."

"He was the last to see her alive. There's still holes, details missing. I'm trying to jar his memory."

"Jack, we have to call it a day."

"What?"

"The investigation will remain active as long as there are leads to follow. There's other shit piling up that needs your attention."

"So we just sit and do nothing? Why, because she doesn't fit within some ethnic priority?"

Lafave looked sternly at Jack and shook his head *don't go there*. "It's been three months. Until we have evidence a crime's been committed, her photo goes up on the wall with all the others. We just can't allocate resources to every child that goes missing. I'm sorry."

Lafave waited till he was sure Jack got the point, then walked off, conversation over. Harrington had a look of relief on his face, but erased it when Jack looked his way.

Jack entered the holding area adjacent to the interrogation room. Harrington followed, leaning up against the wall, hands on his hips.

"We're gonna have to let him walk," Harrington said. Jack peered in at Victor through a large two-way mirror. Victor was muttering something to himself.

"He's irrelevant," Jack said.

"How do you figure?"

"Gut feeling."

Harrington grinned. "The last time you had a gut feeling I lost a hundred bucks."

CHAPTER 3

Nine year old Rebecca Lowell awoke shrieking at the top of her lungs. She threw the blankets off her sweaty body, her flannel pajamas stuck to her moist skin. Her wavy blonde hair was matted to her wet face and neck, beautiful blue eyes stretched wide and bloodshot.

She grasped at her chest, clutching it as if trying to keep her racing heart from bursting out. She took a blurry look around and realized where she was, back in her bedroom, the nightmare receding — they were getting worse.

Her mother, Laura, threw open the door and raced to Rebecca's bedside, pulling her close, comforting her. Rebecca flailed about, still screaming in panic.

"It's okay, I'm here. Mommy's here." Laura cradled Rebecca's tiny body in both arms.

"I can't breathe! I can't breathe!" Rebecca was coughing and shaking, her skin hot and slick to the touch.

Laura gently rocked her back and forth, embracing her tightly. "You're safe. You're in your own room, in your own bed, safe and sound."

These were the phrases the doctor had instructed her to repeat when these attacks occurred. It was all part of the treatment. But this was every night now, and Laura had deep black circles under her eyes to prove it. It had gotten to the point where she would just lie awake in anticipation of the screams.

Rebecca sobbed as her nervousness was replaced by the comfort of her mother's soothing "shhhh" repeated over and over as she rocked her back and forth like a metronome, the same way she did back when she was a colicky baby.

Laura stared up at her worn reflection in Rebecca's dresser mirror. She had short, brittle blonde hair, with a smoker's skin and teeth. She was 27, but you'd guess 37. Her eyes were set deep in their sockets from months without sleep.

"This isn't working," Laura whispered to herself. Nothing was working. None of the doctor's advice panned out. No one had the answers when it came to helping her daughter. She dropped her head, exasperated.

CHAPTER 4

Carl Rosa opened the door just before Jack's knuckle could hit wood. "I saw you pull up," Carl said. He took a step back, allowing Jack to enter.

Carl was of medium build, always clean shaven and wearing a collared shirt. Life as an immigrant from Ecuador was hard; Carl always wanted to make a good first impression. His apartment was small but tidy, the furniture modest, some of it personally handmade, uneven. The kitchen table had two chairs and a small cracked white vase in the middle with no flower. Decoration was sparse, which made the items tacked on the gray walls stand out: Angelina's school photo and a free calendar from Castro's Plumbing.

Jack noticed two stacks of fliers on the counter — one in English, the other in Spanish — next to some empty rolls of tape. Missing person fliers for Angelina, made using the same picture that hung on the wall. It had details of her age, weight, height, what she was wearing, and the date she went missing, July 21.

Jack stared at the word July. He looked over at the calendar, turned to October. It had a picture of a bright orange pumpkin sitting in a field of corn and straw. Angelina surely had turned into a pumpkin by now, and would soon likely be making an appearance in a field somewhere or along the side of a highway. It dovetailed into the unpleasant purpose for his visit.

Jack had assured Carl months ago he'd find his daughter. He realized the moment the words left his lips that he'd fucked up — promising something like that in an effort to console a crying man. Jack saw this visit not only as a professional failure, but worse — as a broken promise.

"Can I get you anything?" Carl asked.

"No, thank you." Jack stepped towards the kitchen. Carl took a plate of crumbs left over from the sandwich he just ate and placed it in the sink. He rinsed it, then turned around as if trying to find something to do next. His anxiousness made it all the harder for Jack.

"So?" Carl asked. Jack wore a poker face that betrayed no emotion. He knew Carl sensed the disconnect. If there was any good news to report, Jack would have answered his call, or phoned back. Instead, Jack chose to come see him in person. Carl sat down.

"They're not going to allocate any more manpower to her search. They're shutting it down. I'm sorry, Carl."

Carl lowered his head and nodded a few times. Jack relaxed his shoulders, it seemed Carl was taking it well. Jack turned away and looked out the window. He caught a glimpse of a young Hispanic woman sitting on a fire escape across the alley, a few floors below. She was nursing a baby at her breast. *In this cold?*

"I don't understand." Carl said hushed, "is she any less of a human being now than she was three months ago?"

Jack was still watching the woman, concerned. "I understand how you must feel."

"You got any kids?"

Jack turned to him. He knew where this was going, but played along out of sympathy. "No."

"You have no idea how I feel."

Jack knew he was going to say that, he'd asked him several times before. Jack allowed Carl the free punch. Had Carl opted to cry on Jack's shoulder, he probably would have let him do that too. But like Jack, Carl was a tough hombre and he wasn't about to let the tears slip in front of another man. Those were reserved, for the ultimate bad news.

Jack did know how he felt. Not in a direct comparison, since it was true, Jack had no children. But he had suffered loss. Unbearable loss. The kind that wipes the smile from your face permanently.

Jack took a step forward and placed his hand on Carl's shoulder. "Carl, given the amount of time that's passed, the chances of—" Jack could feel Carl's muscles tense into stone.

"She's alive. I know it." Carl turned with a jerk and placed his hand on Jack's, gripping it. Carl was a small man, but his palm was like alligator skin, with a grip like a wrestler from years of carrying heavy machinery at his warehouse job for minimum wage. "Jack... you—"

Here it comes.

"You promised me." The words were like a bucket of ice cold water on Jack's head. Jack imagined Carl on his knees, holding his daughter's mutilated corpse in his arms, looking up at Jack — as if how could he have let this happen.

Jack was about to say something when he felt that familiar pinch in his throat; it swiftly traveled down to his stomach and back up to his larynx. He coughed loud and wet, covering it just in time. For a moment, he lost his composure and had to brace himself on the back of Carl's chair to keep from doubling over. It was a raw, painful cough, and his normally pale face turned ketchup red. Carl stood and offered his seat to Jack, who refused.

"I just gotta catch my breath," Jack said, the phlegm and wheezing made him sound like some kind of alien. Carl gave him some space. After a few more stomach churning hacks that looked like he might crack a rib, he grew silent. The fit over, Jack stood up straight.

Carl poured some water into a glass. Jack nodded a thank you and drank a sip. He took a deep breath, apprehensive of triggering another attack, but his body was finished embarrassing him for now.

"I've searched for your daughter as if she was my own. If she's alive, I'll find her." Jack paused — he wasn't finished. This time he insisted on prefacing his words with a disclaimer: "But you need to prepare yourself for the worst."

Jack took some time to sit with Carl and go over all of the things he'd done during the complex process of searching for Angelina. Interrogating witnesses, visiting all of the places she was last seen, questioning the locals, checking video tapes from any surveillance cameras in proximity to where she might have traveled that fateful day. How he used sophisticated FBI databases to search the surrounding cities and states to see if any unidentified bodies had been recovered and lay unclaimed.

Carl sat and listened, but Jack could tell he knew this was just by the book procedural bullshit. The only real hope for finding his daughter alive was a miracle. And there was no investigative police procedure for conjuring miracles. Carl had just as much hope praying, which is what he seemed to do as Jack spoke.

"I have to go now," Jack said, courteously pausing for permission before he got up. Carl nodded and Jack pushed back on his chair.

"Thank you, Jack. You..." Carl shook his hand firmly. "You were the only one who cared."

"That's not true, Carl."

"Yes, it is."

Jack walked to the door. Carl sat back down and resumed staring at the wall. Jack figured he'd probably been in that same position before he'd arrived too, like he was just on pause — awaiting his daughter's return so he could come back to life again.

"This isn't over, Carl. I haven't given up." *Shut up Jack, you asshole.*

Jack closed Carl's apartment door and walked through the hallway. On his way to the stairs he passed a little boy wearing only underwear, standing alone picking his nose. A woman, maybe his mother, was cursing in Spanish behind the door of their apartment.

The little boy smiled a toothless grin at him. Jack slowed his pace — how easy it would be to walk off with this little boy. How far could he get before he would be missed? The boy's vulnerability angered him. Had he become too paranoid?

The work had planted these worms of dread inside Jack's brain; years of picking through the aftermaths of worst-case scenarios. Maybe that was why searching for Angelina kept him so motivated. The possibility, even if remote, she was still alive. A chance for a happy ending.

He entered the street. Two young Dominican men were leaning on Jack's car, talking. They took one look at him and made way, crossing to the other side of the street. Jack looked like he was in no mood to be trifled with.

Jack reeked of cop, thugs could spot him a mile away. He would never have lasted 5 minutes undercover, any self respecting hood would have made him instantly. Jack had this chiseled, purpose-filled face that shouted authority figure. Gather him with any ten men at random, Jack would be the one you'd approach if you were lost and needed help.

As he reached for the handle, he felt another coughing fit well up. He braced, trying not to throw his back out, as his chest tightened. A wave of awful hacking followed that turned his insides out.

CHAPTER 5

The secretary wiped her glasses with an alcohol cloth and checked them for spots. Not satisfied, she rubbed them again.

Rebecca sat patiently in the waiting room chair, her little feet dangling just above the ground. She swung them back and forth whenever she got nervous or bored. The secretary admired Rebecca's blonde hair with a slight wavy curl women would spend extra money for at the salon. Her pretty big blue eyes contrasted the dark circles underneath, puffy and purplish. Her overall complexion was pale, tired, and listless.

She exchanged glances between the sketch pad braced on her knee and the secretary behind the desk opposite her. Every now and again, the secretary's eyes would leave her computer screen and lock with Rebecca's. Rebecca studied the contours of her face, memorializing each line on paper with her chewed pencil. Its swishing point sounded like whispering as it crisscrossed the paper. Combined with Rebecca's intense gaze, it unnerved the secretary a little. She craned her neck to get a glimpse of what Rebecca was doodling. She figured it was probably of her, some cartoonish rendition, with a giant disproportionate head, for sure. Rebecca looked up and their eyes met again. The secretary smiled, but Rebecca kept right on sketching as if she were working to meet a deadline. This was serious business to her.

"Would you like some candy?" The secretary smiled, holding up a bowl of outdated mints.

"It'll give me cavities." Rebecca's pencil didn't break stride. The secretary shifted in her chair and made a "tut" sound with her tongue. She returned to her invoices, and never gave Rebecca another thought.

On the interior door was a plaque that read: *Doctor Leonard Hellerman, MD, Child and Adolescent Psychiatry*. Inside, the doctor sat behind an enormous mahogany desk. The walls were decorated with rows of awards and plaques, enough to convince any parent of a child with a busted mental spring that they'd come to the right repair shop. Leonard was 55, but the hair dye helped him pass for 49. He wore glasses, more for intellectual show than anything else, as if people expected their psychiatrists to wear them like a chef wears a tall hat.

Laura Lowell sat uncomfortably across from him. She looked like she'd rolled off the mattress into her clothes before tying her hair in a knot. She was subtly beautiful; if she made an effort, she could turn heads. She looked like she hadn't made an effort in a long time.

She tapped her fingernails on the arm of the chair, anxious to get this over with. Leonard noticed and kept his speech soothing and metered. He always chose his words carefully, and right now he was being extra careful.

"I think terminating Rebecca's sessions now would be a mistake."

Laura paused before replying. Leonard often spoke slowly and deliberately, with long pauses allowing you to absorb the importance of his words. There were several times she'd opened her mouth to speak during a conversation, only to see his hand go up like a crossing guard, politely instructing her that he wasn't quite finished yet.

"I just don't think this is helping."

"The regressive therapy is working; I think we're close to a breakthrough. In fact, I was going to recommend you bring her in twice a week from now on."

"I haven't slept in weeks; I'm up every night with her now. This whole thing, I hear what you're saying, it's just—"

Leonard's hand went up. "Have you been giving her the medication I prescribed?"

"She's getting worse, not better."

Leonard quickly switched gears, sitting back. "Laura, the best advice I can offer you is to stay the course. As I said early on, these things often get worse before they get better."

"She was fine before we moved here. There's been so much stress; the divorce, the new house, new school."

"Ms. Lowell, Rebecca isn't reacting to the stress of a new environment. Her episodes were triggered by some sort of traumatic event."

Laura straightened in her chair, her lips turned inward.

Leonard continued, "Until we find out exactly what happened to her, we'll never get to the root of the problem."

"Nothing happened to her," Laura said defensively, her eyes now locked with his.

"Look, Laura, if it's the money, I'll even waive my fee."

"Why are you so interested in her?"

"…I want to help you."

Laura abruptly grabbed her coat and stood up. She stammered a moment for the right words, not wishing to be rude.

"I'm sorry… Thank you, doctor."

Laura exited the room quickly, not allowing him the chance to persuade her into giving him any more time with her daughter. She didn't even want to look back for fear he might be following her, which he was.

Laura raced through the waiting room and grabbed Rebecca's arm, yanking her along without stopping. Rebecca dropped her sketch pad on the floor.

"My book!" Rebecca said, dragging her feet.

"Come on, we're leaving." Laura grabbed Rebecca's jacket, adding it to her own under her arm, and bolted from the room.

Leonard stopped beside the secretary's desk, who looked up at him confused. They could hear stomping down the staircase in the hallway.

The secretary came around her desk and stooped down to pick up Rebecca's sketchbook, still open. She saw Rebecca's drawing of her and gasped. It was no cartoonish doodle. It was an anatomically perfect rendering, startling in its detail.

Leonard took the book from her shaking hands.

He flipped through it, stunned — drawing after drawing of artwork worthy of framing in a gallery. "Incredible," he whispered. Over the course of the past few months, Leonard had developed a theory about Rebecca's condition. Seeing this only confirmed he was right. Once again, she'd amazed him, and he cursed himself for only discovering this additional evidence now — too late.

CHAPTER 6

Jack entered his home carrying a briefcase and a small white pharmacy bag. The house was a small three bedroom colonial on a tree lined street, mid block. He'd wanted a quiet neighborhood, far from busy roads. A place where kids could play safely. The house was completely dark inside, the lawn in dire need of mowing.

Inside, every flat surface held the scatterings of case files. When entertaining the rare visitor, Jack spent a lot of time apologizing for the mess while clearing stacks of photos and important notes off the furniture. Jack wasn't much of an outdoorsman or sportsman, although he enjoyed a day of fishing now and then. There wasn't much memorabilia of his exploits, just a few citations and honorable plaques for bravery and citizenship. All work related. The only thing you could tell about Jack from a tour of his home was that he was in law enforcement.

When he joined the department, it wasn't for the perks or family tradition; Jack genuinely wanted to make a difference. After receiving the promotion to detective, he had every intention of becoming the greatest investigator to ever carry the badge, often at the cost of family and relationships, no apologies. Solving crimes and punishing the guilty gave his life purpose.

Jack hung his gun belt inside a closet. He held the door a moment, staring at a never worn navy blue suit, still wrapped in the same plastic he brought it home in. It had cost him over 400 dollars, and was by far the nicest suit he owned. He was saving it for a special occasion.

He closed the closet and took off his shoes. He noticed his answering machine was blinking. It was one of those ancient Panasonics with the mini cassettes. Jack actually had a passion for old school technology, one of his prized possessions was his antique Technics record player.

He looked at the message counter: *2 messages*. Jack frowned with interest. He pressed play.

"There's never been a better time to get term life insurance for only-" Jack skipped to the next message.

"Hi Jack, it's Robert again." Jack's eyes found a spot on the wall and stared, waiting for the asshole to finish. *"I don't know if you're getting these messages, I know how busy you are. Please call me, we need to talk. Something a brother should know anyway."*

Next to the machine was a framed photograph of Jack, SMILING, his arm around a beautiful woman. A smile that would break his jaw now if he tried it.

"We're still at the same number…be really great to hear from you. Trish sends her best. Anyway, if you get this and-"

Jack hit the erase button, almost breaking it. He considered tossing the machine across the room. Instead, he took a deep breath and coughed hard a few times, his cheeks puffing out. The last one hurt enough to remind him to take his pills.

He dropped the small white bag on the kitchen table and tossed around a few stacks of papers until he found a glass. He filled it with water at the kitchen sink, tore open the bag and dumped out a small pill bottle. There was a red warning on the label that read clearly: *Do NOT mix with alcohol.*

He maneuvered the child proof lock according to directions and it popped open after a few tries. He shoveled two pills in his mouth and went to take a drink, stopping just as the glass reached his lips. He tossed the water down the drain and opened the refrigerator.

Inside was an assortment of take out containers, a lonely bar of butter, some cheese and two cans of beer. Jack grabbed a beer, washed the pills down, and grabbed the other can.

He sat down at his table and started sifting through Angelina Rosa's case file. An image of his brother Robert suddenly flashed in his brain and he abruptly cleared the table of its contents in one angry swipe. *Fucking asshole!*

His head blurred and his eyes closed. He felt himself slipping in and out of consciousness. He could hear people talking — distant, muffled, as if he was submerged under water, their voices just above the surface:

"Pulse rate?" a voice called out.

"We're losing him," another replied.

"Blood pressures dropping."

"We're losing him!"

He heard commotion, shouting. The noise gradually began to fade, leaving him in total silence. A soft voice whispered in his ear, "There's a reason."

With those words, Jack opened his eyes and found himself in a field of grass near a giant oak tree. Two people were sitting beneath it, enjoying the shade of it's expansive branches. There was a small pond nearby.

Jack looked up into a bright blue sky, so blue it was almost surreal. Floating below the clouds was a small yellow kite with a white ribboned tail. It swirled in the breeze, then did a few loops. Jack watched it soar and maneuver through the air. It gave him an enormous sense of peace and calm, unlike anything he'd felt in a long time. This place was warm, full of love and happiness.

The playful kite spun and flipped, diving out of the sky. It headed straight for the ground. As it smashed and crumpled, Jack *awoke.*

CHAPTER 7

Rebecca sat in the back of the classroom watching the second hand of the clock tick away the last few minutes of the day. She repeatedly placed her pencil at the top of her desk and let it roll down. She counted tiles in the ceiling, counted the number of letters in words, whatever she could to keep her mind occupied. Sometimes it worked and kept the spells at bay. *Just five more minutes*.

Even on the first day she'd arrived at her new school, the kids sensed Rebecca was different. From the way she spoke using large words, to her incredible artwork that nearly gave Mrs. Lindsay a stroke. The first time the teacher ever saw Rebecca draw, her hands were shaking as she exclaimed, "*Jesus, Mary and Joseph!*" She made Rebecca draw three more pictures that day, watching in awe while the other kids were ordered to read and keep quiet.

The faculty found Rebecca odd, so old in her young shoes, so mature. It ingratiated her with them. It intimidated her fellow students. Rebecca wasn't just an outsider who didn't fit. She was *different*. The worst offense a child can make.

The taunting didn't begin until the spells started becoming a regular occurrence. Rebecca would often scream out for no reason, or use bad language that just didn't belong in the mouth of a nine year old. She mostly didn't remember the episodes after they had passed, but the other children didn't let her forget.

Her mood swings were unpredictable and scary. They had begun a little while after moving here during the summer. She couldn't pinpoint an exact time or place it started, just that she'd never experienced these problems back in Livonia. Things were fine before they arrived here to *start over* as Mommy put it.

It was as if raw emotions were channeling through her. She didn't understand them, but recognized they were originating from within. As the problem metastasized, it started following her to school; poking and disrupting her day like a bad stomach ache. No longer just a night terror, she couldn't escape the horrible, unexplainable thoughts that were polluting her young mind. They were taking a huge toll, aging her, changing her. Isolating her.

Doctor Hellerman had provided some methods and remedies for dealing with the episodes, like letting her stomach expand slowly while breathing deeply or humming a favorite song softly. Sometimes it worked. Other times not. She'd overheard him telling her mother the nightmares were part of some memory she was *suppressing*. Something she'd seen, perhaps recently, that was so horrific she just couldn't face it. That didn't seem to make sense to Rebecca, but she didn't have an explanation for the nightmares. They did feel real, like a memory, like it had actually happened. Something she was reliving — not just dreaming. Her mother disagreed.

The last bell rang and children burst out from each door, racing to get away as if the school building were on fire. Rebecca descended the steps with her head down, avoiding eye contact. *Another day down. Step over the cracks. Shoe lace untied - just keep moving, tie it later.*

Rebecca had one more obstacle between her and the safety of home. The dreaded walk to the bike rack. Once you were out in the yard, away from school faculty, it was every kid for themselves. Rebecca lived a few miles away from school. The first few days her mother had made her take the bus back and forth, but that was worse than prison. It locked her up with no place to run, allowing the other kids 30 uninterrupted (and mostly unrefereed) minutes to torture her at will. So she begged her mother for permission to ride her bike instead.

In her peripheral vision she spotted Jeff and Tommy creeping like two evil henchmen, eager to play their favorite game. Her heart sank as they pulled up right behind her.

"Watch out, she's mental," Tommy said.

"I hear she had to go to a brain doctor," Jeff said, returning serve.

"Yeah, they opened her head, but they couldn't find nothin! Ta doosh!" Tommy's laugh was filled with evil. Rebecca ignored their barbs and kept walking the endless path to the bike rack.

But Tommy wanted some tears. He hopped forward on one foot and gave Rebecca's backpack a shove, knocking her face-down onto the sidewalk. Rebecca caught herself just before she kissed the ground — scraping up her hands a bit, but otherwise okay. Tommy hadn't intended to use so much force, but didn't apologize either. Instead he raised his hand in a victory dance.

Rebecca stayed down, hoping they were satisfied, having gotten their humiliation. They stood over her, cackling and high fiving like their team just scored a goal.

Holly Schmidt, another regular victim of the evil duo's barbs just for her name alone, stood over Rebecca, eyeballing the two hyenas. Holly was very tall for her age, heavy.

"Leave her alone!" Holly screamed at the top of her lungs.

"Holy shit, it's Holly Schmidt!" They sang in harmony. A parent walking with their child saw the commotion and approached. Tommy spit in Rebecca's hair as they jogged away.

Holly offered her hand to help, but Rebecca was too embarrassed to do anything but get up and out of there as quickly as possible. She brushed past Holly, unlocked her bike from the rack, tossed the lock in her front basket and climbed on her bike.

She didn't get 10 feet when the chain broke, sending her pedals spinning out from under her little, white sandaled feet. She lost control and found herself face down for the second time in only a few minutes. All around her, merciless child laughter.

She got back up without dusting herself off, defiantly marching her bike down the street, not looking back. Her elbow burned, blood oozing through her sweater sleeve.

Along the route home was an opening in a fence that led to a wooded area. It cut a direct path to her street that would have shaved about 10 minutes off her trip, bypassing the bridge over Route 101, and the big round about at Redwood Drive. Many of the kids used it. She saw people jogging in there from time to time. She didn't know if Jeff or Tommy used the path to go home, but that wasn't what she was afraid of.

The place gave Rebecca an overwhelming sensation of dread whenever she approached. She always picked up the pace double time to hurry past it, as if whatever dark evil lurking deep within the trees was going to reach out to grab her if she walked too slow. She didn't know why it scared her, but the butterflies in her stomach swarmed when she got close, similar to how she felt just before the spells came over her.

CHAPTER 8

Laura held the phone away from her ear and shook it, her face contorting with frustration. She exhaled contempt for the person on the other line as she lifted the phone back up again, regaining her composure.

"I'm not going to discuss it anymore." She took a deep drag from her cigarette and pulled back the blinds to look out the front window. She saw Rebecca dragging her wounded bike, slamming it onto the lawn. "No, I didn't get it," she said, distracted. "Bullshit."

Laura stabbed out her cigarette in an ashtray on the windowsill. "Yeah, well, what you say and what you do are two totally different things."

Rebecca kicked open the front door and made a beeline for the staircase. Laura followed behind. "I gotta go," she said, pressing the button to end the call. She followed Rebecca to the staircase and watched her disappear around the corner.

"Hey, where've you been? I was worried sick!" Laura heard Rebecca's bedroom door close with a bang. "Becca?" Laura climbed the stairs. She reached for the handle, pausing a moment to calm down, still pissed off from the phone call. She reminded herself how Rebecca need not suffer for her mistakes. For all she knew, the drama and betrayal that sliced their family up the middle was the cause of poor Rebecca's night terrors.

Laura slowly entered the room. Rebecca was seated in the center before a large, white easel. On it, a half finished canvas painting of the maple tree growing outside her window. Adorning every empty space of wall in her room were crooked, hastily tacked up works of art, each one a glorious masterpiece, amazingly detailed. A true prodigy if there ever was one.

Along the floor was an assortment of canvasses, empty bottles of paints, brushes, charcoal pencils. Laura spent a good portion of the wages from her part time supermarket job on Rebecca's expensive art hobby. How could she not? It also kept her quiet. Rebecca never suffered any outbursts while she was occupied with her art. Perhaps the outlet for her expression released those troubling emotions in a more sane and civilized way. Without it, she exploded, especially when immersed in the dull, confining routines of elementary school.

The sun was setting outside, casting a warm orange glow through the room. Rebecca dipped her thin bristled brush into a jar of water. She dabbed it, then dipped it into a jar of green paint, scraping and poking the glass to utilize the last remnants.

Laura loved to watch. She offered no explanation for Rebecca's gift. There wasn't anyone in her family she could trace the artistic gene back to. It was a mystery. A miracle.

Laura wasn't particularly religious, she never took Rebecca to church or felt the need to hand down any family traditions as there weren't any in her family growing up. But she was convinced that if there was a God he was speaking through Rebecca's artwork.

Laura gazed around at the growing collection on the walls. Rebecca's art mostly consisted of still lifes, inanimate objects. There was one of herself that she wasn't particularly fond of, mainly because Rebecca had very accurately captured the wrinkles beginning to form around her eyes. The portrait made her look angry. Rebecca painted it one night after Laura scolded her for not eating her dinner. She remembered feeling self conscious upon seeing it a few days later, wondering if she really looked like that. That one could go, she thought.

"You okay, sweetie?" As expected, she got the silent treatment. "That's really beautiful, what you're doing there."

"Bike's broken," Rebecca said. Laura frowned on one side of her mouth.

"That old bike was broken when I rode it. I'll get you a new one, I promise."

Laura spotted green chewing gum had *somehow* gotten tangled in Rebecca's hair. She'd have to cut it out. *Little fucking bastards.*

Laura placed her hands on Rebecca's shoulders gently. "Pretty soon we'll have to open up a gallery for your collection."

Rebecca turned abruptly to her. "Mom, why'd we have to come here?"

"Rebecca—"

"Everyone hates me here."

"No they don't, sweetie." Rebecca turned back around and continued to paint. Laura sat down on Rebecca's bed and sighed, they'd had this conversation already. She'd tried before to explain the complications created when two parents separate, translating it into Rebecca's nine year old language. Laura didn't have a trade or a real profession. In order to make ends meet, they had no other choice but to move back to Lansing, into the old home she'd grown up in. Laura's father had recently passed, leaving the house to her. By default — not decree, she was his only offspring. The house harbored some tough memories for Laura, many she had worked hard to forget. But it was a roof over their heads for now. And the way things were going, probably for a long time.

Rebecca had visited the house once before, when her grandfather was very ill. She remembered it smelled "yucky" and she was afraid to enter the room where her grandfather spent most of his day staring at the ceiling, writhing in pain. But curiosity won out and she eventually ventured inside. He broke the ice with a joke she didn't get, but he laughed, and the odd sound made her laugh too. Laura had stood outside the door with her hand on her mouth, trying to hide her own sobbing.

Rebecca was very confused and asked her mother why she'd never met him before. *Some things are just too complicated to explain* was all Laura could come up with. A few weeks later he was dead.

They hadn't returned since.

Even though Rebecca was upset about leaving her friends in Livonia, she was actually quite excited to return to the house. She danced around when she realized her new bedroom was much larger than her old one. Her exuberance drowned out a lot of Laura's trepidation about being in "that place" again, and for a while Rebecca gave her the strength she needed to deal with the anguish of the last few months. Maybe they could make it, maybe they could be happy.

But the joy was brief. It wasn't long before the night terrors started. Laura had expected Rebecca to have a strong negative reaction to the divorce and the subsequent domestic upheaval — but this wasn't normal.

Then the school called, asking her to come down to discuss Rebecca's behavior in class. Laura was shocked when she heard some of the stories of what she'd done. The final straw happened during one outburst when Rebecca lashed out at a boy who'd approached her desk to ask to borrow a pencil. Rebecca screamed obscenities and smacked him hard across the cheek. The teacher described Rebecca's eyes at that moment as if she was a demon, possessed.

Laura agreed to let that *incompetent* school psychologist sit with her daughter twice a week. He very quickly threw his hands up in frustration. Those sessions escalated to the hasty recommendation of Dr. Leonard Hellerman, Child Psychiatrist. At Laura's expense, of course.

Not only was Dr. Hellerman also a failure, Laura blamed him for exacerbating the situation. Laura had heard enough these last few months, endured too many bullshit theories on Rebecca's "condition". Rebecca never knew a bad day in her life, as far as Laura was concerned. And Laura was *all too familiar* with what a bad day of childhood was like. She considered herself an authority on the subject, a purple heart veteran of domestic abuse. Sure, Rebecca's father had left them, but statistically speaking, these days that was more the norm than the exception. Nothing accounted for Rebecca's sudden, frightening metamorphosis from normal, well adjusted — even happy child, to the jittery, terrified, profanity spewing insomniac she had become. And while Rebecca mostly couldn't recall details from her nightmares, what she did describe was suffocating in its horribleness.

Laura decided they needed to solve the problem in-house. Rebecca was her daughter; if she couldn't help her, perhaps no one could.

Laura stood up from the bed and moved to Rebecca's side. She caressed Rebecca's red cheek with the back of her fingers. Rebecca let her.

"Warm milk isn't doing the trick, so I brought home some herbal teas from work. Maybe we can try it, hmm? Try and get some sleep tonight?"

"Mom?"

"Yes, sweetie?"

"Who is she?"

"Who?"

"The girl. The one the doctor was asking about? The one I talk about in my sleep? Carmen?"

Laura's lips went tight, the question caught her off guard. She tugged at a loose thread in Rebecca's sweater. "No one." Rebecca seemed unsatisfied with that answer, but went back to her painting.

"Rebecca, everyone has nightmares. Yours are just worse than most, that's all. But they'll pass. I promise." Laura kissed the top of Rebecca's head, embracing her, growing emotional.

Her eyes landed on a framed photograph Rebecca kept on her dresser. There was Laura, her ex-husband Richard - tattooed and muscular, and Rebecca in the middle. All smiling, happier times. Rebecca had drawn a pink heart around the photograph. Laura allowed her to keep it out on display. She didn't want her own pain to become Rebecca's. He would always be her father.

Laura stared at Rebecca's tiny face in the picture, Rebecca *winking* at the camera, something she did in virtually every photograph.

"I'm sorry, baby. I screwed everything up, didn't I?"

CHAPTER 9

Jack had fallen asleep at his desk. The fluorescent lights blinded, like something sharp jabbing his brain. He winced, slowly lifting his head, a piece of paper stuck to his cheek peeled away.

He looked down bleary eyed at his notes, the text started to move like tiny ants. He shook off the cobwebs, trying to pick up where he left off. His last thought had been the realization that he'd read the same sentence over and over. He dragged his palms down his face and leaned back in his chair, any attempt to continue would just be grinding metal. He rubbed his dark, swollen eyes.

He felt each tick of the clock, each second wasted. On his desk was a stack of gruesome crime scene photographs, not for the faint of heart. Even Jack could only stare at them a brief moment before his stomach turned. Beside those was a single picture of Angelina. Her bright shining smile inspired and haunted him at the same time. He dreaded the day he would have to move her picture into the other pile. He pushed himself to continue.

Harrington entered the office.

"Victor's state appointed council threatened a harassment suit if he's questioned again without being formally charged."

Jack turned to Harrington, holding up a report. "Take a look at these."

Harrington flipped through, "Natalie Gonzalez, Cassandra Ruiz... What about them?"

"Both Hispanic, same age as Angelina, each one held captive several months, murdered, then dumped, no DNA, no trace evidence, nothing."

"Gang related."

"No, that's a stereotype. Someone's out there, targeting these girls. Easy prey, illegal, family afraid to come forward to report them missing. Maybe whoever killed these girls took Angelina too."

"What makes you think Sandoval didn't do it?"

"Keeping someone captive takes privacy. Victor lives in an upstairs apartment with seven other people."

"Now who's stereotyping?" Harrington joked.

"There's a chance she could still be alive."

"Held captive?" Harrington said skeptically.

Jack handed him an envelope.

"What's this?"

"Results from the most recent DNA search. No matches. Searched all the border state databases; Ohio, Illinois. At least we know Angelina's not a Jane Doe somewhere."

"What's your point?"

Jack stood up and gazed at his map on the wall. He placed a colored thumbtack into a location. There were several others that he'd used to dot the areas where the other bodies had been found, each thumbtack an *X marks the spot*.

"I got a similar case hit up in Ann Arbor. Lisa Delgado, 18. Same M.O." Jack said as he placed a thumbtack to mark the spot her body was found, standing back to examine the pattern forming.

Harrington slid the report out halfway. Affixed with a paperclip to the front was a picture of a beautiful young Hispanic girl, long black hair. Jack tapped his chin. "That would make four victims."

"You think there's a pattern?" Harrington asked.

"I'm sure of it. I've already arranged a meeting with their department. You should read this."

"Tomorrow." Harrington handed the folder back to Jack. He put one arm in the sleeve of his coat. "I can't even keep my eyes open."

Jack sat down and went back to work. Harrington frowned pitifully. "It's late." He walked back and opened the door to leave. "No one will ever accuse you of not giving your best, Jack." Harrington waited a moment, huffed through his nose, and closed the door. The room fell silent.

Jack could hear the clock tick again. Then a sharp pain in his midsection forced him to sit up straight. He'd grown accustomed to living in constant discomfort, but every now and again the really bad ones caught him off guard. He took a few deep breaths and reached for his pill bottle, hidden behind some books on his desk's hutch. He popped the lid and shook two into his palm. He washed them down with some warm club soda he'd poured a few hours ago and forgot about, grimacing as he waited for them to take effect.

Jack heard footsteps in the hallway headed towards his office. The door swung open, Harrington tossed his jacket on a chair and stepped up to the coffee pot, switching it back on. He glared at Jack, muttering as he flopped loudly into a chair.

"When my wife runs off with the postman, it'll be your fault," Harrington said. Jack heard him whisper *"dick"* under his breath. Harrington's show of solidarity gave him a second wind. He put on his glasses to get back to it when the phone rang.

He reached for it, letting out a groan, his muscles stiff. Jack answered with a tired, raspy, "Hello?"

"Jack?" The voice asked, not sure he had the right person on the line. Jack searched his memory, trying to match a face to the voice, but couldn't quite place it. He cleared his throat again.

"Who's this?"

"It's Leonard. Dr. Leonard Hellerman."

"Leonard," Jack said familiar, wringing out his body with a one-armed overhead stretch that made his spine crack and his shoulders shiver. "They miss you around the courthouse."

"Jack, I need to speak with you."

"…Sure, go ahead."

"It's about your case. Can you come here to my office tomorrow morning?"

Jack paused, intrigued. "What's the address?"

CHAPTER 10

Pain shot through Jack's nervous system like a lightning bolt. The bursts of discomfort were getting more pronounced with each day. He flipped two pills into his mouth before realizing he had no water to wash them down. They were too expensive to spit out, so he swallowed them dry.

He climbed out of his car. It was drizzling, but Jack never carried an umbrella, real men didn't need one. To Jack it was the equivalent of prancing around in a dress. Real men lifted their collar and, if the rain was heavy, wore a hat.

Leonard's office was on the third floor of a modern building with mirrored windows. Jack entered the lobby and slid his finger down the list of companies on the lighted directory. He confirmed Leonard's floor with a tap on his name and office number, *304*.

He pressed the up button on the elevator and waited. A young woman entered the lobby holding the hand of a little boy, about six. Jack smiled lazily at her, and then at the boy, who looked up at Jack with a dark, murderous glare. The elevator door opened with a ding, Jack held it open for them. The boy resisted, so she tugged his arm with a jerk.

She managed to drag the boy into the elevator and nodded her appreciation. Hate radiated from the boy's eyes like he was sick with fever. Jack thought maybe this was where it begins, maybe the evil that kept him employed was manufactured early on. *Could it be that some of these fuckheads were just born this way?* The woman exhaled with a pained look, as if expecting Jack to comment on her "problem". Jack tried to think of something funny to say to break the silent elevator ice. *Let me lock him up now, save everyone the aggravation,* was all that came to mind. A sympathetic raise of his eyebrows was the extent of their conversation.

The doors slid open and he held them again. As they all stepped out, Jack immediately saw an arrow pointing in the direction for room number 304. He turned to the woman, who had wandered in the other direction.

"It's this way," Jack called out to her.

She turned and whirled her hand in the air with an *of course I went the wrong way* flip. "Thanks," she said, aware it probably didn't take much to guess where she was headed.

Jack led the way down the hall. He entered Leonard's office and paused at a few more disturbing sights: a girl kneeling on the floor with her face in the seat of her chair, sobbing. Another boy was hanging upside down reading a book, his finger deep in his nostril, his mother repeating "sit up straight" over and over with monotone uselessness.

"Jack Ridge," Jack said at the desk. Leonard's secretary looked up and made an "*oh*" with her mouth.

"The doctor's expecting you, go right in."

Jack took another glance at the full waiting room and figured this must be important. He looked up and down at Leonard's impressive all glass door, his name etched with calligraphy lettering.

Leonard stood up as Jack entered, but stayed behind his desk. "Jack, come in, come in." Jack brought the noise of the waiting room in with him. "Close the door."

Jack did, and the noise was sealed off completely, leaving Leonard's office library quiet. "You running a nursery?"

"I only treat children now," Leonard said, extending his hand. Jack reached across the desk and shook it. Leonard did a double take upon seeing up close how much Jack's appearance had disintegrated since they last met.

Jack took a brief stroll around Leonard's office, admiring his many awards and certificates. Jack had previously only interacted with Leonard during police investigations. Leonard was a very respected authority on whether a defendant was insane or just faking it. Seeing a framed photo of Leonard with his arm around Muppets at a charity fundraiser for Autism research elicited a rare smirk from Jack.

"Got tired of patients putting you in headlocks?"

"It's less money, but yes, the risks are fewer, thanks for hashing that memory up. Please sit down."

Jack turned and coughed hard into a ready handkerchief. He sat, hoping the spell would pass. After a few more embarrassing hacks, he steadied his breathing, willing the attack away.

"That doesn't sound good."

"You said you have something for me? About my case?" Jack's gaze was very intense, eyes red and watery, a man with little time to waste. It unnerved Leonard; he shifted in his seat.

"I'm not supposed to divulge anything about patients. But I've been following your case, and under the circumstances, I felt an obligation. Can I trust your discretion?"

"That depends."

"Jack, I think one of my patients may have witnessed a murder." Jack sat back, Leonard had his full attention. "She was brought to me suffering from night terrors, erratic behavior, blackouts. The elementary school psychologist referred her. This past month I've been putting the child through regressive hypnotherapy, trying to get to the root cause. Without provocation, she recounted witnessing a brutal attack in graphic detail. The girl she described... matches Angelina's description."

Jack processed it, nodding, his detective's cynicism navigating the likelihood of any plausibility to the claim.

"Maybe she saw something on TV? They don't censor details like they used to."

"If I can recognize anything after all those years of examining witness testimony, it's how to discern the difference between imagination and real memories."

"Who is she? Can I speak with her?"

Leonard stood up and opened a very large metal filing cabinet. "Her name's Rebecca Lowell. Her mother concluded her treatment. I don't think I'll be seeing her again."

He pulled a large folder out and slid the drawer closed with a loud metal slap. He handed the folder to Jack like a priest would hand off a bible to an aspiring scholar of the clergy, hands on top and bottom to prevent the overflowing contents from spilling out. Jack opened it. On top of a thick stack of notes was an audio tape. Jack picked it up.

"The sessions were recorded. Most of the dialogue is random and obscure, but you'll know it when you hear it."

Jack stood up, eager to get past Leonard's dramatic rambling and unearth the truth, if there was any to be had. He had exhausted every lead till it was worn down to the nub, desperate for a break. No matter where it came from.

"Where can I find her?"

"That's not a good idea."

"I'm working against time here. If this is real, I need to speak with her."

"She has no conscious recall of the incident," Leonard said, a strange look of panic on his face, as if he was starting to regret calling Jack in the first place.

Jack sensed something was off. "You said the school recommended you?"

"Jack, I've violated a trust by telling you this."

Jack acknowledged Leonard's appeal for discretion with a nod of understanding. He looked Leonard up and down, realizing how exposed and vulnerable this disclosure made Leonard feel. Jack was familiar with the rule of law in patient doctor confidentiality — in as much as Leonard and others of his kind had discussed it aloud over the years. Especially in cases where they felt a patient could be a threat to the public.

This was more than just supposition by Leonard, he must have done his homework on this and debated the merits of disclosure prior to contacting him. But there was something about the look on Leonard's face, the uncertainty — almost apprehension — that said Leonard was holding something back.

Jack was a master of reading people. He didn't lay claim to any sort of clairvoyance, but being in the detective business you develop a sixth sense for knowing when someone was hiding something. Facial ticks, body language, vocal intonation can often reveal someone's guilt or innocence. And Leonard had a terrible poker face. *Well, Leonard, the box is partially open, there's no going back now.* The baton had been handed to Jack; whatever Leonard knew, Jack would soon discover for himself.

There was a loud pounding on Leonard's door. Jack could hear the natives getting restless outside in the waiting room.

Leonard's intercom beeped: "Doctor?"

"I'll let you get back to work," Jack said.

"Jack, this conversation never happened, okay?"

"You know I can't agree to that."

He opened the door. The boy from the elevator was smashing his head on the other side.

Jack looked up at the boy's mother. "You're in good hands." He looked back at Leonard and saluted his goodbye. Leonard didn't respond, he just stood idle, a nervous expression.

CHAPTER 11

Aaron Phillips loved children. Psychology was a last minute switch when his original engineering major revealed no academic propensity, much to his father's disappointment. But he enjoyed what he did and took pride in it, as much as Jack did in his work. He was a soft spoken man with a haircut from the 1980s, an awkward mullet of dirty blonde hair that actually made him appear the opposite of the hip he believed it to. He was sort of a nerd, but the kids thought he was cool because he never seemed to take anything seriously. Always quick with a joke, or just the right words to diffuse an argument between students. He was well liked by all.

Jack disliked him instantly. First, he greeted Jack with a damp, limp-wrist handshake. Then, he made a bad joke about Jack paying a visit because of his outstanding parking tickets. Aaron added *"Just kidding"* a second later. Jack didn't return his smile.

He'd sat Jack at a long table in the library, taking the seat farthest from him.

"Rebecca's exceptionally bright; off the charts, as we say. When she started here, she seemed fine. Then, overnight, her teachers noticed a sudden change in her behavior. It got to the point where her episodes became a distraction to the class."

"What's wrong with her?"

"I can't say, really." Jack narrowed his eyelids. Aaron continued, "Meaning, I don't know. There's only so much we can offer her here. Doctor Hellerman comes highly recommended."

"Any problems at her last school?"

Aaron shook his head with absolution. "They were surprised to hear about it."

They sat and waited, Aaron was diligent not to make eye contact with Jack, clearly wanting to get this over with as soon as possible. Jack had been vague about his reason for asking to see one of their students, but his credentials checked out. If anyone questioned him for divulging information about a member of the student body, he would just insist he had no choice.

A woman opened the door slowly, stuck her head in, and smiled at Jack. "Mr. Phillips, she's here."

Jack stood up politely as Aaron went to the door to fetch her. He paused, "I'm going to need to document the nature of your visit, detective."

"This won't take a minute," Jack said.

Aaron wisely decided not to debate and left the room. He returned a few moments later with his hands on Rebecca's shoulders, easing her with kid gloves into the room. He turned and kneeled before her.

"Rebecca, this man's name is Jack; he's a police detective." Rebecca stood stoic, unfazed by the situation. "He just wants to ask you a few questions. Okay?"

Rebecca nodded and Aaron led her to the table. She didn't wait to be seated, choosing the corner of the table directly opposite Jack, no fear. Aaron stood behind her. Jack eyeballed him until he got the hint and stepped away. Jack held his eye contact, staring him all the way out of the room.

Once Aaron was gone, Jack turned to Rebecca and managed a gentle grin to try and make her feel at ease. He recoiled slightly at the contrast of her startling blue eyes with the deep, black circles beneath. They almost looked like bruises, they were so pronounced. Rebecca had a weary gape, it reminded him of the look kids had in war torn countries where bombings kept them up afraid at night. He'd also seen that same quiet stare on children's faces as he told them their mothers or fathers had just died. That inconsolable look of innocence shredded to pieces by life's harsh realities experienced way too soon.

Jack saw that same dreadful sorrow behind Rebecca's eyes; he felt empathy, a kinship. Sitting opposite each other, visually, they were two of a kind. Jack liked her instantly.

"Rebecca, my name's Jack Ridge; I'm a police detective. Can I ask you a few questions?"

Rebecca didn't answer. She looked up into his eyes in a way that made him uncomfortable; not an easy feat, considering Jack could stare down the barrel of a gun without flinching.

Suddenly his chest tightened, he felt that tickle in his throat. He coughed hard and loud. *Not now.*

He dug into his pockets quickly for his pills, breathless, like a deep sea diver fumbling for his mouthpiece. He shook two pills into his hand and swallowed them dry. His head and neck vibrated a little from the effort to force them down.

"You take pills too?" Rebecca asked.

Their eyes locked in a staring contest.

"Sometimes." Jack took out a picture of Angelina from his inside jacket pocket.

"Do they make you sleepy?"

"Sometimes. ... Rebecca, this is a picture of-"

"You look funny."

"I do?"

"You look just like my grandfather did before he died."

Jack stiffened a bit, not sure how to react to that. Her comment cut deep, without intention, the innocence of a child. Jack ignored it and continued.

"This is a picture of a girl named Angelina. She's been missing a long time. A lot of people are looking for her. It's my job to bring her home."

He showed Rebecca the picture. She stared at it with indifference.

"Do you recognize this girl?"

She lifted her head and nodded. A rush of hope and

excitement blasted through Jack's body and, for a moment, he felt no pain.

"Where did you last see her?" Rebecca took a good look and considered her answer. She could tell how important this was to him.

"On TV," she said softly.

"…TV?"

She nodded. The air left the room. Jack put the picture back into his pocket, disappointed. "Is there anything else you can tell me?" She shrugged. "Maybe something you felt uncomfortable telling someone else? Her family is worried sick. They're afraid something bad might've happened to her. I promise, if you tell me, nothing bad will happen to you."

Rebecca withdrew, her eyes fished around the room for something to stare at. Jack feared he was losing her. She turned and looked out the window, exhaling through her nose. "Rebecca, I hear you have terrible nightmares. Is that true?"

That got her attention.

"About a girl? About something bad happening?" Rebecca turned inward, like a child when you ask to see the cut on their finger and they clench their fist into a ball of marble.

"Do you think you're having these dreams because of something you saw on TV?" Jack said in his best nice guy voice. No response. "Okay… Well-"

"How do you know I have nightmares? Did my mother tell you?" She caught Jack off guard, he didn't want to say yes or no, and he certainly didn't want to reveal it was her psychiatrist who sold her out, especially after promising Leonard at least an *attempt* at discretion.

"I appreciate you taking the time out of class to come and talk with me, Rebecca."

She shrugged. "We were doing fractions."

They both stood up. "You like math?"

"Not really." Rebecca pushed her chair in like they're taught to do.

"Why not?"

"The teacher yelled at me."

"She did? What for?"

"Correcting her."

Jack smiled and opened the door. Even though the conversation was pretty one-sided and uneventful, his gut told him he would see her again.

Aaron Phillips was waiting just outside. He slapped his hands together with a *glad that's over* smack. "Well, all set then?"

The sun had broken through, children outside at recess played ball and tag; screaming, laughing, calling each other names.

Jack watched them through the breezeway window, enjoying the sound of children's laughter and happiness. A profound longing and emptiness welled up inside, but not enough to sour the moment.

Jack was halfway down the hallway when he realized he had made a wrong turn. He doubled back and caught a glimpse of Rebecca walking back to class. A young boy passed her by, making an effort to bump shoulders with her, hoping to knock her off balance. Rebecca went backwards with a wince, but didn't fall. The boy laughed it up as he skipped down the hallway in Jack's direction. Jack thought about sticking his leg out to trip the little bastard.

CHAPTER 12

It was that transition just after dawn, light gradually replacing darkness. Jack squinted, his eyes still adjusting to the new morning light. He wanted to get to the Ann Arbor precinct early. He found he got more cooperation from people at the start of their shift rather than after their daily routine had engulfed them. Frost covered the ground, the wet conditions making the roads slippery.

On the seat beside him was Leonard's file on Rebecca. He couldn't subscribe to the idea that someone could witness something as horrific as murder and not be able to recall details from the experience. But that didn't mean he wasn't intrigued, especially after meeting her. He'd heard of instances where a person's mind chose to bury traumatic thoughts and memories it couldn't process; he'd done that himself. Part of his job dealt with people who suffered from momentary lapses in reason. Husbands who'd strangled their wives in a fit of jealous rage, then later couldn't recall doing it, denying it even happened. Shit, there were mornings he awoke still holding onto a bottle of beer, unable to remember how he got into bed.

He passed the faded green sign for Ann Arbor and took the exit.

Jack stood in Sheriff Miller's brown wood paneled office,

flipping through the contents of a murder report. It was extensively detailed and annotated. Every crime scene photograph had a cross reference of where it was taken, by whom, during what time of day. Jack read the name on the cover, *Lisa Delgado*. He stood up and spread the documents across the top of the desk.

Sheriff Miller stood in the corner of the room sipping coffee from a giant #1 Dad mug. His kids had painted it for him - 14 years ago. He was completely bald with a wrinkle in his forehead that ran vertically up into his crown, making his head look like a cracked egg.

"Illegal, no family, 'least none that have come forward yet," Sheriff Miller said. "No missing person report was ever filed. Probably scared."

Jack sifted through picture after picture of grizzly crime scene stills. They'd found her body just days after it was disposed of. The carnage in the photographs was fresh, Jack could almost smell the stench of blood and decaying flesh, something he never got used to.

"A runner found her along the side of the road; not even an attempt to conceal the remains. Just left for the elements, stripped naked, no prints, fibers, nothing. The skull was smashed, teeth removed. She was a Jane Doe for a few weeks."

"How long ago?"

"Four years? Cause of death was asphyxiation. Stabbed first, but purposely cut where it wouldn't be lethal. So she'd suffer."

Jack started to write it all down when the sheriff interrupted him. "It's all in the report. I'm not offering any insight the coroner hasn't already made in his notes." Jack put his pen away and started stacking pages of the report.

"Anything unusual or... different in his report?" Jack asked.

"Did find indentations along the bones of her hands and feet. Some kind of sharp wire that cut deeper the harder she pulled. Torturous scumbag. The damage occurred over a period of time, erosive, like when you leave an animal in a cage too long."

"Held over a period of time," Jack said.

"What? Oh yes, that was his assertion too."

Jack searched the report, finding pictures that corroborated the sheriff's account.

"Anything else you can tell me?"

The sheriff took another sip of his coffee and smacked his lips. "A witness saw her climb into a tan car, not sure the model. Claimed she didn't get a good look at the driver."

"Her statement in here?"

"Just the reporting officer's transcript, she refused to file an official one. Afraid we might put her on the next bus to El Salvador."

Jack found several photos of Lisa, posed pictures with good lighting.

"These look like modeling photographs."

Sheriff Miller nodded. "Pretty girl. You say you got four similar cases on your ledger?"

"Three," Jack said, "Angelina Rosa's body hasn't been found. No denying there's a pattern here." Jack closed the folder and looked around the room. "You got a copy machine I can use?"

The morning traffic heading back to Lansing was stop and go. Jack cursed himself for not using the men's room before hitting the road.

He tried to distract himself from his full bladder by processing the information he'd just received. He grabbed a small personal voice recorder from his glove compartment to collect some quick thoughts. His best judgment came with his initial gut reaction, before things became fragmented by theories and alternate scenarios.

He pressed record, pausing a moment to gather his thoughts while his other hand kept the wheel steady.

"Held captive over an extended period of time. Possibly for sexual gratification. Body stripped clean, no trace evidence of any kind. No attempt to conceal the body. Victim was last seen getting into a tan late model car, no struggle. According to the witness, she opened the passenger door herself. Possibly knew her attacker. Pretty. All of them. Preying on vanity, a ruse maybe."

Jack squirmed, keeping an eye open for a clean looking gas

station to pull over and relieve himself. He placed the recorder down next to Rebecca's file. He glanced at her name, written in black sharpie on the label. Curiosity was getting the better of him.

CHAPTER 13

"What did you say your name was?" Jennifer asked again, adjusting the phone.

"Robert, Jack's brother," the voice repeated. *Jack has a brother?* She held her palm over the receiver, debating how to respond. If Jennifer had mastered anything in life, it was the art of small talk. Give her 3 uninterrupted minutes, she'd know your whole life story. She was the one who always remembered the cake on someone's birthday. When you had issues at home, she demanded constant updates on your well being. It was her nature to pry — a trait she felt would make her a good detective someday.

Having known Jack for several years and only just now learning he had a brother seemed, well…impossible.

The caller must have been lying — maybe a reporter trying to get an edge on the competition. The weird part was, this guy sounded a little like Jack, just without the raspy tone. She wondered what else Jack was keeping from her. Like that cough he claims is nothing but a dry throat.

At that moment, Jack wandered past her desk, his arms bursting with paperwork.

"Jack? You got a call on two. Says he's… your brother?"

"Tell him I'm dead," Jack said flatly, never breaking stride. He entered his office and closed the glass door.

Jennifer removed her hand from the receiver. "I'm sorry, he's dead." She looked back at Jack's office, confused. "Just now. You wanna leave a message?"

Jack tossed the case report he'd copied from Sheriff Miller's office onto his desk, dropping Rebecca's envelope on top of it. The cassette tape slipped out, Jack caught it before it fell to the floor. On one side was hand written simply: *Rebecca*, and a date.

He remembered seeing an old cassette player collecting dust around somewhere. He pulled open a few drawers, then checked a tall cabinet in the corner, finding it was buried under a pile of books and stationary supplies. He cleared some room on his desk with his arm, inserted the tape and pressed play.

There was no sound, so he raised the volume. A static hiss, followed by some commotion, the sound of a microphone rubbing on fabric. Then Leonard's voice reciting the date. Jack increased the volume more.

"October 21, session 6, subject's name Rebecca Lowell, 9 years old." Leonard's voice sounded tinny, but he enunciated his words clearly, very procedural-like.

"Initial observations: bright, articulate, but difficulty with social interaction. Suffers from persistent insomnia, stomach ailments, blackouts. Having trouble procuring the source of her distress, so far unresponsive to open dialogue & session Q&A."

Jack fast forwarded the tape a bit.

"I believe the problem is being obscured by a defensive subconscious. Ruled out possibility of parental abuse, however the query is not completely off the table. I'll attempt to probe deeper, possibly regress into early stages of development."

Jack pressed fast forward again, growing impatient. *"That's good, just relax,"* Leonard said, the recording acoustics had changed a bit. Jack could hear another person in the room, breathing. It was high pitched. *Rebecca*.

"Listen to the rhythm of my voice. I want you to count backwards from 10-" Jack hit fast forward once more. Time was precious but he was willing to give Leonard one more chance to impress him with

something. He pressed play.

"*When you were a little girl, what was your favorite doll?*" There was a slight pause, followed by Rebecca's answer, slow and groggy.

"*Mimmy.*"

"*I want you to think about Mimmy, think about the first time you saw her. Think back. Can you see her? Hold her?*"

"*Yes.*"

"*How old are you?*"

"*…Three.*"

"*Are you happy here?*"

"*Yes,*" Rebecca's voice was soft, lispy.

"*Now, let's move to the time you were most frightened.*" Leonard's voice took on a very serious tone, making Rebecca's breathing quicken. "*Remember, they're just memories, you're safe with me.*"

There was a long beat of silence. Jack checked to make sure the machine was working.

"*Rebecca?*"

"*I'm cold,*" she answered, her voice suddenly deeper, shaking. "*I hear a train. It's loud.*"

"*Tell me more of what you see,*" Leonard sounded energized.

"*The river. There's a willow tree. It's all black. Burned. It's falling into the water.*" Rebecca's breathing grew rapid, her words sharp, the way someone gets when they want to stop talking about something, anxious to change the subject. Leonard employed his calming voice to try and soothe her.

"*You're safe with me, Rebecca. I'm by your side. I won't let anyone hurt you. Please, tell me what else you see.*"

"*I'm scared,*" she said, sniffling.

"*What are you scared of? Is someone there with you?*"

"*Yes.*"

"*Is it your father?*"

"*No,*" she said in a hushed whisper.

Leonard mimicked her, whispering back, "*Your mother?*"

Rebecca didn't answer. Jack's eyes watched the wheels of the tape recorder spin around and around, his interest piqued.

"*What happened here, Rebecca? What frightened you—*"

Another long silence. Then:

53

"She's hurt."

"Who? Who's hurt, Rebecca?"

"She's not breathing!"

"Who's hurt, Rebecca? What does she look like?"

"P...pretty. Black hair. There's blood. I see blood."

"Whose blood? Can you describe her?"

"I don't want to look!"

"Please Rebecca, nothing can hurt you, you're safe with me. Do you know her?"

"She has no clothes on." Rebecca began to hyperventilate.

"Stay calm."

"She can't breathe! She can't breathe! Stop it!"

"Rebecca, who are you shouting at?"

"I want to go home!" Rebecca sobbed.

"They're just images, memories, let my voice guide you, protect you."

"No, she's not dead, don't!" Jack could hear Rebecca kicking and flailing about, Leonard struggling to calm her. "No, please, no! Stop!"

"Who is harming the girl, Rebecca? Can you see a face?" Leonard's responses started to sound desperate, he was losing control, and had to shout above Rebecca's shrieking.

"Please don't!" Rebecca started choking. There was a violent crash, like something was knocked off a table and shattered. Leonard's voice got very close to the mic, distorted: "Rebecca, it's okay, you're safe, you're safe!"

Jack anxiously hung on every word, the hair on his neck stood straight.

"Help. Help!" Rebecca was making herself hoarse.

"Concentrate on my voice Rebecca!" Leonard's voice trembled. "On the count of three, I'm going to bring you out. One, two—"

Rebecca let out a blood curdling SHRIEK.

Jack smacked the stop button.

His office fell silent. He'd unknowingly been grasping the arms of his chair so tightly his nails dug right through the fabric. He unclenched his fists — then the rest of his body, with one loud, long exhale.

He looked over his shoulder at his office door, wondering if anyone had overheard the chaos on that tape. There was no group of people pooled in his doorway — as he half expected there to be.

He could hear his own breathing, feel his heart racing. It was like listening to someone actually being murdered. Something only a real killer would have been privy to. A person would have to be cold blooded to not be affected by it.

Jack rubbed the back of his neck, massaging it in thought. He stood up and reviewed a few of the details Rebecca provided before it all went bad:

Burnt tree, a river...the train.

Jack looked up at his map on the wall. He took a fresh blue thumbtack and pressed it home, right where the tracks of the local freight trains crossed the river, deep in a wooded industrial area.

Rebecca's case file included her home address and phone number. Jack had taken the time to look up where they lived, it was only a few miles from the area Rebecca had spoken of. *Coincidence?* Jack didn't dare get his hopes up. If there was an award for most cynical detective, Jack would be the odds on favorite. A glass half empty kind of guy. So it was with a full container of salt that Jack decided to pick up the phone and call Laura Lowell to ask if he could speak with her about her daughter.

Leonard would not approve, might even get hostile, but that was no longer his concern. A human life hung in the balance. Or, at the very least, the successful recovery of a body and closure for Carl Rosa. Perhaps even enough of a lead to catch a killer. But he was getting ahead of himself. First thing's first.

He dialed Laura's number. The phone rang several times, but no answer and no machine. Jack hung up and reached for his coat.

He walked down the hall to the Captain's office. Jack knew he'd gone to the well one too many times, but he had to try. He knocked before he entered. Captain Lafave looked up from his paperwork; Jack was about to ask for something he wasn't going to say yes to, and by the defensive way Lafave leaned back in his chair, folding his arms in front of him, he was thinking the same thing.

"No," Lafave started, shaking his head.

"I want to do another sweep. Different area this time, down by the river. Near the tracks."

Lafave blinked. "Based on what?"

Shit. Think fast. "...Just a gut feeling." Harrington entered, not expecting to see Jack.

"I'm sorry, I'm not authorizing any more goose chases. As it is, they're cutting back on overtime, reducing shifts."

Harrington stood mute, not taking sides.

"What about outside volunteers, the community?" Jack said.

"Tough to rally the troops for these types," Harrington said. "They only come out for blondes."

Jack rolled his eyes, he knew Harrington didn't mean it and was just trying to lighten the mood. He turned back to Lafave, "Captain-"

"I'm sorry, Jack. Unless you have credible evidence to go on? Other than just your gut?"

Harrington made a hand gesture that simulated football uprights, waiting.

"No." Jack said. Harrington imitated the kick sailing wide of the uprights, the sound of a crowd groaning.

"Hey, do you work here?" Lafave shouted at Harrington.

"You wanted the report by three P.M., it's 2:59." Harrington placed a folder on Lafave's desk, tapped it with his index finger and exited the room.

Jack stared at Lafave until he was sure he'd conveyed his frustration, then followed Harrington out the door.

"Look, Jack, I have a lot of respect for you; you've earned it. If you really feel that strongly about this, I'll sign off on it. But it's the last time I'm putting my neck out for you."

Jack nodded his appreciation and closed the door quickly. He didn't want to give the captain any time to reconsider.

CHAPTER 14

Rebecca sat on the lawn, her bike upside down, examining the pedals. Sabotage for sure, she thought. She used a wrench to try and bend the chain guard back into shape, inserting it with precision between the wheel and the metal. Satisfied, she tightened the nut that holds the wheel in place, her nose wrinkled as her cheeks turned red from the effort.

She righted the bike onto its wheels and climbed on. She pedaled only a few feet before the chain popped from its gear. Off she went, face first.

She rolled onto her side and slowly got up, wiping at a grass stain on the knee of her jeans. She crouched next to the bike to examine the flaw in her repair.

"You'll hurt yourself," Jack said behind her. She turned to see him walking up the sidewalk.

"Remember me? We spoke at school?"

"Of course. I'm nine, not ninety." She wiped her cheek with her hand, leaving behind a dark streak of grease and turned back to her work. She banged on the chain guard a few times with the wrench.

"What's wrong with it?"

"I think the chain got stretched."

Jack knelt down. "Here, let me see." He spun the wheel, poking and prodding. "I had one like this when I was a kid."

"Is it that old?"

Jack laughed through his nose. "When I was a kid, your bike was everything. I loved to ride."

"Me too, it helps me think. Or sometimes not to think."

Jack looked up at her tiny frame standing over him, the sunlight made her hair glow. Something about her sorrowful eyes made him want to place his arm around her, comfort her. Rebecca was a complex little girl. An old soul.

"I can fix this," Jack said. He held out his hand. "Wrench?" Rebecca gave it to him. He saw the freewheel was crooked and tried to straighten it. "Looks like someone was messing around with this."

"I know, the rear derailleur is bent." Jack's eyebrows went up. He could see why Leonard held this child in such high regard.

He plied the metal backwards and started threading the chain. "There we go." He turned the wrench, tightening the screws. "So, how's school going?" The words bounced off Rebecca like a rubber ball hitting a brick wall. "Tough being the new kid, huh?"

Rebecca shrugged and looked away. "They all think I'm crazy."

"I was the new kid once. My dad was in the army so we traveled a lot. I was small, prime target." Jack spoke absently, his attention on the bike. Rebecca softened her stance a little. "They teased me, called me names. One day I just decided I wasn't going to let it get to me anymore."

"What did you do?" Rebecca crouched down beside him. He stopped twisting the wrench a moment, giving her his full attention.

"I just ignored them."

"What happened?"

"They pulled my underwear over my head and tossed me in a trash can." Rebecca frowned, not the ending she was hoping for. "But after a while they gave up. The trick is, no matter how bad it makes you feel inside, always stay strong on the outside. And if that doesn't work, there's always option number two."

"Option number two?"

"Yeah; hit 'em where it hurts, then run."

Rebecca smiled. "I like that option better."

Jack continued tightening, his wrist beginning to ache from being wedged in such a tight spot, the spokes of the wheel jabbing him. He threaded the chain and stood up slowly, grimacing.

He righted the bike, straining from the effort. Rebecca noticed, a concerned look.

"There, try that," Jack said. Rebecca climbed on. She pedaled cautiously, afraid of face planting again. This time she kept gliding down the sidewalk. *Fixed!* She looked back and smiled at Jack like he was the coolest person in the whole world. Jack waved her on, *keep going!*

For a moment he wished he was a kid again, he could ride along next to her and forget the world for a while. He got so caught up in the idea, he hadn't noticed Laura walking across the lawn towards him.

"You just saved me a hundred bucks," Laura said — appreciative, but at the same time suspicious of the stranger talking with her child. Jack saw the resemblance in her face, the same blue eyes.

"Mrs. Lowell?"

Laura was caught off guard. "Ms. …Can I help you?"

"Sorry, Detective Jack Ridge." Jack held up his grease-covered hands as an excuse not to shake hers.

"I'm investigating the disappearance of Angelina Rosa."

"I saw something about it on TV." Laura kept one eye on Rebecca, doing circles at the end of the street.

"You recently brought Rebecca to see a Doctor Hellerman?" Laura's friendly demeanor evaporated.

"What's this got to do with my daughter?" Jack could sense her guard going up. He hurried right to the point.

"He ever discuss his concern that what was troubling Rebecca could be the repressed memory of an actual crime?"

"What?" Laura's eyes opened wide.

Jack held up both hands, *hang on.* "Doctor Hellerman used to deal in criminal psychiatry. We worked together on several cases, he provided competency evaluations of defendants we were prosecuting. He's got a lot of experience with witness testimony."

Laura put her hand on her hip, out of sorts. "He never mentioned anything — what right does he have to discuss my daughter's-"

"Anytime there's information that can help prevent or solve a serious crime, disclosure is warranted."

"What are you talking about?"

"Angelina's been missing over three months now. Hard working, good home, stayed out of trouble. Not the kind to just run away."

"Why would Rebecca know anything about it?"

"I don't know." Jack sounded confused himself. Laura shook her head incredulously.

"She never leaves my sight, except to go to school and back."

"You're saying you don't think there's any chance-"

"She would have told me."

"Perhaps she was scared to? Or threatened?"

"I can't believe I'm having this conversation…" Laura clasped her hands together in a prayer-like pose, covering her mouth.

Rebecca was now riding towards them, a big smile on her face. Laura missed that smile.

"It's working great now!" Rebecca shouted.

"Becca, go inside." The smile drained from Rebecca's face. She considered protesting, but sensed the seriousness of her mother's tone. She got off the bike and walked it inside.

"I'll admit, I was skeptical myself," Jack said, stopping shy of revealing just how he came to share in Leonard's conviction. *The tape.* He dared not reveal the level of intimacy Leonard had shared with him about Rebecca's therapy sessions.

"This is ridiculous. She's been having nightmares, some trouble at school. We've both been through a lot lately, what with my divorce, new house, new school. It's hard on a child."

"I didn't mean to press. When you get to the point of frustration that I am with this case, you find you'll listen to anything on the slim chance that-"

"He wanted to prescribe all these pills…"

"Is that why you stopped seeing the doctor?"

"There's nothing wrong with her," Laura said defensively. "Nothing we can't work through ourselves."

"I see," Jack sensed his window was closing. He reached into his pocket and handed her his business card. "Well, if you think of anything, please-"

A violent cough stopped Jack mid-breath. Laura took a step back. "Don't worry, it's not contagious," Jack said through watery eyes in between hacks.

Laura examined his card. "Is this why he was so interested in her?"

Jack took a slow breath, calming. He turned to answer her, "How do you mean?"

"He offered to treat Rebecca for free. Called several times, left messages on my machine, even offered to come here. Don't you think that's strange?"

Jack considered it. "Yes, I do. Please, feel free to call me. Anytime."

Jack turned and hobbled off, clearing his throat. Laura watched him trudge slowly to his car.

"Thanks," Laura called out, "...for fixing the bike."

Jack acknowledged her and kept walking. She turned to see Rebecca peeking out the kitchen window. Her tiny face quickly disappeared from view.

Jack steadied himself on the hood of his car and cleared his throat again. He covered his mouth and coughed hard. Something in his chest felt odd, different. He opened his hand, it was filled with dark blood.

That was a new symptom.

CHAPTER 15

Leonard was in the office working late. The phone rang. Recognizing the number, he allowed the machine to get it.

He let Laura vent into voicemail. Again. She'd called several times earlier, he'd instructed his secretary to say he was out of the office. Laura was furious, and he wasn't ready to address this sensitive subject with her just yet. He might never be.

Of course not, he was a respected physician, and he wasn't prepared to throw his practice away. Not without evidence. Evidence he hoped Jack might uncover.

Leonard knew that once the cat was out of the bag, there was no going back. But he trusted Jack; most who knew Jack did. He was the right person at the right time. Unfortunately, any hope for discretion was now out the window.

Perhaps if he had confided the whole truth, told Jack everything, maybe Jack would have understood the need for circumspection. But the whole truth couldn't be imparted in one sitting; Jack needed a primer to digest all of the information.

Better yet, he needed to witness it firsthand. Otherwise, he'd have just labeled him crazy and walked out, angry for wasting his time.

CHAPTER 16

Jack sat upright on the cold white examining table. He'd been sitting there over an hour and was starting to wonder if they'd forgotten about him. Before he could finish the thought, Doctor Moss entered the room carrying Jack's medical results.

Jack liked straight talk, no sugar, he didn't need his hand held. Dr. Moss, one of the youngest doctors at the clinic, learned early on that Jack was a model patient if you just omitted the bedside manner. And never ask him to sit down.

"It's spreading faster than we expected," the doctor said. Jack swallowed and maintained eye contact. "It's metastasized through your lymphatic system to the lungs." Jack was no doctor, but he had a thorough understanding of forensics and the human body, especially what made you dead in a hurry. His prognosis had been steadily declining for some time now, so none of this came as a surprise. Still, it's never easy to hear your expiration date has been moved up.

"How long?"

"It's hard to say. Everyone's different-"

"About?"

The doctor folded his arms and leaned up against the teal countertop behind him.

"You might want to think about getting your affairs in order."

Jack picked a point on the wall and locked in, his expression blank. The doctor shifted his weight to his rear foot. Jack noticed him leaning back. *Is he expecting me to freak out?*

During Jack's last visit, he'd overheard yelling and screaming in the next room. He learned later the doctor had told a female patient she had just three months left to live. She grew perfectly still (just like he was now), then started shouting, cursing God, throwing tissue boxes, even smashed a glass container of cotton swabs. Jack grimaced. *Not to worry, Doc. You saved me a bullet.*

"What now?"

"Well, there's still the option of surgery. "

"No."

"At this stage there are few alternatives."

Jack looked up at the ceiling, resigned to his fate. He thought about how people often reacted when they learned they were going to die. How they tried to cherish every moment, notice things they never truly appreciated before, the beauty in life. Jack had been immersed in the world's ugliness for so long, he wasn't sure if he could still spot beauty beneath the grime.

For so long he'd dreaded the ticking clock on poor Angelina, how each second was one he could never get back, bringing her closer to certain doom. Now there was a time limit on him.

The doctor took out a pad and began scribbling. "I'm going to give you a new prescription at a higher dosage." Jack slid off the exam table and reached for his slacks, folded over a chair. "I can also contact the department, recommend that you be placed on disability."

"No. Don't do that."

"You're entitled."

"I can't leave, not yet."

"Alright." Dr. Moss continued writing the prescription. "Jack, the final stages can be very…difficult. Is there someone at home to help you out?"

"No."

"No family? Sister? …Brother?"

Jack shook his head. "No one."

Transience

"I know a very good hospice provider. I can put in a good word for you, they sometimes have a waiting list." Dr. Moss signed the prescription and tore it off, extending it to Jack. Jack folded it into his pocket without looking at it.

"Take some time, think about it?"

Jack nodded and the doctor left. Jack finished buttoning his shirt, staring up at an anatomical poster of a man's insides.

CHAPTER 17

Jack's knee smacked into the coffee table as he jerked up from his favorite recliner, still asleep — disoriented, knocking over a collection of standing beer bottles like bowling pins, sending one rolling loudly across the floor.

He blindly threw out his hand to brace himself along the wall, sliding slowly towards the bathroom door.

A familiar voice buzzed on the TV in the corner. As the blood level in his brain stabilized a bit, his eyes started to focus again. He realized what it was that jolted him upright.

It was *his* voice on TV. A reporter was questioning him about Angelina's case in an interview outside the station. Jack was walking fast, and the tiny reporter had to jog to keep up with him.

She asked breathlessly, *"Has there had been any news in the search for Angelina? We're being told that your department has suspended their search?"*

Jack snickered. *You've sure learned how to work the system, Carl. Good for you.*

"We're using every means at our disposal," Jack told the reporter, holding up his hand to block the camera's light.

"Is there anything you can tell us?"

"Nothing at this time." Jack sat into his car and closed the door on the disappointed reporter. She turned to the camera to say

something when the TV clicked off.

Jack tossed the remote on the chair, turned, and a rush of vertigo caused him to stumble a bit. He felt his way inside the bathroom and swatted on the light. His hands found the sides of the sink and he leaned towards the mirror. The fluorescent bulb really amplified his dry, pale complexion. He seemed brittle, far older than his 42 years. He made a pathetic grin, then stuck his tongue out.

"You're defective," he exhaled through his nose, disappointed with the reflection. "You're defective, detective." He laughed morosely.

There were two toothbrushes floating in a small metal holder affixed to the white tile. One was his. The other, much older one, was Sarah's. Dormant for over 12 years. He couldn't bring himself to throw it out. He touched it, it was real. Funny, the things we leave behind, he thought.

He needed so much to talk, unload his problems on someone. Tonight the loneliness felt suffocating. Almost unbearable.

He returned to his bedroom and opened the closet door. He eyed the navy blue suit with an impending look. He lifted it carefully by the hanger, so as not to crease the sleeve. He stepped back and laid it out on the bed, carefully removing the clear plastic.

He took out a clean white shirt and got dressed piece by piece. The same way he dressed for work every morning. Except this suit felt very different. Scary, even — especially the perfect fit.

He straightened his tie, checked the buttons on his sleeves, and laid down on the bed. He folded his arms on his chest, assumed the eternal position and closed his eyes.

He felt his chest rise and fall with each deep breath, the dull pain in his lungs was growing sharp. Another sound replaced his wheezy breaths. The faint voices of paramedics, speaking, shouting:

"Blood pressure's dropping!"
"We're losing him."
"Pulse rate-"
"We're losing him!"

The commotion got louder, scarier, so much so that it no longer sounded like a side effect of too many drinks. It sounded real, in the room right beside him. He shook himself, trying to move, a slow rising panic beginning to take hold. He shook again and his eyes snapped open.

Bright sunlight blinded him, brighter than he'd ever experienced before. He shut his eyes tight, then opened them again, slowly. The bright light was so intense, Jack thought maybe he'd passed on and this was the heavenly glow we're told to expect at the hour of our death. He tilted his head to embrace its warmth.

The intense glare dimmed, allowing him to look around. He found himself in a large open field of bright green grass. There was a slight breeze that felt nice and cool on his skin. He spotted a large oak tree, all alone in the open field. It called to him. Behind it, a string extended up into the sky, attached to a small yellow kite with a red tail. He watched the kite dance and spin in the breeze. *Am I dreaming?* Everything felt so real.

An overwhelming sense of calm and serenity enveloped him. There was no pain, no anxiety, no loss, nothing but peace. He watched the kite lift and soar on a sudden gust of upward air. He lost sight of it in the warm sunlight.

He turned towards the tree. Two people were lying underneath. He took a few energetic steps towards them — needing to know who he was sharing this wonderful oasis of peace and love with. The emotion was so strong, for a moment he thought his feet might leave the ground. Small fragments of pollen floated through the air like tiny dots of stars. He smiled, moving quickly, closer. But the pollen grew thick, clouding his vision.

Up above, the kite spun and dove, twisting helplessly as it came crashing towards the ground with an unnaturally loud smack. The magic serenity he'd felt was abruptly sucked away with a loud ringing noise. The world began to spin and drift away — as helplessly as the kite — disappearing into oblivion, leaving Jack in cold empty nothingness. All that remained was a horrible ringing in his ears. He held them and screamed, "Stop!"

Transience

Jack awoke with a jolt, as if shocked back to life by a defibrillator. He slowly sat up and grabbed his cell phone off the side table. It was *ringing*.

He looked out the window. Still dark out. He checked the clock on the wall, 3 A.M. No good news was ever exchanged at 3 A.M. Not in his world.

CHAPTER 18

Jack's eyelids were heavy, closing like attracted magnets. He swerved, struggling to keep his car in the lane. He hadn't fully slept it off, his blood alcohol still unsafely elevated.

His cell phone rang. It was Harrington, surely checking to see what his ETA was. He let it ring and turned his attention back to the road. His Ford Taurus had crossed over the double yellow line again, this time headed straight into the headlights of a blue Dodge Charger. Jack yanked the wheel to the right, just missing the Charger's grill. The Charger swerved onto the shoulder, kicking up dirt and rocks with a squeal of rubber.

Jack's car skidded and fishtailed back across the yellow line.

"Jesus Christ." He checked his mirror to make sure the other vehicle was okay.

The road curved around a bend, then up a steep incline that caused his engine to jerk and moan, all cylinders grinding to climb the hill. As Jack reached the top and the road leveled out, he could hear the rush of the river. He passed under a train trestle that traveled west, just parallel to the water, criss crossing several times before it turned south towards Illinois.

Jack pulled up onto the shoulder. There were a dozen police vehicles, all with their lights flashing along the entranceway to a wooded area along the busy stretch of road.

Harrington was waiting for Jack in the darkness. A rotating light on the car beside him made his face appear and disappear in flashing bursts of red. To Jack's tired, watery eyes, the image was surreal.

"You look like you can use some coffee," Harrington said, conveniently handing him an extra cup he'd been holding onto. "Might be cold by now."

Jack took a sip and winced. "How far in?"

"About 300 yards."

Jack took a deep breath and prepared his body for what was sure to be a painful walk over uneven, slippery ground. The pain was always worse at night.

"Who found it?" Jack asked, clearing his throat.

"Terry and his people."

"The ones with the dogs?"

"Yeah."

Jack fell in line behind Harrington as the path narrowed, allowing room for others passing in the opposite direction — officers, forensics personnel, and volunteers who had helped in the search. They were being cleared out so detectives could do their job. Jack felt as if he was the last one to arrive. He weaved in and out as they crossed shoulder to shoulder. One bumped his arm, spilling cold coffee onto his sleeve. Jack grumbled an obscenity and tossed the rest in the bushes.

"Anything left for us to sift through?" Jack asked.

"Terry knows the drill, he's been watching it."

There were bright highway construction lights shining in the distance through the trees, creating gigantic shadows that stretched to infinity. As they drew closer, it lit up the entire area like a supermarket parking lot. Radios buzzed and squawked, men with shovels were knee deep into the earth. The whole moment seemed to play out in slow motion for Jack. All he could think about was poor Carl Rosa, and that horrible phone call he would soon have to make.

Jack abruptly stopped in his tracks. The area where they were excavating was directly beneath a large willow tree, split in two from a lightning strike; its trunk charred black. Half of its limbs draped limply across the river's edge, the tips of their branches submerged.

At that very moment, a loud booming freight train whistle screamed out, echoing through the cold night air. Jack took a moment to triangulate his position. Rebecca had described what this scene would look like almost perfectly. Jack subscribed absolutely zero credence to the notion of extra sensory perception, so the idea that Rebecca possessed any clairvoyant capabilities never even entered his mind. Still, the proximity of the location made it virtually impossible for Rebecca to have been able to witness a crime being committed here. The area was several miles from any path Rebecca might have walked to or from school. Her mother let her ride her bike around the neighborhood, but he'd seen how short that leash was. Nothing added up. *So how was she here?* Jack agreed with Leonard, she was remembering something. She couldn't have imagined it. This proved it. But... how? Just Coincidence?

Jack made the long slow walk up to the gravesite that had been recently unearthed. The chief medical examiner at the scene - a heavyset man with thick glasses and coarse gray stubble - approached him somberly.

"Female, 18-19. Body appears fully intact, impressive considering the conditions, length of time."

"Length of time?" Jack looked down at the cadaver forensics was carefully — meticulously — dusting and cataloging every inch of for evidence.

It definitely *was not* what he was expecting to see.

CHAPTER 19

The dawn began to dry off the early morning frost and moisture from the ground. It was warming up but Jack could still see his breath as he stared out across the river, his mind racing.

The forensics team continued their excavation, collecting clues and stuffing evidence into plastic bags. Most of the officers and volunteers had left.

Harrington stood behind Jack and leaned up against a tree, balancing his foot on the trunk. He lit a cigarette and took a deep drag, exhaling with a long, strangely suspicious huff, almost as if he was trying to make his presence known, get Jack's attention.

"Last year I took the boys fishin' up in Roanoke," Harrington began, "not a nibble the whole freakin' day. The kids were bored, driving me nuts."

Harrington took another long sip on his cigarette. Jack remained fixed on the river, and the morning sunrise.

"Finally, I'm just about to call it a day, when BAM! I hooked this Pickerel. Man, what a fight. I got it up out of the water, but the squirmy fucker snapped my reel. Can you believe that?"

Jack turned around, not looking at Harrington, still deep in thought.

"Sucker must have weighed 15-16 pounds."

Jack looked up at a news helicopter circling overhead. The wind from the rotors blew his hair in all different directions. "I have to make a phone call," Jack said. He started to walk back towards the road when Harrington stepped into his path.

"How did you know?" Harrington asked, his stance confrontational.

"Anonymous tip," Jack said quietly as he brushed past him. Jack had a few crazy questions of his own he wanted answers to. Harrington held his hand out, gently blocking Jack's way.

"Okay, but... what told you to have them search down here? In this spot? Lafave said you were very specific."

"Gut feeling," Jack said while looking at the burned willow tree. He brushed Harrington's hand away; he'd been interrogated enough.

Harrington took another dramatic drag on his cigarette, his words filled with smoke, "Just like that, huh? Maybe they should change your title to Jack Ridge, Psychic Detective?"

CHAPTER 20

Carl Rosa decided to take the day off because of intense lower back pain. He'd developed sciatica in his hip and leg, and there were certain days when even getting out of bed was a bitter challenge. When asked to describe the pain, he often compared it to having a root canal done on his spine.

When the phone rang, he debated whether or not to answer it. It was probably the warehouse calling to grill him on why he wasn't at work, tell him how shorthanded they were today — how replaceable he was — and that he needed to take something for the pain and get the hell down there. He decided to let it ring.

He clicked on the TV. A news report was being broadcast from a helicopter. The volume was low, he couldn't quite make out what the attractive female reporter was saying. The headline on the lower third of the screen read: *girl's remains found near Twin Rivers.*

For a moment, Carl forgot all about the pain in his spine. Numbness filled his entire body like one giant shot of Novocain. His heart began to beat faster, thumping so hard he could feel it in his neck.

The ring of the phone suddenly seemed louder, like it was screaming at him. He slowly got to his feet, so numb with fear he could barely feel the floor beneath. He inched towards the phone like a prisoner summoned for his execution, sensing his life now had a very defined before and after. Before this call, and after he heard the words on the other line.

His sweaty, shaking hand grasped the blue receiver and lifted the handset. He stared at it another second or two, then finally put it to his ear. Someone asked "*hello*" several times.

"Yes?"

"*Carl? It's Jack.*"

Nothing would have made Carl happier than to hear his boss's high pitched, whiny voice at that moment.

"...Yes?" Carl said, trembling with dread.

"I wanted to call you personally before you heard about it on the news." Carl's heart sank, his eyes closed. He couldn't decide whether to pass out or vomit.

"Yes?" Carl whispered, sitting down in a chair looking out the window. He stared at the spot on the street below where, as a little girl, Angelina used to skip rope with her friends and sing songs. Tears dripped down his cheeks.

"We found the body of a young girl this morning."

"Oh God..." Carl wiped his face with his hand, going limp, trying to hold on, keep it together.

"We don't have a positive ID on the body yet, but I can tell you — we're almost certain — that it's not Angelina."

It took several seconds for Carl to resurface from his grief spiral. Color gradually returned to his face. The God he was silently cursing moments ago was good and merciful again. Hope lived for another day.

He dropped the phone, placed his hands over his face, and wept uncontrollably.

Jack heard Carl's phone hit the floor. He called out his name once, then hung up. There was nothing more to say.

Jack just couldn't shake the method of how he'd divined this victim's final resting place. But what was even more mind blowing was what the coroner had said. It was so startling, Jack had to ask him to repeat it:

The body they'd found had been dead at least 10 years.

It nearly knocked him over. *10 Years?* Jack stammered mentally with the possibility that whoever killed these girls could have been operating right under their noses for that long. How many more victims could be out there, unrecovered? The scope of his investigation, the magnitude, had become elevated exponentially.

Immediately, Leonard's sessions with Rebecca, the details, became relegated to chance, a lucky guess. Jack didn't want to be dismissive, her account captured on that tape was bone chilling in its realism, he was reluctant to cast aside his gut reaction to what he'd heard. But the estimated date on which this victim apparently met her end made Rebecca's very creative imagination a moot point.

CHAPTER 21

Laura rarely slept anymore, so much as pass out from exhaustion. Even when she was out, she awoke several times, on edge, anticipating the inevitable outburst.

Rebecca offered nothing to make her feel any better. Laura didn't believe she was consciously harboring any secrets from her, despite what Leonard had told that detective. *What a bunch of bullshit.* Rebecca genuinely didn't know or understand who — or what — was preying on her.

There were moments during the day when Rebecca would say or do things that caused some eyebrow raising, but for the most part her outbursts seemed confined to nighttime. Yes, Rebecca was having issues at school, but those were isolated incidents. *Right?*

As ridiculous as what the detective had said was, until she had an alternative, *sane* answer for what was tormenting her daughter, she wasn't taking any chances. The bike, fixed or not, was out of the question. She would drive Rebecca to school for the time being, even though it would make her 5 minutes late for work.

Rebecca didn't argue.

Laura turned a corner, traveling up Connecticut Ave. There was an old church on their right. A man was mowing the small patch of grass in the front. Laura raised the windows — she was deathly allergic to cut grass. Rebecca watched the church go by.

"The statue is gone," Rebecca said.

"The statue?"

"Saint Francis. They took it down," Rebecca said with a hint of sorrow.

"Oh. That's too bad." Laura couldn't remember any statue having been there to be removed. Of course, Rebecca was a kid who paid very close attention to details. She could stare at something for a few seconds, then go home and sketch what she had seen as if developing a film negative. It didn't surprise Laura that her daughter might notice that the landscape revealed a slight imperfection when compared to yesterday.

But how would she know its name? They were Catholic, but she hadn't given Rebecca the opportunity to go to church or have her communion. She was baptized, but that was more of a ritual than anything else.

She also didn't remember taking Rebecca this way to school before... she'd told her to always travel along the side roads, not on a busy main road like this.

"Rebecca? You don't ride this way to school, do you?"

"No. I go down Atlantic, like you told me to," she said, as if wondering why she would even ask such a stupid question.

"Right. That's what I thought."

They reached the school. Laura stopped the car along the curb by the front entrance. Rebecca grabbed her book bag and scanned the yard for bullies, searching for the path of least resistance. She opened the door and stepped out.

"Have a good day, sweetie. Try to have fun, okay?"

Rebecca waved goodbye and headed inside. Tommy spotted her, altering his trajectory to ensure their paths would cross. He stuck his foot out as she passed by, but she didn't fall. Rebecca was ready and had steadied herself.

Laura wasn't ready, and bit her lower lip when she saw it happen. She put the car in park and was ready to get out to strangle the little shit when Rebecca turned at the top of the school steps, waving at her with a strained smile. Laura waved back, her mouth a flat line. Rebecca disappeared inside. Laura waited a few seconds before putting the car in gear, still squeezing the steering wheel.

Rebecca made her way through the hall, avoiding eye contact. A friendly voice penetrated her defenses and she looked up.

"Hi," Holly said. *How brave to risk humiliation*, Rebecca thought. She smiled back.

"What, are you friends with this weirdo?" Christina said. Held back in first grade, Christina was tall and as beautiful as she was evil.

"Are we friends, Rebecca?" Holly asked.

For a moment Rebecca wasn't sure if Holly was hoping she'd answer *no* just to bail her out, or if she was standing her ground, even sticking up for her. Holly also didn't have many friends, but from what she knew, Rebecca figured Holly couldn't care less what the other kids thought of her.

"Yeah, we're friends."

Holly turned back to Christina. "I guess we're friends."

Christina made a face like she smelled something foul and walked away shaking her head. "Psycho…"

Holly walked with Rebecca to class. "Don't let those jerks get to you," Holly said. Rebecca nodded. It wasn't the first time she'd gotten that advice.

CHAPTER 22

Sam Cheung was considered one of the best forensic pathologists in his field. He had thick black hair and wore silver rimmed bifocals. He stood alongside Jack, examining the bones of the deceased girl. Sam pointed with a serrated blade to the area around the clavicle and jawbone. Jack leaned in.

"The hyoid bone was crushed. Here and here, see? Powerful hands."

The skull was tilted backwards, mouth open, as if frozen in a silent scream. Sam walked around the table, removing the tarp that covered the victim's lower extremities. He'd cleaned the excess dirt and residue from the cadaver. The bones had acquired a yellowish color from the years of decay.

"These marks on the fibula and ankle were caused by some sort of restraint, a wire. Lab's testing the residue." Sam pointed to each mark as he described them. "She pulled so hard to break free, it dug right through the skin, serrated the bone."

"Held captive?" asked Jack. Sam nodded.

"Same as the others." Sam lifted the foot of the victim. "There's trauma to the patella and feet. These indentations here were caused by being kept immobile on a hard surface for an extended period of time. The ulna and radius in the right forearm were shattered, possibly from blunt trauma, a fall maybe."

Jack examined the remains, trying to envision what the girl once looked like. For a brief moment, he became introspective. He saw himself lying on that cold table, someone poking around at him. Only there would be no question what did him in.

Jack's eyes drifted over the bones. He looked at the pale flesh of his own hand, then back at the skeleton. *Soon that will be all that's left of Jack Ridge.*

He drifted inwardly long enough for Sam to notice. He cleared his throat and Jack looked up.

"You okay?" Sam asked.

"Yes, I'm sorry-" Jack said as he erupted into a coughing fit that echoed loudly in the cramped, white tiled exam room.

"Sounds serious."

"Continue." Jack wiped his mouth with a folded handkerchief. Sam moved back up towards the skull.

"No cavities. These missing front teeth weren't from poor hygiene." Jack exhaled painfully.

"How long on an ID?"

"Still waiting on dental. If she's US, it shouldn't take long. If the caregiver's abroad, might be a few days, a week, maybe more."

"The coroner at the scene estimated she'd been down there possibly 10 years."

"Yes, at least that." Sam removed his glasses to rub his eyes, leaning on the table. "The years of decay make it hard to determine ultimate cause of death. But it doesn't appear to have been quick and painless."

Jack stared long and hard, his brain spinning. The press would want to know, first and foremost, the source of the information that led him to discover her remains. He had no answer for them. None that made sense anyway.

CHAPTER 23

Jack sat in his office and watched the clock; it was almost 11 A.M. He was so certain the body unearthed would be Angelina's, he'd made peace with the end of his tenure as detective while scaling that hill. When he learned it wasn't, it was like he'd gotten a reprieve. A second chance. It spurred him to work even harder, smarter.

The pain was like caffeine, keeping him awake. He shook two pills into his hand. Then a third. It was so unbearable now, painkillers were becoming like candy. And they really weren't doing much for him. The doctor offered to up his prescription to something more powerful, but the side effects prevented him from driving, concentrating. Right now that wasn't an option.

Harrington entered, carrying a printout. "I took the over on Denver last night. Drinks are on me."

Jack put his bottle of pills away discretely, behind the most recently printed edition of the Police Procedural Guide for Collecting Evidence.

"Oh, I forgot," Harrington said, "you don't go out. You don't socialize at all, do you?"

"Is that it?" Jack asked, holding out his hand. Harrington tossed him the printout.

"Her name's Carmen Muniz, she was 19." Jack's eyes gravitated towards the smiling picture of Carmen at the top. A face to the bones. Plain, young, sweet; she resembled all the others.

"Carl said she was held captive, several months or more," Jack said.

"If you're right, then this guy's been getting away with murder for over ten years."

"I know I am."

"Press is going nuts. The Captain's phone hasn't stopped ringing all morning. Everyone wants to know how her body was found...Jack."

"I was hoping we could keep it out of the press for a while."

"I can run a play fake, but that will only buy us a little time."

Jack read through the document some more, there was a listing for a next of kin, *Hester Muniz,* with an address. "This guy likes to have his way with them. Take his time."

"A power thing?"

"Maybe. It means Angelina might still be alive. This girl, Carmen, parents been notified yet?"

"I don't think so," Harrington said. Jack stood and reached for his coat. "Oh, you volunteer? Good."

"He didn't bury the others, made no attempts at all to conceal their bodies," Jack said. "Why this one? What was he afraid of?"

"Maybe it was his first? He was less cavalier?"

"Maybe she was too close to home. Which means he'll be nervous we found her." Jack collected the report, tucking loose pages back inside the folder. He headed for the door.

"They want to do the press thing this afternoon," Harrington said. "I'll try and stall, what should I say?"

"You love to talk."

"Only about football."

"Tell them we have nothing to go on. That there doesn't seem to be any connection to the other murders. Let him think he's safe." Jack left the room in a hurry.

"Hey, you still haven't explained how you found the body!" Harrington listened to Jack's footsteps get farther and farther away. He pushed up out of his chair and walked over to Jack's desk.

He'd spotted Jack hiding something behind a book when he first walked in. He moved it and discovered Jack's pills. He picked them up, squinting to read the prescription. Harrington was no dummy, he knew it was a heavy painkiller. Jack had never complained of pain, never betrayed a wince. But apparently Jack didn't only look like shit, he felt like it too. Harrington was confused and, at the same time, impressed.

He put the bottle back, careful to lean the book in place just like he found it.

CHAPTER 24

Jack pulled up to a crowded housing complex. The tenants were mostly a cluster of Hispanic groups: Dominican, Ecuadorian, Puerto Rican. He checked his handwritten address, matching it with the street sign across the road. Woods Avenue. *Right place.*

He took a moment to collect his thoughts. Even though Carmen had disappeared over a decade ago, there was no doubt her family hadn't enjoyed even one day that wasn't clouded by the horror of not knowing what became of their sweet daughter. Some things in life you can never move past, never forget. *Like Sarah.*

Not a day went by he didn't think about her face, how she felt in his arms. Twelve years, but the pain was still fresh. He would trade every day he had left, and every day he'd spent since, to hold her just once, hear her voice one more time.

The only difference between Carmen's parents and Jack's loss was that Jack knew the fate of his wife. Now they were about to learn Carmen's, or at least half of the story. The other half, the part where Jack brings her killer to justice, was still being written.

He took a deep breath, exhaling hard and loud, and climbed the cracked cement steps that led to apartment 3G. He glanced at the picture of Carmen from the report then tucked it away in his pocket and knocked.

There was loud shouting coming from an apartment upstairs. Jack looked up, waiting for a piece of furniture to burst through an open window and land on him. Jack knocked again. Finally, the door opened.

Hester Muniz, 50 years old, a little heavy, but not unattractive, opened the door. Jack saw the resemblance immediately, and his heart ached.

"Yes?" Hester said with a warm smile.

"Mrs. Muniz?"

"Yes?"

"I'm Detective Jack Ridge."

Hester sat on the end of a twin bed, wiping her eyes. She had led Jack into Carmen's old room, which was just as she left it. Jack was taking a brief tour; examining pictures, trophies, keepsakes, there was even a hairbrush, Carmen's hair still entwined.

"All these years I pray she living her life somewhere," Hester said, sniffling.

"I'm very sorry for your loss." Jack turned to admire a painting on the wall. It was a still life of a bowl of fruit, truly breathtaking. There were others, a sunset at the beach, one of a dog, all incredible renderings.

"She love to paint. She was so talented. Her father work himself into the grave to keep us here. She get scholarship for her art, he was so proud."

Hester's words made Jack feel even more remorse for the loss of someone so gifted.

"They're beautiful," Jack said quietly.

"I see that pretty young girl on TV all the time. They never once mention Carmen when she disappear."

"I read her report," Jack said. "What can you remember about the night she went missing?"

Hester shook her head and wiped her eyes again. She stared at the floor. Jack gave her a moment. She sighed softly and collected herself.

"We had a fight. I pray and pray she come home. All these

years, I beg Jesus, please, just let me speak to my baby one more time. Tell her how sorry I am."

"Who else lives here?"

"My husband, he die two year ago." The levy burst, Hester could no longer contain the tears as the emotion overwhelmed her. She moaned with grief, making the moment even more uncomfortable for Jack.

He noticed a strong smell of perfume, and... wet dog. A large white collie entered the room and went straight for Jack; pawing at his leg, licking him. Jack politely rubbed the dog's head, glad for the interruption. It sliced through the emotional pall that had engulfed the room, letting the air back in a little. Even Hester turned her attention to the dog.

"Faucet, no!"

She stood up and grabbed the dog by the collar, leading him outside. She returned after a moment and closed the bedroom door tightly. The dog scratched at it a few times.

"Sorry."

"It's okay," Jack wiped the dog's slobber off with his handkerchief.

"Carmen name him Faucet, his nose always running."

Jack approached a dresser across the room. There was a framed photo of Carmen at her high school graduation. He picked it up to take a closer look. Carmen was dressed in her cap and gown, a large gold cross around her neck. She had her arm around a young boy, about ten years old. "That her brother, Francisco. He join the army."

Jack put down the photograph and picked up another one. This one showed Carmen wearing a white sundress with orange flowers, smiling with a wink, her arm around another young girl her age. Jack had to take a closer look to confirm it, but he was certain the other young girl posing with Carmen was a young Laura Lowell. Jack turned and held the picture up for Hester to see.

"Who's this?"

Hester squinted. "...Her friend from school, I forget her name."

Jack studied the picture, half wanting to confiscate it under his jacket. He placed it back down and turned to find Hester standing right behind him.

She leaned over and unhooked something from around Carmen's framed Communion photo.

She cupped the item in her hands, extending them out towards him. Jack stared into her glassy eyes.

"This was Carmen's." She took Jack's hand and placed a gold cross on a chain into his palm, closing his hand to make sure he couldn't refuse. It was the same cross Carmen had been wearing in the graduation photo. "Go with God. Bring justice for my daughter."

CHAPTER 25

Out in the schoolyard was a hidden alcove where Rebecca could sit quietly, hidden from view until recess was over. There were two large silver doors where food deliveries were made each morning, otherwise, no-one went in or out. She could relax undisturbed, out of sight of the other children.

She'd swipe a piece of chalk from the teacher's board and sit and draw on the cement. Once in a while, an aide would peek around to check if she was okay. They would smile and Rebecca would smile back.

Normally the teacher's aides would shoo children away from there — they didn't like it when a student wandered off where they couldn't see them. But they understood Rebecca was having a hard time adjusting, and that she wasn't up to any mischief.

Rebecca was on her knees sketching madly today. The dream last night had been one of the worst. She could remember the woods, screams, a girl lying on the ground — a terrifying man with his hands around a girl's neck, squeezing, his eyes blank like a mannequin's. She'd tried to run, but couldn't move, as if rooted to the spot.

She fought to remember his face, wanting to memorialize it in chalk, hoping if she stared at his image long enough it wouldn't be scary anymore. But she couldn't focus, couldn't quite get the memory correct to her satisfaction. She huffed with an exhale of frustration.

The last thing she remembered from the dream was a feeling of being sucked up into something, like a giant vacuum came along and she was a tiny piece of dirt. The feeling was horrifying, like falling upwards, and she shuddered every time she thought about it.

She hadn't slept through the night in so long, an ache started developing in her head. It receded slightly when she closed her eyes — which she tried to do often, irritating her teacher who had to keep reminding her to please pay attention.

She held her eyes shut, drifting off, the noise of laughter and shouting became just a drone in the distance. She took a deep breath and exhaled slowly.

Thwack! A large rubber ball smacked off the brick wall behind her head, snapping her eyes open. Tommy collected the rebound and wound up again, aiming it right between her eyes.

"Look what I found!" he said with a grin that showed every tooth in his mouth. "I thought they locked you up in the basement during recess, freak."

He released the ball with a grunt. It missed her by inches; Rebecca flinched and covered her face.

"Reba the retard," Tommy sang repeatedly. He lobbed the ball again, not as hard this time. Rebecca reached out and caught it reflexively. Tommy's expression went dark, furious.

"Give it back!"

Rebecca threw the ball to her right, it bounced down a stairwell. Now Tommy would have to get permission, and probably an aide, to go fetch it. His face burned bright red, similar to the way his father's did whenever Tommy's mother bested him in an argument. His father's response was to throw her against the wall, while Tommy and his younger siblings watched helplessly from the staircase.

"You stupid shit!" Tommy shouted, approaching. Rebecca hurriedly tried to erase her sketch. Tommy marched over and stepped on her hand.

"Ow!" Rebecca squealed. Jeff and a few others overheard the sweet sound of suffering and rushed over to join in the fun.

Tommy stepped back and saw the chalk dust sketch. "What, you gonna draw us a picture?" Rebecca tearfully massaged her squished fingers. Jeff moved in and knelt beside her, getting right in her face.

"I think she's gonna cry," Jeff said, dribbling spit like some mad dog. Rebecca pushed him and, because he was kneeling off balance, he went tumbling backwards. Several kids laughed out loud, which made Jeff want to hurt Rebecca more. Rebecca knew staying on the ground would leave her vulnerable to his assured counter attack. She stood up, her back to the wall.

Tommy clenched and whirled his fist as if he might strike her, but stopped just short of landing one. "I ought-a kick your face in!"

Christina saw what was happening and skipped over, followed by a few bottom feeders.

"Nobody likes you, retard," Christina said.

"I don't care," Rebecca said, keeping her chin up. Christina recoiled at her defiance and got right up in her face, shoving her.

"Think you're so smart, don't you?" She grabbed Rebecca's shoulders and pushed her again, hard. "No one likes you." She went to do it again, but Rebecca pushed back. A look of stunned disbelief on Christina's face.

The crowd of children *"oohed"* like a bloodthirsty mob. Rebecca thought about what Jack had told her the other day. Maybe if she just ignored them, they would leave her alone. She relaxed her shoulders.

Christina took a running start and shoved Rebecca again, the back of Rebecca's head slammed into the brick wall. Rebecca's eyes welled up from the shock and pain. She rubbed her scalp, but showed no fear.

Tommy and Jeff joined Christina, pushing and pulling Rebecca like toddlers fighting over a rag doll. Rebecca fought to stand her ground. There was a familiarity about the violence that unleashed waves of hysteria inside her. Her skin got numb, her mouth dried up, she felt dizzy.

The crowd thickened, growing louder and riotous. They shouted taunts and encouragement to Tommy and his gang of thugs.

"Grab her hair!" one said. Christina obliged and they all tumbled to the ground.

Holly pushed her way through the crowd. Rebecca was trapped under the pile, only her small feet visible, kicking and stomping. Holly screamed at the top of her lungs, "Leave her alone!"

A scrawny boy with glasses who was hyped up and cheering like he was a spectator at a wrestling match shoved Holly back, "Shut up!"

"Stop it! They're hurting her!" Holly wailed.

Rebecca could hear Holly's cries through the taunts and shouts. It gave her strength to keep fighting.

"Hold her down!" Jeff screamed. Christina grabbed Rebecca's face and neck. The sensation sent waves of terror through Rebecca's body and she lost all bearings — *was this just another nightmare?*

Something flashed before her eyes, a bright white light that made everything around her vanish like water vapor in the wind. The world began to spin, it made her sick and nauseous.

She could still feel hands around her neck — but the children were replaced by a dark figure hovering over her, menacing, terrifying. She could smell his breath. His darkened face was a blur, but his shape was familiar. She could feel his dirty, blistered fingers wrapped around her throat. She could smell blood, in her mouth, up her nose.

Her windpipe squeezed shut, she couldn't get air into her lungs. Her eyes bulged. She tossed and flailed about like a fish out of water. Tommy and the others saw what was happening and let go. They stood up and backed away.

A teacher's aide finally spotted the melee and pushed through the sea of tiny onlookers, blowing her whistle for them to make way. "What's going on? Break it up!" she shouted. Christina and the others quickly adopted somber expressions, nervous about the damage they had caused.

"We didn't mean it," Christina insisted, her voice now timid and innocent.

"We were just kidding," Jeff added.

Several of the other children, who moments ago were screaming for blood like a mob of striking teamsters, burst into tears at the grim reality of their bullying.

Rebecca's eyes had rolled back into their sockets, her torso lurching and sputtering, in the throws of a violent seizure. The aide, who had only just volunteered for the job a few weeks ago, stood helplessly for a moment, clueless. She knelt beside Rebecca and put her hand on her chest, as if trying to wake her from the spell. Upon her touch, Rebecca lashed out wildly, striking the aide across the cheek.

She recovered and cradled Rebecca's head to keep it from smashing on the concrete. She held her tightly as Rebecca's body quivered and trembled, so harshly, one of her shoes flew off. The aide blew her whistle again, a long breath, loud like an alarm.

Rebecca had lost all contact with the outside world. In her mind, she could see trees, branches, water. The vision spun faster and faster. Everything dripped red, as if bathed in blood. She felt herself slipping away, further and further, all sensation draining from her body. Soon there was only the cold darkness.

CHAPTER 26

A blinding circle of light roused Rebecca. It moved from one eye to the other. *How strange...*

"Just follow the light. That's it," said a soft voice. A nurse peeled open Rebecca's eyelid again and shined a penlight into her pupil to watch it dilate. Rebecca winced, her reaction made the nurse smile, she was going to be okay.

She blinked, groggy, the bright white room started to come into focus. There was a doctor and several nurses hovering over her, adjusting wires. Her arm felt sore; she looked and saw a needle in her skin held with a bandage, with a tube that connected to a bag filled with fluid, dripping. *This isn't the nurse's office.*

An announcement over a PA asked for a doctor to please come to the ER immediately. Outside, a man was wheeled by on a gurney. *What happened to me?* All at once every muscle in her small body flexed and tensed. She started to panic.

"Just relax, Rebecca," the nurse said, gently rubbing her shoulders, easing her back down.

Hearing her name calmed her a bit. The voice was soft, like her mother's, and her thoughts immediately went to her. *Where is she? Does she know how to find me? Did something happen to her, too?*

"Shhhh," the nurse could see Rebecca's anxiety growing. She

caressed her forehead and held her hand. The nurse's touch was warm, her skin smooth. A sharp contrast to the rough, blistered fingers that had tried to choke Rebecca to death moments before.

CHAPTER 27

There he was again; about 35, brown hair, clean cut. Nice smile. He would always find a reason to search endlessly for something wherever Laura happened to be stacking shelves. But so far, he hadn't had the courage to speak to her.

She turned to look in his direction and he darted his eyes away. She tried to time it — catch him looking. His quick head turn made her laugh. It was nice to be reminded that she was still an attractive woman. Still alive. Even though she'd stopped caring about her appearance, her face bloated and listless from so many sleepless nights, it hadn't affected her innate beauty. Her visible condition, her sad eyes, brought out the protective impulses of some men.

But her life revolved around Rebecca now and she was fine with that. The divorce had steeled her resolve; she needed to make sure Rebecca's environment remained stable. It was more of a priority than her own loneliness.

Laura crouched down to organize the bottom shelf, leaning in and reaching to the back to retrieve outdated boxes of cereal, pulling them to the front. She took a large stack of current ones and placed them on the shelf above, in order to pull the older ones out.

The manager, Ted, a shrimp of a man who made up for it by shouting when he spoke, passed behind her, making sure to admire her shapely rear end.

"The sugary cereals go on the bottom shelves Laura. So the kids can see it? Beg their mothers to buy it?"

"What do you think I'm doing?" Laura looked up — the handsome man had left. As Ted reached the end of her aisle, she flipped him the middle finger.

"Eyes in the back of my head!" Laura knew he hadn't seen what she did, he just knew everyone hated him and assumed it. She pulled boxes off the shelf and turned their labels to face front, pushing the newer, fresher dates to the back.

"Laura?"

Laura crawled back out from under the shelf and looked up again, this time at Amy, a cashier with braces and her hair in a bun. Amy liked to time her 15 minute breaks to coincide with Laura's, so she could bum cigarettes.

"There's a phone call for you."

"For me?" Laura sounded nervous.

"Yeah, from the hospital."

CHAPTER 28

"I'm looking for Rebecca Lowell, she was admitted here?" Jack said. He drummed his fingers impatiently as the admitting clerk looked up Rebecca's name on her computer.

"Pediatric wing, 4th floor," the woman said. Jack pushed off the counter towards the elevator. He tapped the up button relentlessly until the door opened.

He entered the pediatric wing, spotting Laura at the other end, pacing. She seemed deep in thought, biting her nails, still wearing her Super Saver apron. Jack knew that slow despondent creep across the floor. It reminded him of that day. The worst day.

He slowed his pace, not wanting to add additional stress. Were they more acquainted, he'd have opened his arms to offer a consoling hug. Instead he put his hands in his pockets and attempted to look as non-confrontational as possible. He called out to her:

"Ms. Lowell?"

Laura furrowed her brow. "What are you…?" she trailed off.

"I tried to find you at your job, they told me you were here."

"Why? What's going on?"

Jack looked into the room where Rebecca was sleeping, a nurse was adjusting her IV.

"I was just about to ask you."

Laura's shoulders drooped, she exhaled exasperation.

"She got into a fight. Bunch of God damn animals."

"Is she okay?"

"I don't know. When I find out who it was, they're gonna be missing a few teeth."

Jack looked at his shoes, searching for a way to somehow segue into his *other* question. He didn't want to corner her, make her feel ambushed, but time was short.

"Ms. Lowell, we found a body — a girl, down by the Twin Rivers."

Laura covered her mouth. "I'm sorry. Is it-"

"No." He rubbed his chin, unsure how to proceed. "The location we found the body... the circumstances, they match Rebecca's account."

"Account? What account? I don't understand."

"Neither do I."

Laura shook her head irritably. "Look, I told you, there's no way Rebecca could know anything about any of this."

"I agree," Jack said. Laura's head jerked up. "The girl we found... was murdered about 10 years ago. The victim's name was Carmen Muniz." Laura's face went pale. She turned and looked in at Rebecca, asleep, helpless.

"Carmen..." Laura cupped her nose and mouth, absorbing it.

"She was 19. I visited her mother's home this afternoon. I saw a picture. You knew her, didn't you?"

Laura nodded, still stunned.

"So, you can understand, I have a few questions I need to ask."

Laura kept nodding, not taking her eyes off Rebecca.

"Ms. Lowell, I think all of these murders are connected, which means this guy has been killing for a lot longer than anyone suspected. Whatever you know about Carmen — her disappearance — I need to know."

"I don't know anything about it. We lost touch. I-"

"Then how does your daughter know so much? You see my dilemma." Laura took a few steps, putting distance between them. "Look, this guy is still out there, another girl is missing. If you know something, if you're protecting someone?"

Laura looked at Jack like he had grown two heads.

"Mrs. Lowell?" a third voice interrupted the standoff.

Laura turned to see the doctor who'd calmed her down earlier, when she burst into the room in hysterics upon seeing Rebecca all wired up.

"Yes?" Laura said, her priorities shifting, tuning Jack out.

"I'm Doctor Harris, we spoke earlier."

"Is she okay?"

Jack took a courteous step backwards.

"She's doing fine. She had a seizure. Has she suffered any before?"

"Yes, several."

"For how long?"

"Just the last few months really."

"Is she on any medication for them?"

"...No," Laura said, guilty.

"Well, I'd like to keep her here a little longer, for observation. Run a few tests, try to get a more definitive answer for what's causing them."

"Can I see her?" Laura asked. Doctor Harris acknowledged Jack with a look, then turned back to Laura.

"*You* can." The doctor walked Laura into the room. Jack watched from the doorway.

Rebecca tossed and turned, mumbling in her sleep. A nurse stood at her bedside, monitoring her vitals. Tears dripped down Laura's cheeks as she gently grasped Rebecca's small fingers.

Everyone listened closely as Rebecca's words grew clearer, more pronounced. Laura couldn't make any sense of it, but recognized some of the words. She'd heard them before. Jack watched intently.

A Hispanic orderly entered the room, wheeling a very large garbage can on a cart. He retrieved a small trash container from inside the bathroom and dumped its contents. He replaced the plastic bag and set it down beside the toilet.

"What's she saying?" Laura asked.

Doctor Harris shook his head, unsure. "I don't know."

The orderly turned his cart towards the door. "She's praying." All eyes turned to him, then back to Rebecca.

"Praying?" Laura asked, her face a question mark. Jack didn't speak Spanish, but understood a few words. As they listened, Rebecca's speech grew more audible and clear:

"Santa Maria, Madre de Dios, ruega por nosotros, pecadores, ahora y en la hora de nuestra muerte. Amen." Rebecca repeated the phrase over and over, louder and louder. Laura watched with wide eyes.

Jack quickly withdrew his notepad and started jotting down what she was saying. He wrote the same sentence twice before he recognized she was repeating herself.

"Does your daughter speak Spanish?" Jack asked.

"No." Laura said quickly. Doctor Harris listened, confounded by what was taking place.

"What about your ex-husband?" Jack asked.

"He can barely speak English, much less a second language."

The doctor leaned over Rebecca, taking her pulse, holding her head to see if she was feverish. He whispered something to the nurse, who drew the curtain around Rebecca and Laura with one quick swipe, cutting Jack off.

CHAPTER 29

Jack stormed into Leonard's office, the secretary following right behind him.

"I'm sorry Doctor Hellerman, he wouldn't-" Leonard held up his hand.

"It's okay, Mary." Leonard had been expecting Jack. He waved her away and she closed the door. Jack stood across from his desk, rain dripping off his jacket.

"Something very strange is going on here," Jack said, his gaze intense, the same he used on suspects during interrogations. Leonard had to avert his eyes. He spun his chair 45 degrees and looked towards the window at the falling rain.

"I risked my practice by confiding in you, Jack. I was trying to help you." Jack saw the morning paper on Leonard's desk, he picked it up. On the front page was an article about Carmen. The headline read: *Body of girl missing 10 years found.* Underneath the headline was a picture of Carmen, the same graduation photo Jack held in Carmen's bedroom.

"There's something you're not telling me."

"There's a lot I haven't told you."

"I'm listening."

Leonard turned and finally looked at Jack. "I've already said more than I should have."

"We're not leaving this room until you-"

"You told the mother. You didn't mention the tapes, did you? I never even let *her* listen to them."

"No, but she's not stupid. How else could I have gotten Rebecca's account of the murder? You were right, her descriptions were vivid."

"A credible recollection, not a vivid imagination."

"It's not possible... How?"

"You mean, how could a nine year old girl describe a murder that took place... before she was even born?"

Jack slapped his palms flat on Leonard's desk and leaned in. "The river, the train, that tree — it's just as she described, not another like it in the whole damn world. How could she have known? Where'd she get it from? Even the method of death." Leonard remained calm.

"You heard the tapes; that wasn't her imagination re-creating something she overheard. She was there."

"That doesn't make any sense!"

"They've positively identified her body?"

Jack nodded. "We couldn't release it otherwise."

"And you've visited the family."

"What's going on here, Leonard?"

Leonard sat back and drew a deep breath. The office intercom buzzed: "*Doctor, you have a call on 1, Mrs. Burke has a question about her son's prescription?*" Leonard ignored the page.

"I've exposed my practice too much already."

"You called me. I could cite you with obstruction."

"But you won't."

"Why?"

"Because you want to know just as much as I do."

Jack studied Leonard a moment. He took a seat, not breaking eye contact. The two stared at each other a long while.

"I saw something yesterday I can't explain," Jack said. "No one could."

"*Doctor? Mrs. Burke's on 1, should I tell her to call back?*"

Leonard jabbed at the button on his intercom. "Mary, clear my afternoon."

Leonard walked Jack into a room lined with file cabinets and thick, expensive mahogany bookshelves that looked like they'd been passed down for generations. The room was a complete mess, as if ransacked by thieves. Books, papers, entire drawers removed, notes hastily scribbled down and scattered about, nothing in its place. *Well, Leonard, we have one thing in common.*

Jack stared out a grimy window that hadn't been washed in years. It was lunchtime. The rain had scaled back to a soft drizzle. People were racing around, going about their daily routines. *Inside here, madness...*

Leonard swiped a stack of folders off a chair. "Here, sit." He closed the large door and grabbed another chair, pushing it up to a table stacked with books and notes. Several times he opened his mouth to speak, then hesitated, unsure of where to begin.

"I haven't got all day," Jack said.

Leonard rubbed his hands together. "At first I was convinced I was looking at a clear cut case of some sort of abuse, physical — mental. I noticed she had these marks on her neck — the mother said they were birthmarks. I was suspicious."

Jack listened quietly, intently, desperate for Leonard to get to the damn point. But something about the drama in Leonard's delivery forced him to hang on every word.

"No matter what I tried, I just couldn't get Rebecca to open up. I suggested regression therapy to the mother. She agreed."

Leonard got up and went to the window. It was open a crack and he pressed it down, shutting out the street noise, quieting the room.

"The sessions began normally. But as I regressed her further backwards, she became very distressed. I knew I was getting somewhere. Then...something happened. Something that altered my entire belief system, not just as a doctor, as a human being."

"Get to the point."

"Do you believe that the complexity of our bodies, our world... our universe, is too great to be just mere coincidence?"

"Never thought about it." *Liar.*

"You a religious man?"

"Stop dancing around the subject."

"Well, I'm Jewish; my faith doesn't allow for the possibility of transmigration of the soul. So you can imagine my dismay when this nine year old girl began to recount, in wrenching detail, how she was brutally attacked and viciously raped. She went so far as to describe the pain of having her windpipe crushed, blood rushing out her nose and ears. You can see why I hesitated about telling the mother?"

"There has to be a logical explanation."

Leonard walked over and opened a file cabinet. "There are two explanations. One is the possibility of transmigration, where the soul exits one body after death and enters another."

"You're talking about reincarnation?"

"Yes," Leonard replied, locking eyes with Jack to make sure he knew he meant it. "The other is demonic possession. However, I gravely doubt that a demon would supply a young child with intimate knowledge of the problems a Dominican immigrant faces in a predominantly white American high school. Or fond memories of another loving family and mother. The evidence of xenoglossy alone was convincing enough."

"Xenoglossy?" Jack asked. Leonard grabbed a folder from the cabinet and closed it.

"Fluently speaking a language you've never heard before." Jack sat back, Rebecca's episode at the hospital repeating in his memory. "To my knowledge, no one in her immediate family speaks Spanish, yet I had to translate almost half our session."

"It's just not possible," Jack said, but he couldn't deny that as incredible as it sounded, there was no rational explanation for how Rebecca knew what she knew. He had no choice but to remain open-minded for the moment.

Leonard returned to the table, placed the folder down, and began rifling through it.

"She even went so far as to recall her fear of dying *unclean* for God. I'm sure I don't have to elaborate. Does that sound like the imagination of a nine year old to you?"

Leonard removed a report from the folder. "The attention to

detail and the forensic pathology with which she described her experience of death virtually eliminated any possibility of an overactive imagination. But I still wasn't convinced."

Leonard placed a printout on the table. "I looked into the identity of this girl Carmen she described. I found her listing under missing persons." Jack looked closely, it was a copy of Carmen's report.

"I've seen it."

"I knew if somehow her body was found, it would prove beyond a doubt that what Rebecca was telling me was real."

"So you called me. I find the body, give your research credibility. Unbiased validation?" Jack's tone turned Leonard around.

"Do you have any idea how important this is? If I can prove it irrefutably, it could rewrite Judeo-Christian dogma as we know it!"

"You're crazy."

"Of course I am."

"Why didn't you just tell me the whole story from the beginning?"

"I thought it would be better for you to experience it firsthand. Only then could we sit and discuss it like rational human beings. Clearly, it's had the same effect on you as it did me."

"You knew this had nothing to do with my case, didn't you?"

"If it has nothing to do with your case, why then are you backtracking your investigation as if these crimes are related?"

Jack folded his arms. It was obvious he'd been used. But what difference did it make? Leonard was right, he *was* just as interested. Maybe more. There had been a murder, just like Leonard said. One mystery was solved, with a new one introduced. Leonard was also right not to tell him beforehand. He would never have even listened to the tape. Jack wanted to believe that Rebecca's story - Leonard's interpretation — could be real. But complex twists were for TV drama. The real world was ugly and sad, and rarely extraordinary.

"In the following weeks I did some research. Doctors who'd risked their practice to publish articles on their experiences, ones I would have normally dismissed. Now they had a profound resonance. I discovered that an overwhelming majority of these children recalled suffering through a painful, untimely death. Usually very violent and traumatic. There's nothing more traumatic than murder."

"What does it prove?"

"Do you remember your dreams?"

Jack shook his head, "Not really."

"But I'm sure in your line of work, you've awoken on several occasions from a terrible nightmare."

Jack nodded. Leonard removed his glasses and rubbed the sides of his nose. "Most of us pass away having lived out our dull, normal, boring lives; lives many of us might want to forget. But should you be taken before your time, perhaps stabbed and strangled as you repeatedly begged for your life, that might be too painful to ever forget. We lose most of our childhood memories, but we retain the painful ones in intricate detail. Many of my adult patients come to me because they're plagued by traumatic events from their adolescence. Most of us have difficulty living with just the problems of this life."

Jack looked at Leonard a long time. "You really believe all this?"

"It took a while to discard my scientific ideals, but after your discovery by the river, how can I dispute it?"

Leonard unwrapped the file he took from the cabinet. "I've always been fascinated by stories of how some children come out of the womb with the uncanny ability to speak and read before they can walk. Or to draw and paint— " he removed Rebecca's sketch pad and tossed it across the table to Jack, "with the skills it takes many artists a lifetime to acquire."

"Something in the brain chemistry," Jack said, feeling as if he was defending rationality itself. He picked up the book and flipped through Rebecca's work. His eyes widened, each sketch was more brilliant than the last. His resistance was wearing thin. "She drew these?" Leonard waved his hand, *that's nothing.*

"1962, in Glasgow, a five year old child was placed in front of his aunt's piano for the first time at a party. The child proceeded to belt out excerpts from Beethoven's Appassionata. Neither of the parent's came from any musical background, they didn't even own a piano. A noted physician who attended the party documented the case. There are hundreds of these on file."

Jack flipped to a charcoal rendering of Laura. Her face was neither happy nor sad. The detail was extraordinary, he couldn't turn the page, transfixed. He examined each hand drawn line.

"Most of the children documented seem to lose the ability to recall these memories after age six. Coincidence that this age coincides with the onset of the childhood latency period? I now believe this regression is the stage where old and new merge, and the soul accepts its new identity. But in extreme cases, perhaps involving murder, violence — it scars the soul. It doesn't recede. In Rebecca's case, her episodes were triggered when she arrived in Monroe County. New to her — grievously unforgettable to Carmen."

"What about these people who get hit in the head and suddenly remember what the weather was like every day of the year for the last 20 years, or can suddenly memorize entire volumes of encyclopedias?"

"Photographic memorization is far different from being able to recall something you've never been exposed to."

"If it was her own death she was describing, why was Rebecca talking in the third person?"

"She was recalling the moment of detachment from the physical state. Looking down at her own body, unable at that point to make the distinction of self, since we had yet to make that connection. She didn't *know* it was her own body."

Jack stared at the floor. Leonard waited for his reaction, expecting him to roll his eyes. But Jack was stoic, sincere. Leonard seemed relieved; Jack was the first person he'd confided his theories in and he had fully expected ridicule. Instead, Jack was curiously intrigued, even if skeptical. At least he was still in the room. Still listening.

Jack finally looked up. "The tape you gave me of Rebecca. It seemed like parts were missing."

"They're not missing..." Leonard returned to the file cabinet and retrieved his cassette recorder.

CHAPTER 30

Jack watched from the window as Leonard's secretary exited the building. Leonard had given her the rest of the day off.

Leonard sat at the table, a tape playing. It was a different session and much more intense than the previous one Jack had heard. Some of the material was tough to listen to. Rebecca recited very adult situations through her tiny young voice. Sexually violent, horrific situations.

Rebecca's fragile voice cracked on the recording: "*I can't! I can't,*" she repeated, sounding so helpless, "*Please!*"

"*Rebecca, detach yourself!*" Leonard's voice was clear on the tape, in control. "*He can't hurt you!*"

"*No! Oh God!*" Rebecca shrieked as if being defiled, violated. She began to choke. Her suffering, even if just recollections brought to the surface with dexterity by a doctor's skilled coercing, was excruciating to bear witness to. Jack winced with every scream. The experience was real and heartbreaking.

"*You're safe, Rebecca. They're just images!*" Leonard's voice assured, "*I want you to move away from here. Go back, before this happened. How did you get here?*"

The tape fell silent for a moment. Then Rebecca's voice reappeared, but different, deeper, not her own. "*Mi madre y yo tuvieron una pelea.*" Jack recognized the deeper tone of her voice from the hospital. He watched Leonard quickly sift through his notes. He found the right page and began translating for Jack:

"…My mother and I had a fight."

"*Ella piensa que soy no más larga una virgen. Pero no es verdad. Estoy limpio. Es una fantasia que compuse.*"

"She thinks I'm no longer a virgin, but it's not true. I'm clean. It was a fantasy I made up.*"*

"*Pienso que mi hermano lee mi diario.*"

"I think my brother read my diary."

"*Me escondí debajo de mi tocador.*"

"I hid it under my dresser."

The tape went silent again. Only Leonard's voice, "*Rebecca? Rebecca? Can you hear me? Rebecca?*"

"*It's raining,*" Rebecca said, "*I don't want to go home. I'm scared.*"

There was another long silence. Jack looked at Leonard, wondering if that was all there was. Leonard shook his head, there was more:

"*Rebecca? Rebecca?*"

"*Trusted him…*"

"*Who, Rebecca? Who did you trust?*"

"*Lied to me.*"

"*Who?*"

Rebecca's started to choke on the tape. "*Oh, God, please… No!*"

"*Who is trying to hurt you?*"

"*Catch her. Catch her! No! Stop!*"

Jack clenched his teeth as Rebecca's sobs grew so loud the sound on the tape started to distort.

"*Rebecca, breathe! Breathe!*" Rebecca started to calm down, her breathing slowed. "*That's it, breathe, deep breaths, good girl. Float past this. What do you see?*"

"*It's dark. My hands are tied. Legs hurt. My hair is wet. Blood…my blood. Can't move. Can't move!*" Rebecca grew hysterical again.

"Enough, shut it off," Jack said.

"Not yet, it's important. You must listen," Leonard raised the volume on the player.

"*Try, Rebecca, what is this place?*" Rebecca sobbed, her emotion palpable.

"*There's a light,*" she said sniffling, "*a window.*"

"*Can you see out the window?*" A brief silence.

"*I see a road.*"

"*What else?*"

"*It's getting dark. Church bells,*" she said, her voice now soft as a whisper. Jack made mental notes of every word, every detail.

"*Where are you? Can you see a location?*" There was another brief silence. Again Rebecca's voice was replaced by a lower, more raspy sounding one.

"*Bendito es el fruto de tu vientre, Jesús. Santa María, Madre de Dios, ruega por nosotros pecadores, ahora y en la hora de nuestra muerte. Amén.*"

Leonard put his glasses back on and scanned his notes, "...Holy Mary, Mother of God, pray for us sinners now...and at the hour of our death."

"*The fruits of our labors...find Jesus on the hill,*" Rebecca said in English, her voice groggy, hoarse.

"*Rebecca? ...Rebecca?*" Leonard stopped the tape.

"She just kept rambling prayers after that."

"What does it mean?" Jack asked.

"You're the detective."

"She never gives a name? Something specific?"

"In one of our sessions, she only responded to the name Carmen. She never names her attacker. But I believe she knew him."

Jack's legs had stiffened from sitting too long. He placed his hands on the armrests of the chair and pushed himself up. He took a few steps, deep in thought. Outside the window, the sun had set, the street lights were starting to turn on.

"Doesn't amount to much more than chance," Jack said finally.

"No. That's too dismissive."

"A bizarre coincidence."

"There are no coincidences," Leonard said firmly, a little frustrated.

"The mother, Laura, she knew the victim. They were friends."

"Some believe there's a synchronicity between birth and death, life and loved ones, remaining within the same circle, changing roles, learning, growing. Who are we to know these things?"

Jack turned to Leonard, "Why burden a little girl?"

"Perhaps Rebecca is God's way of rectifying an oversight."

Jack wondered, *would God ever rectify the oversight on him?* He wasn't so narrow-minded as to think his life — and life as a whole — was some cosmic mistake, a random event. He honestly felt there was a plan. He just felt slighted, out of the loop about what that plan was. Jack took full responsibility for his lot in life, but some things were out of his control, and it was *those* events, the ones that were left up to the fates, that always seemed to land penny-head down. He could have used a little help then.

But what about innocence? If we're all part of a bigger picture, then why allow harm to a child like Rebecca? Maybe it was a second chance to right a wrong? For Rebecca's everlasting soul to find justice. *Could it be possible?* If she was working through emotional baggage that spanned lifetimes, then she had been given a second opportunity to understand it, learn from it, even grow. If so, then maybe there was a chance for Jack too. To learn from this life. Jack was intrigued, not just for justice — unprecedented, supernatural justice — but for all the other aspects the concept opened up. He started to feel something he hadn't felt in a long time.

Hope.

"So what now?" Jack asked.

"If it is the same killer as the evidence suggests, then you have to dig deeper. Find Carmen's killer, you'll find Angelina."

Jack turned from the window and moved to the table. He popped the tape from its player. Leonard didn't protest. He grabbed Rebecca's sketchbook. "I'm taking this too." Leonard pushed his chair out.

"Jack, if word of our discussion, the nature of it, were to get out, it could... my practice would be-"

"Don't worry. I have no intention of humiliating you. Or myself."

CHAPTER 31

Laura held the tea bag between her finger and the spoon, squeezed the last ounce of flavor out, and tossed it into the waste basket.

She stood in the middle of the kitchen and pulled her white robe about her, thoughts of a hot bath in her future. She leaned against the edge of the countertop and took a sip of her tea, savoring it. She felt a pinch in her shoulders and shrugged, trying to release the tension a little.

Atop the refrigerator sat a bottle of rum. She jokingly considered spicing her tea with a little spirits to take the edge off. Jokingly, because Laura didn't drink alcohol. Ever. It was how some people dealt with problems. How her father had dealt with them. It wasn't how she was going to deal with them.

The rum wasn't hers. Like many other remnants left behind after her father passed away, she hadn't gotten around to clearing it out. Yet, she did consider it for a moment. It was a sign of how dark things were getting. How desperate.

After they'd returned home from the hospital, Rebecca spent the majority of her time up in her room, painting. She burned through all of her supplies — twice, sending Laura running back and forth to the art supply store.

Rebecca's artwork seemed unusually abstract lately. Random splashes of color, with no thoughtful structure or purpose. It was odd, since her work was normally so intricately detailed. But the last few days, she just dipped and waved at the canvas.

Laura thought maybe it represented the confusion in her head, putting on paper what she couldn't verbalize. Random thoughts and emotions that made no sense, the canvas some kind of cathartic outlet.

The screams were still keeping her awake. Laura knew something had to give soon, her nerves were redlining.

Laura entered the living room, sat on the couch, and turned on the TV. Another news report; Carmen's murder was being discussed in detail. They showed a smiling picture of Carmen, her high school photo, then ran images of her body's discovery, the ongoing police investigation. Laura sniffed and swallowed audibly. She dabbed at a tear, not realizing Rebecca had entered the room. She fumbled for the remote, zapping it off.

"What was the name of the girl they were talking about?" Rebecca asked. From the look on her face, Laura could tell she'd heard it, she was just looking for confirmation.

"I didn't hear," Laura said, getting up to move to the kitchen. She picked up a dish in the sink and began rinsing it. Rebecca followed her.

"Did you know her?"

"Who?"

"The girl? The one on TV?"

"...No."

"Then why were you crying?"

Laura poured dishwashing liquid onto a sponge, nearly scrubbing a hole in the already clean plate. "I wasn't crying. My eyes itch. It's the dust in this old house. I have to get to that."

Rebecca opened the freezer and nearly climbed in to grab the tub of ice cream, dropping back down on the linoleum floor with a loud thud.

"You didn't finish your dinner."

"Yes I did."

"You just pushed it around your plate." Rebecca scooped some chocolate into a bowl. "You can scoop that right back in the tub, it's too late for ice cream. I'll warm some milk for you instead."

Rebecca sneered and turned up her nose at the mention of it. She took a clean glass, still dripping from Laura's hard work, and leaned over the sink, brushing Laura aside. She filled it with tap water and headed for the staircase.

"If you want water, sweetie, there's cold water in the fridge."

"It's to clean my brushes."

"Then you could have taken a dirty glass."

Rebecca disappeared upstairs. Laura stopped washing the dish. Under normal circumstances, she'd say it's too late to be up painting; it was time for bed. But she didn't remember what normal was anymore. And she was appreciating the silence. *Long may it last.* She heard Rebecca's door close. She put her head down and sighed.

Laura went to the den and stood amongst a few boxes that were still waiting to be unpacked from the move. She reached into one and upended the contents, sifting for something. She pulled out a small spiral bound address book. She opened it.

Inside under M was an old entry for Carmen Muniz, with a phone number. Her name was circled with a heart. Laura turned a few pages and a worn, yellowed photograph slipped out. She held it up; it was a picture of her and Carmen, snapped by a friend at Lakeview Park after a ride on the roller coaster. They were both shouting something, she'd always loved the candid smiles on their faces.

She stared at her 15 year old self, her hair so much longer and blonde then, Carmen's hair so dark next to hers. They were like contrasting pieces on an Othello board. She was reminded of an odd moment while giving Rebecca a bath, back when she was about two years old. She was toweling her off when Rebecca commented how she preferred her with long hair, asking why she cut it short. But Laura had cut it short a few years before Rebecca was born. Rebecca never knew her with long hair. Laura figured she must have seen pictures of her. She never really tried to rationalize what she'd said, she just remembered it being weird at the time.

Laura smiled at the picture. Fond memories, stored for safe keeping years ago, floated to the surface. Her eyes welled up. She didn't realize how hard she was gripping the photo until the edges started to curl inward from the pressure. She placed it back in the book and opened her mouth to breathe again, emotional. She tucked the book back into the box and folded the top over.

Each step creaked as she climbed the staircase. The old house had a real personality, especially at night. Every floorboard made a sound, every door had its own unique whine. Rebecca's was especially loud.
Laura opened it as slowly as she could to mute the sound. Rebecca had climbed into bed herself. Peacefully asleep, she seemed so alone. A wave of guilt washed over Laura, she felt useless.
"Sleep, baby. Just, please sleep," Laura whispered.

Laura crept back into the living room and lay down on the couch. She checked the clock on the wall, 9 P.M. She closed her eyes.
The house was silent. Laura's thoughts drifted to work, doctor bills, all the things she was putting off. She could hear the wind wheezing through a small crack in the sill. It breathed a lonely song. She, too, felt lonely. She tried to block it out of her mind — *how selfish* — with the way Rebecca was suffering. The emptiness of her situation was like pangs of hunger with no food to satisfy it. No other adult to talk to, confide in. No one to unload her problems to at the end of the day. No strong shoulder to lean on, gentle hand to caress her cheek and tell her it was going to be alright. No one to share her burden.
She drifted in and out. Thoughts became moving images, dreams. She entered a rare, peaceful sleep.

Something itched at the tip of her nose, she scratched it and suppressed a sneeze. She looked over at the clock on the wall. 1 A.M.
4 hours?

It felt like she had only closed her eyes for a moment. She snapped up off the couch and went to the kitchen to check the clock above the sink.

1 A.M. She rubbed her eyes. "Shit..."

Her thoughts immediately went to Rebecca. It was the longest she'd gone without waking the dead with her blood curdling shrieks. Laura headed for the stairs quickly.

As she opened the door to Rebecca's bedroom, Laura had to silence a gasp. Rebecca was wide awake—sitting up in bed, her eyes big and dark, her stare almost catatonic. The sight gave Laura a shudder.

Rebecca's vacant eyes slowly turned, finding Laura in the doorway. Her glare made every hair on the back of Laura's neck stand up straight.

They stared at each other a few moments. Rebecca didn't blink, no expression at all, like some animatronic doll with no soul.

"...Becca?" Laura said, as if asking permission to speak to her daughter in there, half expecting some demon to answer.

Rebecca slowly raised her hand towards her chest, gently feeling around her throat. "I can't find my necklace," Rebecca said, soft and monotone.

Laura stood frozen in the doorway. She swallowed. "...What necklace, baby?" Rebecca didn't answer. "Becca? What necklace?"

Rebecca's eyes were open, but she wasn't present in the room. Her spirit was somewhere else — speaking to someone else. The fact she was currently staring at Laura was mere happenstance.

Laura sprinted down the hall to the bathroom. She threw open the medicine cabinet and grabbed the bottle of pills Doctor Hellerman had prescribed, the ones that were supposed to help Rebecca sleep — the ones she'd stopped giving her. *They never worked before, what makes you think they'll work now?*

Laura desperately shook two into her trembling hand and filled a Dixie cup with water. She caught a brief glimpse of the black circles under her eyes in the mirrored cabinet. She closed it, afraid Rebecca's ghostly image might be standing behind her waiting to shout *boo!*

She raced back down the hall and re-entered Rebecca's bedroom. Rebecca was now on her back, sound asleep. Eyes closed this time.

Laura crept towards her. She slowly extended her hand to pull Rebecca's blankets up, half expecting her eyes to suddenly *pop open* like at the end of some B horror movie. But they didn't. Laura ran her fingers gently through Rebecca's wavy hair.

She watched her a moment, then gazed around the room at her artwork. The paintings took on a slightly different appearance in the dim glow of the night. Rebecca's easel was off to the side, turned away. *What's she trying to hide?*

Laura inched towards it and snuck a peek.

The picture of the tree had been replaced with a portrait. In the soft light, Laura couldn't quite make it out. She turned it silently towards the window to better see in the moonlight. It was a pixel perfect replica of Carmen.

Laura covered her mouth. She looked down at her feet and noticed she was standing on top of yesterday's newspaper. Rebecca had spread it around to prevent ink from damaging the floor. Carmen's picture was visible on the front page. The headline read: *Missing girl's body found after ten years*.

The portrait seemed so lifelike that Carmen's voice — her memory of it, came rushing back. Laura looked at Rebecca, still asleep. She quietly picked the newspaper off the floor and walked out of the room, closing the door behind her gently.

Laura returned downstairs and entered the kitchen. She flipped open the wastebasket lid, crumpled the newspaper and tossed it in - right on top of Jack's card, the name slightly blotted out from her recently discarded tea bag. She reached in and retrieved the card, wiping away the smudged brown tea stain with her finger. Jack's number was still legible.

CHAPTER 32

Jack took two pills and was going to return the bottle to its hiding place behind the book, but the pain was especially bad today, so he tucked them into his front pocket.

He sat forward at his desk and picked up his pen, placing it firmly between his teeth, before pressing play on the tape machine. Leonard's voice cued up.

"Rebecca?"

"It's getting dark," Rebecca said in her deep other voice, *"Church bells. I hear church bells."*

"Where are you?" Leonard asked. There was a brief silence, the tape player's motor buzzed and squeaked.

"Santa Maria, Madre de Dios, ruega por nosotros pecadores, ahora y en la hora de nuestra muerte. Amén. The fruits of our labors… find Jesus on the hill… find Jesus…"

Jack pressed rewind. He listened to that passage again. The first part sounded like a prayer, but the other part felt more like a warning. It was vexing him. He replayed it over and over.

"Ahora y en la hora de nuestra muerte. Amén. The fruits of our labors… find Jesus on the hill… find Jesus." Rewind. *"Find Jesus…"* Repeat. *"Find Jesus."*

It almost sounded to Jack like she'd reverted to Rebecca. She wasn't reciting prayer, she was observing something in the moment. To his ears anyway. He was about to press play again when the phone rang. He'd been playing the tape very low — keeping his word to Leonard. The interruption of the quiet made the phone's ringer seem terribly loud.

"Hello?"

"Detective Ridge?"

"Laura. How are you?"

"Not so good."

"What is it?"

"You still want to talk?"

"Very much," Jack said, sitting up straight. He hadn't noticed that his office door had crept open. Someone stood behind him waiting patiently for his conversation to finish.

"I'm home, can you come here?" Laura asked.

Jack checked his watch. "It's about 6 o'clock, I can be there in an hour?"

"That's fine."

"Okay. Thank you, Laura." He hung up and leaned back in his chair, chewing his pen as he began to formulate all of his questions in his head; there were so many.

"Heard you were dead."

Jack spun around in his chair, startled. Robert stood before him. He was neatly dressed, with a long tan coat and a white dress shirt. He resembled Jack, only younger. Jack's expression turned cold as ice.

"What are you doing here?" Jack said, his jaw clenched.

"You don't return my calls."

"We have nothing to talk about."

"All these years and we have nothing to talk about? At least-"

"Get out," Jack said with a calm that belied his volcano of emotions underneath.

"I just thought you'd like to know… you're going to be an uncle. Trish is pretty far along now. We tried for years. I guess God finally decided we were ready."

Jack stared through him, his gaze like a magnifying glass in the sun, burning a hole into Robert's being. His hatred was palpable, he had to fight to suppress the urge to leap out of his chair and strangle him.

Robert returned no such malevolence towards his brother. He stood silently, itching at a deep old scar above his left eye.

Jack turned his back and started stacking and shuffling papers for no reason.

"We're gonna be relocating to Austin," Robert continued. "Got a good job lined up." Jack took a deep breath, adjusting his collar, straining to retain his composure. "Trish has family there so it works out great." Jack balled his fists and bit down. "You know how it is when people move very far away. You say you're gonna come visit, but...well, I guess with the way things are, you and I might never see each other again."

Robert leaned forward and tossed a small invitational envelope onto Jack's desk.

Jack's eyes found it.

"We're having a little get together, a little celebration. It would really mean a lot to Trish and me if you could make it." Robert wiped at his mouth, waiting for Jack's response. Jack didn't move. He might not have even breathed during the awful silence.

"Jack... there isn't a day goes by I don't feel sorry about what happened."

Jack spun around, venom behind his eyes. "Are you finished? Are you through?" Jack spoke so harshly it set off one of his coughing fits. He hacked three or four times brutally, his eyes bulging, veins surfacing in his neck and forehead. Robert leaned forward to help, but Jack's watery eyes screamed hate — maybe even *death* — if he took another step closer.

Robert instead took a step back in retreat. "Alright." He turned and opened Jack's office door. The din of the station spilled in, breaking the silence, letting in air.

"Hope you change your mind, Jack." Robert exited and closed the door. Jack sat motionless for a few moments. He abruptly turned and slammed his fists down on his desk, scattering neatly stacked papers in all directions.

Jennifer was walking by at precisely that moment and witnessed Jack's tantrum through the glass windows of his office. Jack reached for his jacket and nearly opened the door into her.

"Sorry, Jen."

He hurried past, not allowing her time to ask if he was okay.

A few moments later, Harrington entered Jack's office. "Jack?" He scanned the empty room, gradually making his way over to where Jack hid his pills. A glance over his shoulder, then he moved the book. But the pills were gone.

Harrington turned to leave when he noticed the old tape player on the desk, half buried beneath a mess of paper. Jack had scribbled some notes on a pad next to it.

The Fruits of Our Labors. Find Jesus on the Hill. Church Bells, diary, dresser. Rebecca, Carmen, Santa Maria - Madre de Dios.

Harrington pressed play, Leonard's voice audible:

"I find the evidence before me incontrovertible. More and more my conclusions not only seem plausible, they seem the only logical explanation. There are so many levels of human consciousness that have yet to be explored. The same must be true of the different levels of existence, quantum theories, allowance for the human soul. My belief system has been challenged on every level, but I find my conclusions becoming more and more supportive for accommodating the theory of transmigration of the soul from one incarnation to the next. Perhaps even time is not how we perceive it. Perhaps we are the observer, and our bodies the vessel. Is it any more delusional than the concept of sending files wirelessly through the air from one electronic device to another would be to a man in 1850? We accept that we can transmit documents and information invisibly through space, why then not our essence too? Because we are organic? I think Rebecca might represent the greatest advancement to human evolution. Spiritual evolution-"

Harrington stopped the tape, a queer look on his face. He checked over his shoulder a second time, then sat down and pressed play again.

CHAPTER 33

Laura stood at the back door, watching Rebecca on the same old rusty swing set she used to play on as a little girl. Its antique frame ached loudly with each movement. Jack stood behind her in the kitchen, small pad and pencil in hand.

"He actually said that?" Laura asked.

"He's convinced himself."

"That's why he wouldn't leave us alone. He needs his own head examined."

"I've known Leonard a long time; he's always been a very rational person."

"He had no right discussing my daughter's condition with you."

"He confided in me because he trusts me. He knew I would keep things confidential. He knew about my case and made the connection. He was right."

"But he never ok'd it with me."

"He didn't tell me the whole truth either. Pieced most of it together myself. I had to back him into a corner before he spilled his guts."

"And what do you think?"

Jack took a moment. It was the first time she'd seen him under bright fluorescent lighting. She noticed how gaunt and pale he looked, how brittle. "...I don't know. What I do know is whoever murdered Carmen went to great lengths to make sure she was never found. Without Rebecca, she wouldn't have been. She gave precise details about where the body would be discovered, how Carmen was murdered."

"That's why he involved you? To prove it?" Laura said.

"Yes. But he also knew based on my current investigation that whoever killed Carmen was probably still at large. The information was mutually beneficial."

"You believe it too," Laura said disappointedly.

"I believe the same person that killed Carmen took Angelina Rosa, yes. Based on the killer's M.O., I think there's a remote chance she could still be alive. But there's no time. I need you to tell me everything."

"That's not what I meant."

Jack took a few steps towards her. "Laura, I saw a picture... of you and Carmen. You knew her, you were friends. So either there is something to all of this... or you're not telling me the whole truth."

Jack's sort-of accusation brought about an awkward silence. Laura turned away and looked out at Rebecca again, snapping the cohesion of their conversation. Rebecca had stopped swinging, her legs dangling listlessly. Laura sat down at the kitchen table and sighed.

Jack took her place at the door, watching Rebecca. Rebecca looked up at that very moment, staring back at him as if some psychic connection existed between them. Her dark, sunken eyes seemed to beg pleadingly: *help me, because no one else will.* In that instant there was a unique bonding between the two.

"We were best friends in high school," Laura said finally. Her words activated Jack's hands, he quickly jotted them down on his notepad. "I left home when I got pregnant. Never graduated. I remember, I got the news about Carmen while I was in the hospital. Her mother called, said Carmen had run away, asked if I knew where she might have gone since we were thick as thieves. But after I moved away, I'd lost touch with Carmen. She was very religious, she was upset with me because —*you know...*"

Jack noticed a small framed picture of Laura and Rebecca in autumn, Rebecca dumping leaves on her mother, both smiling. "Have you ever spoken to Rebecca about Carmen?"

"No."

"Maybe she overheard something. Kids can have incredible imaginations. Especially bright ones like her."

"Never."

"You say this all started when you moved back to Monroe?" Laura reached for her cigarettes, then remembered Jack's cough. He had been suffering another spell while standing outside her front door. He'd waited for it to pass before ringing the bell. She pretended not to know he'd been standing there. He was clearly very ill, making a poor attempt to hide it. She placed the cigarettes back, she could wait. If things got too heavy she could use them to chase him out.

"At first, Rebecca seemed to be handling the divorce okay. I thought this place could be a new start for her. For us." Jack was staring at her expectantly. Laura brushed her bangs from her eyes and continued, "This was my father's place. Promised myself I'd never set foot in here again."

Laura rubbed her forehead, she felt a migraine coming on. The door opened, Rebecca walked in. Jack took note of her sullen, exhausted face, even the muscles in her jaw looked tired and limp.

"Hello," she said to Jack.

"Hi, Rebecca."

Rebecca turned to her mother. "Can I have some ice cream?"

"Later." Laura motioned with her head for Rebecca to leave the room, this was adult time. Rebecca took another look at Jack, then gave her mother a devilish smirk. Laura knew what that look insinuated, and hoped that Jack didn't put two and two together. The conversation was already awkward enough.

Rebecca trod upstairs, stomping loudly in protest. Laura listened to the footsteps. She knew if she didn't hear the bedroom door click that meant Rebecca would be at the top of the staircase, eavesdropping.

But the door clicked, satisfying her. She didn't bother to check, so she wasn't aware that Rebecca had actually perched herself along the railing, straining to hear.

"Have you ever observed any behavior like the kind Leonard described?" Jack asked. Laura tilted her head, thinking.

"The other day we took a different road to school. We passed by a small church. Becca asked what had happened to the statue. The one where children would pose for photos after first communions. She was so insistent."

Jack sat down across from her. "I didn't think much of it at the time, but later it occurred to me — it was Carmen's church we passed. Rebecca had such a frightening look on her face, like she was someone else for a moment. But that doesn't prove anything."

"Maybe your coming back here is what set Rebecca off, triggered a memory?"

"Rebecca has nightmares. She's upset."

"Yes, but-"

"Look, there's nothing you can say to make me believe she witnessed Carmen's murder. Or was Carmen. Or whatever that lunatic told you."

"Then how do you explain what happened at the hospital?"

Laura's eyes opened wide. "You *do* believe it."

Jack leaned back. He placed his notepad and pencil on the table. "My job gives me plenty of reasons to assume life has no meaning. So I'd be lying if I said I wasn't intrigued." Laura shook her head defiantly. "Laura, *you* called *me*, remember?"

Laura bit her bottom lip. She wanted so desperately to unload everything on someone. It had been so long since she'd had a normal, adult conversation. She'd experienced enough negativity in human beings to be able to recognize when someone was genuine. And something about Jack felt real and true. She couldn't ever remember a time when her ex-husband sat across from her and truly listened. Had they shared even one night of coherent discussion, they might still be together.

"Why'd you call me?" Jack asked.

"Last night, I went in to check on her. She looked at me as if I was a stranger. My own daughter. I got scared."

"I think whatever power granted Rebecca this window into the past did it for a reason."

"It has to stop. I can't go on like this." Laura hung her head. Jack studied her, trying to envision what Laura was like during happier times. He felt for her.

"Maybe there's a way we can help each other."

"How?"

"The type of criminal I'm hunting often has a pattern to the way he operates. Comfort zones, familiar places, the type of victim he chooses. Every other girl was unceremoniously dumped in plain view. But Carmen was different. He buried her body. He was more careful. I think he knew her. Maybe she was his first. Like I said, without Rebecca we'd have never-"

"If you think I'm going to let that doctor-"

"No. No, I just want you to take a ride with me. I want to bring her somewhere, see if something happens. Maybe jar more memories like the church."

"What good will that do? She doesn't understand what's happening to her. How can she help you?"

"All I know is I've made more progress with this case in the three days since I've met her than I have in the last three months. Maybe she knows more than she realizes, it just needs something to…stimulate it to the surface."

"She's been through so much already."

"Maybe facing this problem is what she needs." Laura rubbed her eyes, then clasped her hands around her nose and mouth, resting her elbows on the table.

"Think it could help?"

"I think there's a voice inside her crying out. She's suffering. If she can help solve this case, if her ordeal can help save another life, it will all mean something. Maybe we can right a few wrongs."

She looked Jack straight in the eye. "I just want my daughter back. She's all I have left, I don't want to lose her too."

"Then you'll bring her?"

Laura drew a deep breath. She looked up towards the staircase behind her, then back at Jack with uncertainty. "I don't know. I'll think about it."

Just then a loud crash jolted them upright. Laura leapt from her chair and ran out of the kitchen. Jack followed.

Laura raced up the staircase so quickly she'd scaled it before Jack could even reach the bottom step. "Rebecca?" she cried out.

Laura burst into Rebecca's room, but she wasn't inside. "Rebecca?" She listened for an answer. She heard water running and moved quickly towards the bathroom, passing Jack on the staircase.

"Is she okay?" Jack asked the blur racing past him.

Laura opened the bathroom door. The shower was running, steam filling the room. The mirror was shattered, shards of broken glass littered the sink and floor. The striped blue plastic shower curtain was drawn.

"Rebecca!" Laura threw back the curtain, taking a few rings off the rail with it.

Rebecca was curled up in the corner of the tub, half naked. There was blood mixing with the water. Laura traced the bleeding up to Rebecca's hand.

"What did you do?" Laura cried.

Jack stood in the doorway. "Can I help?"

Laura held Rebecca's bleeding hand under the water. "Why did you break the mirror?"

"I don't want to go to any more doctors."

"Come on, stand up." Laura helped Rebecca stand. She reached over and turned off the water, then grabbed a hanging towel and briskly dried off her trembling daughter.

"I'm not crazy," Rebecca said, as Laura wrapped one towel around her body, then grabbed a smaller one to wrap around her bleeding hand.

"No one said you were crazy." Laura pressed the makeshift bandage tightly. "It's not that bad, hold still. What were you thinking?"

"I heard you talking," Rebecca said, looking past Laura at Jack standing in the doorway, watching them through the steam.

Laura looked over her shoulder at Jack, then turned to Rebecca. "No, that's not what we were talking about."

"I don't want to go to any more doctors," Rebecca spoke softly, but defiantly.

"Detective Ridge was just asking for our help."

Rebecca pulled her hand away. The look on her changed, a darkness suddenly consumed her.

"No one helped me," Rebecca muttered, staring right at Jack.

"Rebecca?" Laura asked, again wondering who had just traded places in there with her daughter.

"No one helped me! No one helped me!" Rebecca shouted. Laura threw her arms around her, trying to comfort her. It only incensed Rebecca more. Rebecca shrieked, "Don't touch me!"

Jack took a step inside. "Laura, can I help?"

"Maybe you should go. I need to be alone with her. I'm sorry." Jack respectfully stepped backwards through the wafting clouds of steam and closed the door.

He moved down the hall, passing Rebecca's bedroom. He stopped to peer inside, briefly admiring her artwork. A portrait of a little girl caught his eye. The girl was smiling, a simple smile, the detail miraculous. The serenity of the child's expression in the picture contrasted the wrenching shrieks coming from the bathroom. It prodded him to keep moving.

As Jack walked downstairs, he heard Rebecca's voice change, the same way it had done on the tape. "Nadie me ayudó!" he heard her shout. She repeated it over and over. Jack knew enough Spanish to translate: *No one helped me.*

Jack felt as if the words were directed at him personally, verbal daggers in his spine. As he neared the front door, he wondered if Angelina was screaming the same thing at that very moment.

He exited the house, letting the silence of the night air wash over him. Not too many things stressed Jack out, but he was shaken. He exhaled, watching his breath form clouds in the cold night.

He made his way towards his car, the frozen grass crunching beneath his shoes. He looked back at the house, two silhouettes struggling behind the upstairs blind. This wasn't finished. Laura wanted the truth as much as he did.

Jack opened his car door, steadying himself as he eased his body into the seat, the pain especially harsh tonight. He wasn't sure if the discomfort he was feeling was from illness or guilt, but it ached in his shoulders, ribs, and heart. He shut the door and dropped his head back against the headrest.

"…Christ."

He closed his eyes, trying to meditate the pain away. He turned his head left and right, shifting his body to find a comfortable position until the pain subsided. He opened his eyes and found himself staring at Rebecca's sketchbook on the passenger seat. He reached for it and flipped through a few drawings. There was a sketch of what looked like an angel hovering over a small sleeping child. The jagged lines made it appear rushed, but its entirety was exquisitely detailed and brilliant. Jack ran his fingers along the drawing, tracing the outline. It wasn't just her talent that he found incomprehensible, it was the depth of her expression, the layers of substance within each of her renderings. Her talent was unquestionable, but it was the inspiration behind the hands that moved him, the breadth of her spirit. Her drawings reflected experience, understanding, maturity.

Jack closed the book. He knew his next move.

CHAPTER 34

The hallways of Monroe's College For the Arts were lined with brand new tile and brick. Sculpted archways connected each intersecting hallway. It smelled new, Jack figured it must have been recently renovated, the school having been around for generations.

What Jack found it curiously devoid of was — art. Nothing hanging on the walls. Nothing to say this was a building for creative types, no examples of their work. Maybe that was more for elementary schools, something for the parents to admire during meet the teacher night. This was a respected establishment of cultured artists who didn't need to hang their masterpieces along hallway walls. Jack searched for room 17.

He stopped and asked a student, who pointed back the way he came. He had passed it.

Jack entered a classroom with a dozen work stations, each with an unfinished sculpture sitting on top. The room itself was filled with all types of artwork — abstract, modern, classical — all demonstrating various degrees of skill. Some clearly didn't belong, others were quite good.

A teacher was replacing paper on painting easels. Her brown hair was up in a tight bun, though a few rogue curls had broken loose around the temples. Jack guessed her age at about 35-36.

Another teacher was washing paintbrushes at the sink in the back of the room. He had on a very worn striped flannel shirt that was stained with paint and clay. Jack pegged him at about 10 years older.

Class had just filed out, Jack would have to move quick or they'd have the perfect excuse to cut short his visit when the next group arrived.

"It's never too late to discover your talent," she said to him, smiling, pulling paper through and latching it on each station at a hurried pace.

"I'm not a student," Jack said with a foolish grin.

"I know. In order to take my class you have to be accepted. The trials are rigorous and if you possessed the talent, youd've known...already."

"You were about to say long ago?" Jack said. She stammered a moment. "It's okay, I have no ego left to bruise," he said with a grin. Once she realized she was off the hook, she smiled back.

"How can I help you?"

"Helen Strauss?"

She nodded. "Mmm, that's me."

"Detective Jack Ridge." Jack flashed his badge and her smile turned upside down. Jack saw the other teacher approaching, surely curious as to the nature of his visit. "I'd like to ask you a few questions about a former student of yours. Carmen Muniz?" Helen nodded, understanding now why he was there.

"Carmen..." she said, full of sorrow.

"You're the detective who found her. I've seen your face on TV," the other teacher joined in. Jack stood waiting for an introduction. The teacher reached out his hand. "Oh, Michael Ketcher."

Jack shook his hand, it was coarse with pottery dust. "So you've heard."

"Yes," Helen said.

"You both knew her?"

"One of the best students we've ever had," Helen said, turning to Michael for corroboration. He was quick to reciprocate with emphatic nods of agreement.

"Oh jeez, without a doubt; we see so many students each year," Michael said, "but few as naturally gifted as Carmen. That painting there on the wall is hers." Michael pointed over Jack's shoulder.

Jack about-faced to see a stunning portrait of the Virgin Mary hanging on the back wall of the classroom. So lifelike, it was as if you could reach in and touch her. It captivated Jack. He himself had only seen this level of artistic talent *once* before. Did that verify Leonard's hypothesis? Or simply demonstrate that he occupied a very small corner of the world and needed to get out more.

"Some of her work still hangs in the gallery downstairs," Helen said to the back of Jack's head.

Jack turned and exchanged glances between the two.

"Do either of you remember anything bothering Carmen before she disappeared? Was she having problems with another student?"

"I can't say," Helen said. Jack waited patiently for her to elaborate. "Well, it was so long ago."

"Carmen was always engrossed with her work," Michael said. "She often stayed late after class. I don't think things were too happy at home for her."

"In what way?"

"Just an assumption." Michael shrugged.

"I see, but otherwise, she wasn't a troubled student?"

"Not when she was in here, she wasn't," Helen said. She drifted past them towards Carmen's painting, standing before it reverently. Jack joined her and they admired it side by side. Michael leaned on a desk behind them.

"All that talent, gone forever..." Helen said.

Maybe, Jack thought. But that was way too long a conversation.

The hallway began filling up with noise; a wave of students was approaching. The first few entered the classroom, talking loudly, as if outdoors. They were followed by two more, then three more, and soon the class was full and buzzing.

"Well, I appreciate your time. Both of you."

"Of course," Helen said.

"Anything we can do to help, please," Michael said. Jack turned to leave — got a few steps — then swiveled back around.

"Oh…one more thing." Jack opened his briefcase and took out Rebecca's sketch pad. Helen and Michael gathered around, curiously.

"I have a friend whose daughter is also an aspiring artist herself. Would you mind taking a look at these?"

"Not at all," Helen said. She turned the book so both she and Michael could see. They flipped through a few of Rebecca's drawings, each one eliciting the response Jack was expecting.

"They're exquisite," Helen said.

"What school does she attend?" Michael asked. Jack paused for dramatic effect.

"Eastbrook Elementary."

Helen looked up at Jack, her mouth open. The noise in the classroom was getting very loud, lots of chatter and paper rustling, Helen had to raise her voice, "A child did these?"

Jack nodded. Helen and Michael flipped through a few more pictures with a look of shocked disbelief. Jack watched their expressions change with each page. "Have you ever seen work like this from a child that age?"

"How old did you say she was?" Michael asked.

"Nine."

"I've read about it, never actually met one with this kind of talent so young," Helen said. "The attention to detail… incredible."

"So you'd say it's very unusual for a child this age to be able to do this kind of work?"

"She's a once in a lifetime talent," Helen said. *Once in a lifetime… Once in a lifetime.* Her words echoed repeatedly in Jack's brain.

"We'd love to meet her," Michael said.

"I'll see what I can do," Jack said, but that's precisely what he wanted — a third party opinion. He put the book back in his case and tried to serpentine between students to get to the door. He paused to take one more glance at Carmen's painting.

Once in a lifetime…

A great amount of Carmen's art was religious in nature, Jack recalled, remembering the words Rebecca spoke: Santa Maria Madre de Dios. Find Jesus. *Find Jesus...*

CHAPTER 35

Jack put his wipers on the fast setting, but they only smudged the rain in arched streaks. He hunched over the wheel, pressing his nose to the glass, trying to find a piece of windshield he could see through. The interior was all misted up, so he used his sleeve to wipe clean a small patch.

He pulled up to the church on 17th and Connecticut Ave. The building was situated just a few feet from the busy road, with no parking lot except for a small driveway where the church bus parks to unload passengers. Jack circled the building to find a spot. On his second go round, he lucked out; a small minivan's headlights went on. Jack put his signal on and waited for it to pull out. He held up the traffic in one direction and soon a car behind him blared its horn. Jack flicked a switch and a blue light spun to life on his dashboard, shutting the impatient driver right up.

The minivan pulled out — a little fast — probably out of fear of Jack's show of authority. Jack parked and sat a moment, waiting for his legs to fill with enough energy to get out and make the trek inside. He was compelled to remove his gun from its holster and place it in his glove compartment. He looked around to make sure no one was watching. He just didn't feel right about bringing a loaded weapon into church.

He looked out his driver's side window at the rain dripping down the glass. It reminded him of tears. His thoughts drifted back to that terrible night. How the rain was cold and heavy, just like tonight. He'd come outside to his car — he could no longer bear to sit inside that awful waiting room. He sat and watched the rain cascade down the window, just like now. He could still remember the smell of the hospital hallways. A chemical smell, some sort of cleaning solution or disinfectant. Whatever it was, its nauseating odor had made him angry and desperate. It was a constant reminder that he was in a place of life and death, blood and medicine. In there he had no control, forced to sit idle, helpless. Jack was a man of action — the waiting was toxic for him. He had to get out, get some air.

He remembered how hard it was to finally get up the courage to open the car door and go back inside. He feared the awful news awaiting him, news that would change his life forever. Soon he would know how those other people felt, the families he'd comforted. The ones he'd watched crumple in agony to the floor. The kind of pain no words can soothe. You simply have to step back and let them grieve. He wondered how he would react. Would he fall away? Weep openly, make a scene? Opening that car door was the hardest thing he'd ever done.

He recalled taking the news calmly. He didn't scream. He cried, but not enough to turn heads or make others uncomfortable. He took it like a man, internalizing the pain.

Maybe it would have been better if he had let it all out. Instead, he simmered slowly over the years, letting the anger and hurt eat away at his insides until it was no longer just keeping him sad and miserable. It was killing him. Soon it would consume him completely and, in a shallow self pitying way, he looked forward to death's absolution. *But did it have to be like this?*

It was too late for him. But there was still time left to do something good for someone else. It was that noble idea that flexed the muscles in his hand. Jack opened the car door and stepped out into the rain.

He flipped up his collar and headed for the entrance, stepping over a deep puddle that barred his path along the sidewalk. He crept around it onto the mushy grass, which sounded like squished applesauce beneath his shoes. A few drops penetrated his collar and dripped down his bare neck, through his undershirt, down his back. He shuddered, vibrating his lips like a sputtering motor, *brbrbrbrbr*.

He climbed the steps and pressed the door — only to collapse into wood, face first. He leaned back and pulled it open like you're supposed to, hoping no one saw his gaffe.

Inside, the church vestibule was quiet. He gently eased the door closed behind him, muting the sound of the driving rain. It was so quiet, Jack could hear his own breathing. He wasn't a regular churchgoer. Though baptized and put through the motions growing up, it never took. He respected all religions — he'd never take either side of the argument — but he never found a place for it. And his profession only served to drive the notion of a benevolent God from his beliefs. Still, he respected a person's right to worship.

He stepped gingerly, not remembering all the protocols for being inside a house of worship. Especially one in session — which it was, judging by the serene music emanating from the congregation area.

He opened the door to the nave quietly, not wanting to call attention to himself. No one turned around. A funeral was being held, a priest performed a sermon. Most of the mourners were Latino. Jack took a seat in the back and waited.

He looked around at the proceedings with a dour expression. How long before he would be here? Would anyone show up? Sure, he'd get the classic policeman's sendoff. But not the lavish kind reserved for those taken in the line of duty. His immediate station would probably attend, if only out of respect.

What about loved ones? Family and friends? Jack could be quite the chore to be around. Any family he stayed in touch with merely tolerated him. He understood why. So his passing would simply be a procedure, a chore that had to get done, like cleaning up the dishes after a meal. That last thought amused him in a macabre way.

He envisioned his casket filled with ice and beer. They could pay their respects and grab a cold one on their way out. At least everyone would have a good time.

Mourners slowly walked past the closed casket, paying their respects. Jack knew who was in there. That was the reason he came. He searched the crowd for her — and there she was – Hester Muniz; draped in black, head down, sobbing on the shoulder of the man sitting next to her. This was Carmen's funeral, 10 years belated. Jack listened to the priest's sermon:

"In our terrible grief, we thank you Lord for bringing closure to Carmen's family. We take comfort in knowing that Carmen now sits beside your only son Jesus in Heaven. Jesus cradles her in his arms and she feels no more pain."

The priest stepped down from the pulpit and placed his hand on Hester's shoulder. She looked up at him reverently, kissing the side of his hand. He whispered some words of comfort to her, then turned to acknowledge the man she was holding on to. Jack could see now he was a young man, 22 maybe. Dressed in full military uniform.

As the mourners exited quietly, a few noticed Jack sitting there, a puzzled look on their faces as they passed him by.

Hester leaned over Carmen's casket, placed a kiss on the lacquered wood, then knelt and did the sign of the cross. She erupted in a fit of tears; the young man had to help her up to her feet. He walked her back towards the exit.

Jack swallowed, maybe this wasn't the best time to talk with her. But she noticed him right away.

"Detective?"

Jack stood up and nodded. "Mrs. Muniz. I was wondering if I might speak with you some more."

"What's this about?" the young man said, his tone adversarial. Hester placed her hands on his to silence him.

"This is my son, Francisco." Francisco and Jack exchanged glances. "Jack is the one who found Carmen." Hester's tone demanded he respect the detective. Francisco softened immediately and extended his hand. Jack took it.

"Not all the credit is mine," Jack said — no intention of divulging the other deserving party. "I realize this isn't a good time, but maybe if I could stop by your home? When it's convenient."

"Of course, anything."

"We should go, they're waiting," Francisco said, giving her wrist a gentle tug.

"Si, okay." She turned to Jack. "Goodbye. God bless you."

Hester and Francisco exited, leaving Jack alone with the priest. His name was Father Carlos Gonzales, he had a stocky build, and thin black hair with graying along his temples. His face was gentle and disarming. Jack could see how someone like him was just the right person to deliver a message of peace during sorrow, or blessings during joy. In a way, they were both public servants, but for his own reasoning, Jack saw himself as the dark one in the room. Even though Jack fought on the side of good, he was constantly immersed in the dark side of his fellow man, whereas this servant of God saw only the goodness in people.

The priest collected bibles from the pews. Jack approached him.

"Father, my name's Jack Ridge, I'm a detective-"

"I know who you are," he said with a warm smile catching Jack off guard, "Thanks to you, Carmen's spirit can at last rest in peace."

Jack tilted his head, not necessarily agreeing with his assessment. "Then you don't mind speaking for a moment?"

"How can I be of help?"

"How long have you been with this church?"

The priest looked up at the ceiling, calculating in his head. "Eh, I'm 58 now. So, 26 years, I think."

"Carmen was a member of this church?"

"I know her family a long time." The priest continued to collect prayer books as they spoke. He motioned with his head for Jack to step aside so he could collect the ones behind him. He continued to the next aisle.

"Do you remember anything unusual about her before she disappeared?"

"Not that I can remember."

"Maybe she confessed to something? Was anything bothering

her? Trouble at home, maybe?"

The priest turned to Jack, the casual demeanor in his expression gone, replaced with a sudden formality.

"She was a devout member of this church. Her mother still is."

"I'm sure of that. You didn't answer my question."

"Dead or alive, there is a sanctity of confession I will not violate. But I can tell you she never gave her mother a day's trouble. And I know she always wanted the best for Carmen. It was not easy after her husband passed. The sadness became too great for him, the Lord called him home."

"Carmen's murder is part of a larger investigation now. Another girl is missing. Her name's Angelina Rosa."

"We are all well aware of it in this community. I know Mr. Rosa, he's a good man. We both emigrated from Ecuador. I lit a candle with him to pray for Angelina's safe return." The priest motioned towards several burning candles near the entrance. He picked up two more prayer books, the stack almost up to his chin.

"Can I help you with those?" Jack asked.

"Gracias." Jack took half of the books into his arms. The priest walked over and opened a storage drawer by the side of the stage. He bent over and placed the stack inside. Jack did the same.

"You think these cases are connected."

"I know they are."

"You will catch this devil before he takes another beautiful child?"

"I hope so."

The priest stared at Jack as if sizing up his ability to make good on it. He nodded, as if to say, *I believe you will.* "Is there anything else I can do for you?"

Jack tucked his pad and pencil away inside his front coat pocket and shook his head. "Thank you for your time."

As Jack walked towards the exit he noticed a white statue of St. Mary on a pedestal. He hadn't noticed it on his way in. He turned to the priest. "Actually, there is one more thing. The statue outside, where is it?"

The priest stared at Jack blankly. "Statue?"

"By the side entrance, near the street?"

The priest scratched his head. "Not that I'm aware of."

Jack waited a moment, then shrugged his shoulders. "My mistake." Jack moved to the door.

"Detective," the Priest called out, "there was a statue - The Sacred Heart. Some vandals defaced it, we had to take it down. But that was years ago."

Jack was silent. He opened his mouth to say *thank you* when a sudden cough burst from his lungs, nearly doubling him over. It caught him by surprise; he quickly fished for his handkerchief. He found it — covered his mouth — and just let it out. Five long, wet hacks that echoed through the rafters of the church's high ceilings.

The priest took a few steps towards him, but Jack waved him off, signaling that it would pass. It finally did. Jack straightened up, inhaling slowly, making sure it was safe to breathe again. He wiped his mouth with the handkerchief and opened the door. "Sorry, excuse me."

"Detective," the priest called out, "have you found Jesus?"

Jack paused, "I'm still looking."

Jack exited the building and turned his phone back on. There was a text waiting for him. It was from Laura, just two words:

We're ready.

CHAPTER 36

"Does your car have a siren?" Rebecca asked. Jack looked at Laura, sitting in the passenger seat, then into his rearview mirror at Rebecca in back. She was sitting slouched over, her elbow on the door, chin resting on her fist. She seemed disinterested, maybe just making conversation. But Jack played along.

"It's not that type of police car. But I have this-" Jack flipped a switch and his blue spinning lamp came to life. It got a tiny smile from Rebecca. He turned it back off and returned his focus to driving.

"Rebecca, the dreams you keep having… about the girl. What can you tell me about them?" Jack didn't want to sound like another doctor, probing. He wanted to sound like a friend — which he was, his tone very conversational.

Rebecca glanced in her mother's direction.

"It's okay, sweetie," Laura said.

"It's like I'm dreaming, but when it's over, the feelings — they're so real."

"How do they make you feel?"

"Sad. Afraid."

Jack turned a corner and headed into an urban neighborhood. The streets seemed to narrow, houses got smaller, closer together.

Laura looked around, familiar with the area.

"The man in your dreams, does he have a name?" Rebecca's shoulders tensed as she drew inward. "If you saw his face would you recognize him?"

Jack could feel Laura's eyeballs on him. He turned his attention back to the road, withdrawing the question.

"They're just dreams. They're not real," Rebecca said. Jack knew it wasn't *her* talking, she was repeating something her mother had said — probably repeated — over and over, hoping to make it true.

Jack checked his mirror and was surprised to find Rebecca staring back at him, as if to say *you're right, I don't agree with what she says. They are real. Maybe you'll believe me.* More and more, Jack felt a bond growing between him and Rebecca — *kindred spirits.*

"Where are we going?" Rebecca asked. Jack looked at Laura. *You didn't tell her?*

"Rebecca, how would you like to be my deputy for the day?" Rebecca sat up with a smile, as if he'd said how would you like some ice cream.

"Okay. How?"

Laura was interested in his answer too.

"We're going to stop at a few places, and I want you to tell me anything that comes into your mind."

"Like what?"

"I don't know, anything. Doesn't matter."

"Doctor Hellerman asked me to do that too. Said some words, then asked me to tell him the first thing that came into my mind."

Jack nodded. He stopped at a red light adjacent to a park. It had swing sets, benches, a basketball court. There were a lot of tough looking teens hanging out.

"I know this area," Laura said, "we used to come here a lot after school." Some of the teens started cursing, pushing and shoving each other. Fists started flying. "Not much has changed."

Jack drove another half mile and pulled into a parking lot adjacent to the railroad station and a motel. Laura looked back at Rebecca. A folder on Jack's back seat was spilling its contents — several 8x10 gruesome crime scene photographs had slid out onto the seat. Rebecca was peeking through them.

"Oh dear God," Laura said with a gasp. Jack spun around.

"Sorry." Jack swiped the folder off the seat and shoved it back into his briefcase, snapping it tight. Laura opened her car door angrily and got out, slamming it. She opened Rebecca's door and collected her. Jack hung his head, feeling awful.

He got out and caught up to them, Laura had opted to walk a good 20 feet from the car, not knowing which direction they were headed, she just needed to put space between them at that moment.

"I'm sorry, I didn't realize—" Jack said.

"Let's just get on with it," Laura said, not angry with him, just shaken by what she had seen. Jack motioned for them to follow him.

"This was one of the last places Angelina was seen," Jack said, as he led them towards the motel. Laura held Rebecca's hand tightly. "Angelina answered an ad for a job at this motel. I've already interviewed the owner and his employees, they claim they never spoke to her. So there's a possibility this was just a pre-arranged meeting place for something else."

"Why bring Rebecca here?" Laura asked Jack discreetly.

"I thought maybe… if there's some kind of connection."

"What do you mean?"

Jack rubbed the back of his neck. "I don't know, really. Maybe both victims might have disappeared the same way, you know? Maybe there's a common link, perhaps this spot. It's the kind of place where a lot of people come and go without questions asked. A lot of drug dealing, prostitution."

"Carmen? Not on your life."

"Maybe she was lured here somehow. Look, all of this is a shot in the dark." Jack knew he sounded like he was grasping at straws, and he was. He had no idea where to begin, he was just after something that might trigger a reaction from Rebecca. Something like he'd heard on the tapes. Rebecca looked bored and tired, dragging her heels.

"Is this where I'm supposed to tell you what I'm thinking?"

"Yes."

Rebecca put her hands on her hips, as if concentrating real hard. "Okay." Her innocence lightened the mood.

They entered the motel. All three stood at the entrance. It was dark inside, a thin ream of smoke escaped from behind the counter. A man poked his head out, he recognized Jack and frowned.

"Anything?" Jack asked Rebecca. She looked around, a bit confused as to what she was supposed to be doing.

"No," she said, disappointed.

This was a stupid idea. Jack panicked, not wanting Laura to think this was the best he had and pull the plug. He didn't drag her out here just for this. He needed a better idea, fast. "Okay, come on," Jack hurried them out.

CHAPTER 37

Jack sat across a table from Rebecca in his office. She stared intensely at a book of photographs — mug shots of known criminals and suspects. Laura stood over Rebecca, holding their coats under her arm. She kept looking at Jack, he could tell the fuse of her patience was burning short.

When Jack had suggested they go to his office to review some photographs, Laura immediately resisted, but Jack assured her they were nothing like the graphic ones that slipped from his briefcase, so she reluctantly agreed.

Jack turned the page to the next black and white picture, an older man with a bald head and a scar on his chin.

"Take your time, Rebecca," Jack said. Rebecca inspected the picture intently. She shook her head. "Okay." Jack turned to another mugshot.

Jennifer walked by Jack's open office door, peeking in curiously at Rebecca and Laura. Jack spotted her and got up, heading her off at his doorway.

"What's going on?" Jennifer asked.

"Something you need from me?" Jack's body language like a door closing in her face.

Jennifer paused at his curtness. "Another relative you've never mentioned? Ex-girlfriend and your illegitimate offspring?"

Jack moved forward, backing her out of the door.

"Don't you have things to do?"

"I just came to tell you Harrington was looking for you." Jennifer looked around Jack at Rebecca. "Kid's too cute to be yours anyway. Is she the one?"

"Is she the one what?"

Jennifer realized she had opened her mouth too wide. "Oh, nothing."

Jennifer hastily retreated back into the hallway. Jack watched her suspiciously, then returned to his seat across from Rebecca, who was looking at the next picture with one eye closed; concentrating, feeling important. She seemed to enjoy helping out. The photo was of a man named Espinosa, a leathery face with a tattoo below his eye and one on his neck.

"He's ugly," Rebecca said.

"Rebecca." Laura poked her in the ribs.

"Yes, he sure is." Jack grinned. "Anything?"

"Mm-mm, no," Rebecca said assuredly. Jack turned a few more. "No... No."

He turned to a white male with a long nose and one eye larger than the other. His name was Bishop. Rebecca stared longer than the others. Jack's eyes locked.

"Something?"

Rebecca took her time, studying. But then shook her head "No". Jack emptied his lungs in frustration. Rebecca turned the page to the next mugshot herself. Then another, and another, occasionally stopping for second glances, but not much interest or familiarity with any of them.

Jack waited, hopeful. He realized this was probably going nowhere. Needle in a haystack, if that. He was expecting Laura to begin tapping her foot any minute, surprised by her patience. Instead, she turned and began snooping aimlessly around Jack's office.

"I'm going to go outside for a sec," Laura said. She fished around in her bag and pulled out a pack of cigarettes.

"We'll be here," Jack said. Rebecca turned some more. Jack sat and watched. His thoughts drifted, Jennifer's ribbing lingered in his head. He imagined what his life might have been like had things been different. Coming home after work, unconditional love bursting from the front door, lollipop in mouth, hair in pigtails, hugs and kisses. Someone to miss him when he was gone, smile at him when he was feeling low. Helping with math homework. Laughter.

Jack got up and took two pills from his shirt pocket and poured himself a cup of water.

"Thirsty?" Jack asked.

"Nah," she said, not looking up from her work.

He opened his desktop drawer and fished around, finding a half eaten pack of lifesavers. "How about some candy?"

"It'll give me cavities."

He looked up at his map, focusing on the red thumbtack where Carmen's body was found.

"Rebecca?"

"Yeah?"

"You like hiking?"

"What's that?"

Laura came back in the room, smelling of smoke. Jack held on to his answer. "So?" Laura asked, meaning, *are we finished?*

"We're ready," Jack said.

Laura held open Rebecca's coat so she could slide her arms in. Just then, Harrington entered the room, bursting at the seams when he spotted Rebecca.

Laura took note. "We'll be in the car," Laura said suspiciously, pulling Rebecca along with her out of the room.

"Was that the arteest?" Harrington said with a grin. Jack wanted to knock it right off his face.

"That's right..." Jack replied curiously.

"Jack, I know you're pressing because you feel you have some kind of moral obligation or something. But... we all know how this is going to end."

"It's not over till we find a body."

"What are you gonna use next, a divining rod?"

A sudden realization hit Jack. He turned and spotted the

cassette player, left out in the open. *The asshole had listened to the tape!* Now Jennifer's slip of the tongue made sense.

"I'll tell you what that is, Jack. Dumb luck. Like that prick who had us running in circles in the Mitchell case; all he needed was to touch her undergarments, remember?"

"Didn't have *me* running in circles."

"Whatever, even more to my point. Hard work, facts, intelligence solves cases, isn't that what you said? Solid detective work, not superstition? Remember? Imagine what the press would say to this."

"I don't care what anyone thinks. All I care about is finding Angelina. Stopping him before he can kill again."

"And you think this little girl's story is gonna lead you to his front door? She has a bad dream, describes some very common landmarks, the dogs get lucky and voila, it's supernatural! Come on, man. You're a glass is half empty kind of guy. Lately you've been a glass is empty, broken on the floor kind of guy."

"You don't know the whole picture."

"I think Hellerman has spent a little too much time with psychotic patients. You better be careful, it might be catching."

"At this point, I'd rub two sticks together if I thought it would make fire."

"You're wasting your time — this nut's had his way with Angelina, chopped her into little bits. All we can do is wait for him to do it again, pick up a fresh scent."

In his gut, Jack knew Harrington was right. But the idea of doing nothing, just waiting around, had a reek of failure that was suffocating to him. Jack was a man of action. He needed to keep moving. He waved at Harrington's words like he could no longer stand the sight or smell of him.

"I think it's also time you sat Mr. Rosa down and fed him a truth sandwich, too. He needs to start accepting reality. Calls here 10 times a day. Got the press hounding the Captain, tossing around accusations of racism. They know which buttons to push."

"If it was my daughter missing, I'd be doing everything in my power too. Whatever it took." Jack went to step past Harrington, but Harrington simply broadened his muscular shoulders and took up the whole door. He wasn't letting Jack leave until his point was made.

"We all want to see this case solved. But this is no time to fall down the rabbit hole. Her father needs to prepare for the worst; you're just making it harder, sending the wrong message." Jack's mouth tightened, his clenched teeth bared like a snarling dog.

"What message? Hope? That's his flesh and blood. He's not gonna give up just because you quote him a God damn statistic. Giving people bad news doesn't seem to affect you, does it? That's because you've never been on the receiving end. Never experienced true loss. Personal loss." Jack pushed his way into the hallway. Harrington called after him.

"That's not true. I've experienced loss. I took the under on the Saints/Packers last Monday."

Laura stood outside the station waiting for Jack, sucking on another cigarette and deftly wafting the smoke to keep it from blowing in Rebecca's direction. Rebecca was climbing up the steps to the precinct and jumping off, over and over.

Laura was convinced nothing she tried was going to be the magic bullet that was going to solve Rebecca's problem. The school counselor, Doctor Hellerman, Jack; none of them had any answers. Facing her fear, as Jack had said, turned out to be just Jack throwing darts at a board. She knew what he was trying to do — hoping he'd experience a moment with Rebecca like she'd had when they passed the church. But she was the one who had to take Rebecca home tonight and stay up waiting for the screams.

Jack exited the station, an apologetic look on his face.

"What took you so long?" Laura asked.

"Sorry. Let's go."

"Where to now?" Rebecca asked.

"Hiking."

Laura raised her eyebrows, *what?*

CHAPTER 38

Jack led Laura and Rebecca along a dirt path through a thickly wooded area, just a few hundred yards from the main road.

The sun began to set, casting a crimson glow that back-lit the clouds. Its colored beauty forced Jack to slow his pace, hold his look a little longer. He wondered how many more scenes like this were reserved for him in his abbreviated future. How many more moments of tranquility and peaceful reflection did he have left to savor?

"How far?" Laura asked.

"Not too far; right over this hill," Jack said, continuing forward. Laura followed, pulling Rebecca to keep pace, her shoes seemingly filled with lead.

Jack looked down and noticed Rebecca's face had turned pale, she seemed anxious. Jack watched her scrape off a chunk of tree bark with her fingernail, nervously.

"You alright?" he asked.

"I'm sorry, I'm not much help."

Jack patted her head. "That's not true, police work is all about trial and error. You've helped me narrow my search. That's what detectives do. You'd make a great one."

That put a doubting grin on her face, which was quickly erased by the fear welling up inside her. Rebecca had somehow managed to smother her dread to accompany them into the wooded area. She had an overwhelming fear of traveling beyond the thin guardrail that separated the road from the dark woods, which stretched from the highway several miles — all the way to the small, one way street that led to her school. Kids would often cut through to the mart to stuff their jackets with pop and chips. She could have gotten home quicker using the shortcut too, instead of walking the long way round, up over the bridge. But she didn't dare. And worse, she didn't know why. The answer was buried deep in the recesses of her mind, only the lingering emotion of whatever *it* was lay near the surface.

It was that burning question that kept her from running. She needed to learn what secrets lie beyond, even if she dreaded the answer. And she may never have another chance to be flanked by protective adults, escorting her through the darkness, shielding her from what dangers lie in wait. But the suffocating rush of fear and anxiety was multiplying exponentially now. She felt lightheaded and dizzy, her tiny heart pounded in her chest.

She looked up at Jack, slowly leading the way. He made her feel safe, she liked having him around. She sensed her mother didn't mind so much either.

They neared the crime scene, police tape still lined the trees in the distance where Carmen's body had been unearthed. The rush of the river was louder here, its steep incline created an increase in velocity as it smashed against the rocks, enough to drown out the roar of the highway. The noise whooshed in Rebecca's ears. She became aware of her heartbeat, the pressure made her neck throb. Laura felt the tension in Rebecca's clammy hand.

"Sweetie?" Laura asked. Rebecca could only manage to look up at her, the color rinsed from her cheeks.

"Right up here," Jack said. To Rebecca, it sounded like a warning, or maybe like a carnival ride operator — *here we go!* — just as he pressed the button that launched you up the coaster's ramp, careening towards certain doom.

They trudged through a swampy portion of grass, recently churned into mud by police car tires. Yellow crime scene tape spread out in all directions like a spider web.

Rebecca broke free of her mother's grasp and ran ahead.

"Rebecca?" Laura shouted, but Jack held her back.

"No, let her."

Rebecca approached the burnt willow tree, split in two, its submerged branches creating a giant fork in the river, collecting leaves and trash. Jack and Laura stepped behind her.

Rebecca stood in awe, something she had only dreamed was now standing before her, as if she'd conjured it into existence. And then a horrifying thought occurred to her. *If this was real, then what if he was too?*

"Look familiar?" Jack asked. Rebecca looked back at him, her face white, her body shivering with fear. Feelings of Deja Vu and panic rushed to the surface, her face a merry-go-round of emotions.

"Tell us what you're feeling?" Jack asked.

"I don't know." Rebecca's voice was trembling.

Laura reached out to touch the tree.

"This is where she was found. Right here," Jack said. Laura jerked her hand back, as if she'd touched something dead.

Jack placed his hand on Rebecca's shoulder and knelt down before her, eye to eye. "This was the place you described to Leonard?"

Rebecca jerked away, but he held onto her gently.

"Let go," Rebecca said.

"Rebecca, the other night, you said something to your mother about a necklace. You said you couldn't find it. Do you remember that?"

"She doesn't even remember me coming into the room," Laura said.

Jack reached in and pulled out Carmen's gold cross. "Does it look like this?" He held it up for Rebecca to examine.

Rebecca took the necklace. Her eyes went glassy, her mouth open. Jack had managed to pull something out of a dream. Rebecca recognized the necklace, the memories were a blur, but the emotions attached to it engulfed her. She knew in her heart this once belonged to her. "This was mine…"

Laura stepped closer. "What is that?"

"It's my necklace. Jack found it."

"You don't have a gold necklace like that." Laura turned to Jack, eyes sharp. "What do you think you're doing?"

Jack slowly stood up. "I just wanted to see-"

"This was Carmen's, wasn't it? And you're giving it to my daughter, for what? To convince her she's crazy? This isn't what we talked about. I wanted to help her, convince her none of this was real, but you're trying to convince her it is! You're only concerned with this case, not with my daughter."

"That's not true-"

"Carmen was my friend. But she's dead. She's dead! My daughter is alive. I foolishly thought this might help her. I thought if we did this she'd see that nothing would happen, that none of this was real and she was okay. So we could work through the nightmares. But you believe — you're trying to trigger some past life memory to solve this case. It's bullshit! And I'm a fool for agreeing to it, thinking this could help. I must be losing my mind."

"Mom?" Rebecca said, her eyes wide and hurt, her lips quivering. Laura looked back at her. "You knew her? You knew she was real?"

Laura took Rebecca by the hands. "Sweetie, I was going to tell you-"

"You lied to me. It's not in my head. I'm not crazy. She was real, her name *was* Carmen. All this time. You lied to me, you LIED to me!"

Rebecca turned and ran.

"Rebecca!" Laura shot Jack a look that could kill as they both gave chase after her through the woods.

All at once, Rebecca's world began to spin. Her windpipe clamped closed, like some force was pushing her head down. She started gasping and fell to her knees. Laura and Jack quickly surrounded her.

"Rebecca?" Laura shrieked, witnessing her daughter spasm and sputter. She grabbed her by both forearms and crouched down.

"Mama! Mama...lo siento. Lo siento!" Rebecca shouted. Her voice wasn't her own. Her eyes went all funny and distant. She saw flashes of something, like a waking dream, dirty hands reaching for her. Her body became heavy, the blood rushing from her head. Her eyes glazed and she fell head first into Laura's arms.

"Oh God, Rebecca!" Laura held Rebecca like a clamped vice, as if a swirling storm funnel was trying to wrestle her body from her grip.

Jack held onto Rebecca's twitching legs. Rebecca stared blankly up into the trees, her eyes lifeless, as if her body were just a shell. Then suddenly her eyes went wide, she shivered, staring intently upon something only she could see, something terrifying.

Then, as if a silent bomb exploded inside her, Rebecca let out a spine ripping, banshee-like shriek that made all the birds in the trees scatter. It nearly knocked Laura over like a punch to the gut.

Rebecca shielded her face reflexively, as if fending off an invisible attacker, her screams growing louder, more frightful. Laura had been through this every night with her, but never so pronounced, never so lucid. And this time, even with her eyes locked on her daughter's, Laura couldn't calm her, rouse her from whatever evil force was torturing her mind. Rebecca was wide awake, screaming, and Laura could only look on helplessly.

Rebecca convulsed so hard, spit started dribbling down the sides of her mouth. Laura cleaned it off with her fingertips as Rebecca's nose started to drip blood.

"Rebecca!" Laura's terror turned to anger, she turned and raged at Jack. "What the hell did you do?"

Jack swallowed hard. "Nothing. I had no idea-"

"You had no idea? You show her God awful pictures of dead bodies, criminal mugshots, put that fear inside her head. You bring her to the gravesite of a murdered girl, show her something she used to wear! What next? Show her the knife she was stabbed with?"

"No."

"What the hell is the matter with you? What did you expect to happen? She's a child!" Laura's rage reduced Jack to an open mouthed statue, frozen, dead inside. One good tap and he would have shattered into a thousand pieces. Guilt curdled his stomach, his brain went tilt. He wanted to get it over with and die right there.

Rebecca stopped twitching. She rolled towards Laura's breast and calmed. Then her eyes slowly opened and looked up at Laura. "I found you. I missed you so much. I'm not angry anymore." Rebecca's eyes were trancelike. Laura's face twisted with confusion.

"Rebecca? Rebecca?" Laura's voice was urgent but calm, she didn't want to startle or frighten her into another episode. Rebecca closed her eyes again.

"I can breathe again now," Rebecca said. Laura began rocking her back and forth.

"Yes, you're okay. You're safe. You're safe. Oh thank God..."

Jack reached out to touch Laura's shoulder, but then pulled back, unsure. He got up on one bended knee as Laura scooped Rebecca into her arms.

Laura placed Rebecca's head on her shoulder and carried her away in a sprint; no clear direction, she just wanted to get away from Jack. Jack followed sheepishly.

"Laura, I'm sorry, please."

Laura marched a few more yards and stopped out of exhaustion.

"Just take us home... please take us home."

Rebecca coughed and opened her eyes. Red had replaced the pale milk color of her cheeks, the spell subsiding. Getting her away from the river — the gravesite, seemed to help.

Laura pushed Rebecca's hair out of her face. She stroked her forehead a few times, smudging a little dirt. "Sweetie? Rebecca?"

"Mommy. I'm so scared."

"Let's get you both home," Jack said.

Jack held out his hands for Laura to pass Rebecca to him. She did — reluctantly. She could carry her no further.

The three of them made their way back towards the road. Not another word was spoken.

Jack, you asshole...

CHAPTER 39

The young woman crossed her legs, pulling her thin yellow sundress up above her knee, exposing it to the air — and to prying eyes. Her skin was soft, her hair light blonde, tied behind her head in a ponytail. *Ripe fruit.*

He guessed she was about 23. Pretty - not a stunner, *but she'll do.* He checked the left hand. No ring.

She thrust her tongue in and out the hole of her straw, an iced coffee, Hazelnut. He'd stood behind her in line, overheard her order. He hadn't followed the girl into the coffee shop. He was there to get one himself, a tea actually. Black tea with milk and sugar. Lots of sugar. He despised coffee. Too bitter. He liked sweet things.

He made sure to seat himself where he could observe her, so happy she decided to stay. Then a friend joined her, followed by another, and soon they were three beautiful strangers sitting together, unwittingly blurting out intimate details about their private lives.

The blonde's name was Teresa Mason, like the British actor. Thinking that helped him commit it to memory. He didn't overhear them say her name — how often does someone use a person's name during a conversation, especially a close friend.

Unless it's someone you haven't seen in years and you need to reassure them you still remember who they are.

He gleaned her name from the ID badge dangling around her neck — a pass code key that allowed employees re-entry to secured buildings. She wore it like a piece of jewelry for all to see. Nothing wrong with that, except that it helped add a piece to a heinous puzzle for preying eyes. *Teresa Mason, works at* — he squinted to read — *...UIC?* UIC Industries was a software firm located in Midland Park Square, a group of buildings situated on a large campus, all corporate offices. Most had very nice places to eat right in their buildings, but not good coffee.

He tried to tune out the rest of the background noise to listen in on their back and forth. He overheard one of her friends mention she'd run into Randall yesterday. *You remember Randall, that geeky dork who used to follow you around with his tongue hanging out? 11th grade?* Teresa shrugged and made a face like she hadn't remembered until now. She laughed and asked what he was doing. *He's a successful broker now,* the friend said. *He's definitely got money — he was driving a BMW.* Teresa's head tilted, her tongue poked at her straw again.

She slurped down another gulp of Hazelnut iced coffee and turned to look at the strange, ugly man staring at her from across the cafe. His annoying gaze had started to wear a hole in her blouse. He turned away, nonchalant, and pretended to be looking at something important on his phone. She didn't notice he was covertly snapping pictures of her and her friends.

Teresa turned up her nose in disgust, disregarding him. Her friends were too busy yapping to even notice. She re-joined the conversation and asked what Randall looked like now. The friend described him, said *he'd asked about her.* Teresa lit up with a grin full of perfect white teeth. The other friend, a heavyset one wearing a leather jacket two sizes too small for her, told Teresa *you should meet up with him, might finally snap you out of your funk over Paul.*

He had all the information he needed. He took one more look before he left; starting at her ankle, drinking in her bare skin, past the knee, over the thin dress that hugged her curves, to her face, committing it to memory. He felt sympathy for the repressed men who had to work alongside her, confident they must be straining in their seats whenever her tight frame passed their cubicles by. He licked his lips — a new project awaited! *In this life, you need to take what you want, boys.*

He pushed out his chair, tossed his half full tea into the trash, and exited the shop.

He climbed into a large white van. On its side read: *Baxter Mills Inc. Bonded Cleaning Services.*

He could still see her through the coffee shop window. He reached under his seat and dragged out a laptop, he wanted to jump onto the networking sites before he forgot all the details. Was he close enough to pull from the shop's wifi? He saw two bars, good enough. He agreed to the pointless terms of service page and started typing.

He searched the name Teresa Mason first. Quite a few hits came up. He scrolled until he found one for Lansing. There were three actually, but only one with blonde hair. He clicked and her picture enlarged. There she was.

Check.

She had an open page, allowing anyone to see her history. Too easy. He did a quick search and discovered that she went to Clearview High in Windsor Township, graduated seven years ago. Hmm a little older than he thought. His judgment must be off. He liked them younger. As they aged, they often grew wiser to their own mortal vulnerabilities. The young ones walked the earth in ignorant bliss. Still - *ripe fruit.*

He clicked off the page and did a search for Clearview High, then ran a search of alumni. There she was, wasn't she cute? He typed up the name Randall, hoping to only find one. *Lucky me.* Randall Peterson. He was a dorky looking boy. *Wonder what he's doing now?*

He searched and discovered Randall works for Martin Mitchell Investments. Lives in Annandale. Nice address. And sure enough, on the corporate website for Martin Mitchell, there was a contact page for him, with a nice-sized photo. He right-clicked and downloaded it.

He went back to the social networking site and expertly created a new page, using a fake email address for confirmation. He wasn't worried about them tracing him, since the computer was stolen from a plumbing job he did weeks ago in Bridgetown, plus the public wifi camouflaged his IP address. *One step ahead.* Some idiots don't even put a pass code on their devices. This one did, but he was able to crack it. Five minutes on Google.

He created the fake page for Randall Peterson. He even found his actual page, and was able to download current pictures of him for authenticity. *Too easy. Oh look, he does drive a BMW.*

About 4 minutes later, he'd put together a fake page that even Randall couldn't decipher was phony without scrutinizing every detail. And the only thing he got wrong was the date of birth — it wasn't listed, so he guessed.

He then sent out friend requests to hundreds of people he never met, knowing most just clicked yes because the more connections you had, the cooler you were. He knew before long he would be loaded.

He brought up Teresa's page and sent a friend request. He also sent a message, telling her about how he had just run into...*shit, what was the other girl's name?* He scanned Teresa's posts until he found a picture of the fat one with the tiny leather jacket. There she was, squeezing her fat face into the picture, blowing a kiss. A simple mouse over and: *Natalie Krycia.*

Check.

He updated his message to let Teresa know how he had just run into Natalie, *you remember, our friend from high school? She said she still spoke to you, and that you were still local!* He then let her know how anxious he was to meet her and re-connect over coffee. Maybe they could go share a Hazelnut iced coffee, which was his favorite.

Was that too slick? He decided it was, and deleted that part. He could save it for their next conversation. He sent the message and waited. And waited. He started up the van to go to his next appointment. He shoved the stolen laptop under his seat and drove off.

He whistled while he worked that day; excited, anxious. He replaced the flange bolts on a toilet with a spring in his step.

After work, he passed a public library. He parked and hustled inside, they were closing in 5 minutes.

He grabbed a seat at the computer tables and surfed to his fake page. She had accepted his friend request, even though he only had 35 friends. He would mention how he is very picky about who he connects with, hence the low number. She also responded to his message. She couldn't believe it was him after all these years, and she couldn't wait to catch up.

Checkmate.

CHAPTER 40

"This won't take long," Jack insisted. Hester took the hint and stepped back out of Carmen's bedroom into the hallway.

"Take all the time you need."

"Thank you." Jack waited until he heard her footsteps reach the kitchen. He shut the door, but didn't seal it. He didn't want to seem obvious.

He scanned the room. He knew exactly what he was looking for — where it would be — *if* it was there. He took a step towards the dresser with trepidation.

Hester adjusted her chair in the kitchen, the scrape on the linoleum froze Jack in his tracks. He didn't want her to catch him doing what he was about to do. How could he honestly explain what he was searching for, its possible location divined through a child's subconscious. He was only there to leave no stone unturned. Even a stone as ridiculous as this. There was no way it could be there. *But the river, the necklace, her reaction!*

Let's get this over with.

He stared once again at the framed picture of Carmen and Laura. There was a small, cheaply made green jewelry box with three tiny drawers, one of them open. Jack touched it, closed it with his fingertips. There were a few trinkets from the Caribbean, a Dominican flag in a glass cup, a hairbrush and a small plastic sewing kit on a shelf. He glided his fingers along the comforter of her still-made bed. There was a thin layer of dust that had collected over the years. Jack swished his hands together, brushing it off.

On top of the dresser was a broken lamp, a few scattered CDs, and some dried up painting supplies. Jack crouched down on one knee and braced himself against the side of the dresser. It was old solid wood, not pressed board, with a hand carved pattern along the bottom that had small arches forming a point in the center. He examined its craftsmanship. *Quit stalling.*

He took a breath and reached his hand underneath. His fingertips pierced through a spongy substance that was probably an ancient collection of spider webs. He wasn't squeamish and kept feeling around. Nothing. He kept one ear trained on Hester in the kitchen, any slight rustle and he'd have to abort the mission.

He flattened the side of his face against the floor and reached all the way under, swiping his hand back and forth like a windshield wiper across the entire nether region of the dresser. Empty.

He retracted his arm and leaned on the dresser for balance. He opened the top drawer and fished around through her delicates. He opened the middle — tossing the contents impatiently.

The bottom drawer wasn't on its hinge correctly, something blocking it from closing completely. He bent down and reached inside when the bedroom door opened. Jack didn't hear it.

It was the dog, Faucet. He licked Jack's face, surprising him.

"Stop it," Jack whispered, pushing him away.

"Detective? Everything all right?"

Jack spun his head around. Francisco was standing in the doorway. Jack pushed himself up to one knee, fumbling for a quick explanation as to why he was disassembling Carmen's furniture.

"Yes, I was just — did your sister share her room with anyone else?"

"No."

Jack nodded, as if the question was an important one. "I

wanted to thank you for all you've done," Francisco said, offering Jack a hand. He eased him back up to his feet. Jack was impressed, Francisco was small in stature, but he easily lifted Jack with his strong grip. "My mother's suffered so much. This week was the first we've seen her somewhat... at peace... in a long time. For years she's been on about asking Jesus for another chance, hoping against hope to see or speak to my sister again, that she might be found alive. But mostly it was the not knowing. Now, I think she can stop worrying and accept the truth. My family can't thank you enough."

Thank Rebecca, don't thank me.

Francisco took Jack's hand and shook it. His military forged grip was like iron. Jack tried to think of something to say, but couldn't come up with anything appropriate, so he simply nodded.

"Just one thing, how did you ever find her body? She went missing so long ago."

Jack stammered, "It's complicated, I-"

"I guess that's your job."

"Yes," Jack said, relieved Francisco didn't press.

Hester entered the room. "Francisco, leave him, he needs to work." Hester pushed him out by the shoulders as if he was still seven years old. She waved at Jack and closed the door, sealing it.

Jack waited a beat, long enough for one breath, then sprung into action. He pulled out the bottom drawer and reached inside.

His fingers found something and his eyes went wide.

Wedged into the sleeve of the wood was something hard. Jack felt a cold chill slide down his spine. He pulled it, and it came free. It was a hard cover book, leather bound with a tiny lock, wrapped closed with rubber bands and what looked like a stretched out hair tie. He held it with reverence, disbelief. He knew it hadn't moved since it was last placed there, and he was sure no one knew it was still hidden there but him. And Leonard. *And Rebecca.*

If he did the right thing, told Hester about his discovery, it would be a challenge to take it with him, examine it. She'd never allow something so precious and sacred to leave the boundary of her home. But it could hold a clue, maybe several. No time to debate the morality of taking it. He slid it into the large inside pocket of his jacket.

Now for the other issue.

It was there. It was actually there. Just like she described. A girl's ramblings under hypnosis had led him to find something that transcended death. Jack's hands trembled. This must have been what Leonard had felt like when he read about Carmen's body being discovered. Jack felt a sudden rush of blood to the head and had to place his hand on the bedpost to stabilize his rubbery legs.

He took a moment to gather himself, then exited the room. He passed right by Hester in the kitchen and headed for the front door.

"Can I get you something to drink?"

"No, thank you," Jack said, not making eye contact. She got up quickly and followed him.

"You're leaving?"

"Yes, thank you again." Jack opened the front door and let himself out. Hester stood in the doorway, open mouthed, afraid she'd done something to offend him. He hadn't even asked her one question.

CHAPTER 41

Jack drove a few blocks until he was a good safe distance from Hester's apartment building. He pulled over along the side of the road.

He sat parked for 10 minutes, just staring at Carmen's diary on the seat beside him. He ran his fingers along the worn leather binding; conflicted, curious. The implications of it even existing made it seem like some religious text, ancient.

He caressed the tiny brass lock that held it closed. He could have broken it with a good squeeze of his thumb and forefinger. But doing so felt like such a violation. He picked it up, held it firmly with both hands, then tossed it back down again.

"Shit."

He drummed his fingers on the steering wheel for a few moments, then snatched it back up again with purpose. "Forgive me…"

He broke the tiny seal. The writing was all in Spanish. Some of the pages had tiny drawings in the side margins. He flipped through a few and a photo slipped out. It was a picture of Carmen and a young man, smiling — a photo booth picture, the kind you'd get at the mall or amusement park. On the back was written CM & VR in a heart. Jack flipped to the last entry. It was dated a week before she was reported missing. He struggled to decipher a few words, but his Spanish was rudimentary at best: hello, goodbye, bathroom — and all of the curses shouted at him while interrogating murder suspects in the inner city. That was about it.

It was getting late, if he didn't hurry, it would be dark soon. Jack circled the block several times, scoping out the locals, looking for a potential volunteer. After assessing the candidates — a man in his undershirt drinking beer on his stoop, a couple arguing outside their apartment, two men working on their car, he returned to a group of 13-14 year old girls, singing clever rhymes while skipping double dutch rope in the street.

He took a moment to debate what he was doing. Several officers back at the station spoke Spanish and could easily translate this for him. But the content of the book, its circumstances, exposed him to ridicule, especially with Harrington, who'd made him question his own judgment. When it came to humiliation, Jack was risk averse.

He rolled down his passenger side window, leaning over. "Excuse me!" he called out to the girls. They didn't hear, so he called out again, "Hey, excuse me!" One of the girls waiting her turn looked back at him: *You talking to me?* "Hi, yes, can I talk to you?"

She had thick wavy brown hair and wore cut off shorts with a half shirt that had the word *precioso* bedazzled on the chest. She cautiously approached his car, leaving a good two feet of distance. Her friends paid him no mind and kept their routine going, jumping with perfect timing while the two others spun the rope faster and faster, chanting their song.

She leaned in. "What?"

"I was wondering if you could help me out?"

A hand on her hips, suspicious. "You lost?"

"No, listen, I'll pay you ten bucks if you-"

"Fuck off-"

"No, it's not like that. I just need you to help me read something."

"Why, you stupid?"

"No - well yes, I am, but this is… I don't speak Spanish, and I have this book I'd like you to read to me."

"What makes you think I speak Spanish?"

"A hunch."

She curled her lips and looked back at her friends. "This gonna take long?"

"Depends on how fast you can read. No, it won't take long, just a few minutes."

Jack put his car in gear and pulled over to the side of the road. He turned off the motor as she opened the door to climb in.

Jack got out of the car and walked over to a nearby stoop. She made a face like he must be crazy. She got back out, slamming the door.

"What you doin?"

"Never get into a stranger's car," Jack said as he slowly sat down on the stoop, the pain making him look like an old man. He tried to hide it, but she noticed. She also noticed his gun holster as his jacket shifted.

"You're a cop?"

"Detective."

"What's the difference?"

"More paperwork. Sit."

She sat down beside him, wondering why she agreed to this. He handed her the book.

"This looks like someone's diary." She opened it and flipped a few pages. "You're not supposed to read these," she said with a sly grin, but serious.

"It's okay, it's not supposed to exist. Can you read her handwriting?"

"She drew these pictures? Man… they sick, oh shit."

"Can you read it?"

"I'm reading it."

"Out loud?"

"Which page?"

"I don't know. Just read."

"Today was cloudy. I stubbed my toe on my bedpost, it hurt so bad. My little brother won't stop singing that stupid song-"

"Skip to the next page." Jack twirled his hand in a rush.

"I miss my papa. Haven't seen him for a few days, he is working nights again."

"Next one."

She mumbled, straining to read the first few scribbles. *"January 12. Ummm, to a, to see it hanging there, knowing so many people could admire it for years to come. My papa was so proud, I came in first place. I got a gift; free dinner for two at Cafe Gianna's. I gave it to my father, to take my mother. He works so hard. He cried when he saw it. He touched my name at the bottom. He's been back there three times since it went up. He tells me, this is just the beginning."*

"Skip to the final entry," Jack said.

She flipped to the last written page. *"April 17. Today in class a man posed nude for us to paint. I know it was not a sin, but I felt ashamed. Like I do when I have those feelings. Victor gets angry at me. He scares me sometimes. I love him with my heart. I want to love him with my body-*ooh, this is getting good."

"Just keep reading."

"I want to love him with my body, but I don't want to lose the love of the Lord. My mother would kill me if she knew. How can something so beautiful be such a sin?"

"She mention Victor's last name?" Jack asked.

The girl read a few more sentences to herself, mumbling as she scanned the lines.

"No, but there's a phone number next to this, look."

Jack took the book back and stood up. "Thanks." He handed her ten dollars and walked back to his car.

"This girl gonna get pissed if she finds out you read her diary?" Jack opened his door and climbed in.

"No, she'd dead."

The girl shivered and wiped her hands on her jeans, grossed out.

CHAPTER 42

Rebecca crept past Laura, asleep on the couch in the living room. She had taken some aspirin and dozed off while watching TV, still on with the volume low. Rebecca moved through the kitchen to the laundry room in back.

Inside were stacks of boxes, some opened, some still sealed with box tape since the move. She'd seen her mother carry a small book into this room and return empty handed. Her mother had been crying, unaware she'd been watching her from the staircase, which gave a clear view into the kitchen and the entrance to the laundry area if she crouched down under the metal railing.

Rebecca went to the open boxes first. One was filled with clothes of hers that she no longer fit into, *donate to Goodwill* was scribbled on the side. Another had pots and pans in it. Rebecca moved that box aside and something in it shifted, making a loud noise. Rebecca froze and listened for her mother. She waited a good minute before she continued, opening another box that was filled with old photo albums. The first one was a flip book from Disney World. Rebecca was just 3 or 4 years old. She had no memory of going, but from the photographs it looked like she had fun. She wondered why she had so much trouble remembering things from when she was younger.

She opened her parent's wedding album. The first picture was a large color print of the two of them, happy, kissing. She puffed out her cheeks and frowned. She quickly closed it and moved it aside. There were some loose pictures at the bottom. She gathered them up and flipped through one by one. Most were of her mother when she was younger. Her hair much longer than it is now. There was one of her grandfather. He looked angry in the photo, his eyes going in different directions.

Then she found a small black phone book at the bottom of the box. She recognized the binding — *this was the book her mother was holding*. There was a picture inside. It was faded, but she could clearly make out her mother with her arm around the girl from the paper. Carmen. It was all true. *Why did she lie to me?* The betrayal made Rebecca feel very alone.

She recalled the doctor asking her a question after the third or fourth session:

"Rebecca, tell me, who is Carmen?"

He said she had told him her name was Carmen while she was under. She had no idea who he was talking about, she had no memory of that name or who it belonged to. Certainly no memory of ever saying it.

After their last session, she came out of it to find the doctor was sweating and very nervous. When she got up from his comfortable couch, she noticed the small green lamp that normally sat on the table beside her was on the floor, smashed. That was the last time she ever sat alone with the doctor.

The following visit, the doctor brought her and her mother in his office, all serious like. He asked her mother if she knew who Carmen was. Her mom got all fidgety, turned to her like she'd said a curse word or something. Her mother said to wait for her outside with the secretary. A few minutes later she came out all upset, grabbed her arm and said they were never coming back. She wouldn't even let her go back to pick up her sketchbook.

She had waited two days, until her mother stopped muttering to herself, to ask her who the doctor was talking about. Who was Carmen? She sensed her mother was keeping something from her. She'd always sensed it. Then the report on the news. *Why would she lie? Was she scared of her nightmares being real?*

She flipped through the book to C, but found no entry. She flipped to the M's and there it was, the name Carmen Muniz circled with a heart. She placed the book on her lap and repacked the box, closing it. She clutched the book and returned to the kitchen. She sat on a tall stool with a round red cushion and picked up the phone.

The drone of the dial tone made her shiver nervously. She swallowed, listening a moment to make sure her mom wasn't up and about. She dialed the first few digits, her small fingers trembling. The terror was making her head ache, but her curiosity was so intense she decided facing the inevitable was her only choice. The pain and fear would be there anyway.

She finished dialing, hesitating before inputting the last number. She pressed it, sending the signal whisking along its way, then held the phone with both hands — waiting.

She looked over her shoulders several times, making sure the coast was clear. She checked the clock over the sink. 12:30 A.M. She hadn't slept a normal schedule in so long, it never occurred to her that whoever answered on the other end might not be too pleased to be getting a call this late, regardless of who was on the line.

It rang once, twice, three times… four times. Rebecca went to hang up when she heard a click.

"Hola?" a voice said. It was Francisco. Rebecca sat silently, her mouth open, but no words. "Hola? Hello?" he said again.

"¿Quién es, Francisco?" Hester's voice said in the background, nervously. The sound bounced around in Rebecca's ears - she recognized it. She opened her mouth wider, but again nothing came out. Rebecca could hear the phone change hands.

"Hello?" Hester said, clearing her throat, still groggy. Rebecca pulled the phone away from her ear in terror, but curiosity pushed it right back, fastening it to her head. "Hello, who is this? Nada, no one."

"…Hello," Rebecca said, breaking her silence.

"Who is this? Why are you calling me like this? Habla!"

"…Momma?" Rebecca whispered into the phone. Hester went

silent.

"Rebecca?" Laura's voice spun Rebecca around, she immediately hung up like a young child caught looking at dirty pictures, slamming the pages closed. But she missed the base. Laura stood at the entrance to the kitchen in the darkness, bleary eyed, her robe open.

Laura approached and grabbed the receiver from her hand. "Who are you talking to?"

Laura lifted the phone to her ear. "Hello? Who is this?" Laura could hear sobbing, and then a click. "Hello? Hello?" Laura hung it up. Rebecca looked away, unable to make eye contact.

"Who was that?" Laura turned Rebecca around, lifting her chin. "Rebecca, who was that? Who were you calling this late?"

Rebecca just stared. Laura saw her old phone book and the photograph sitting on the counter. She grabbed Rebecca's shoulders. "Rebecca, who was that on the phone? Who were you calling? Answer me!" Rebecca jerked away and took a few unbalanced steps backwards, confused, frightened. Her mother knew exactly who she was calling.

Rebecca's eyes went dark, cold. Immediately fear gripped Laura tightly, not wanting to endure another episode like the one by the river. She backed off, softening her tone.

"Sweetie, talk to me."

"I have to go," Rebecca said. Laura reached for her, but she pulled away, taking a few more steps, but not really going anywhere.

"Baby, what are you talking about?"

"They must be so worried," Rebecca whispered. Laura crept towards Rebecca slowly, the way someone tries to approach an animal without spooking it. "Who? Who's worried, sweetie?" Rebecca just stood there, an epiphany was washing over her, pieces of a puzzle locking into place.

She turned away from Laura and grabbed her head, a tremendous pain suddenly swelled inside. It was the realization of truth, the anguish of being lost, of death, and then of being found, reconnection, longing and fulfillment — all of these emotions swirling inside her, slamming her fragile mind. Emotions without the clarity or perspective of where they emanated from. Emotions without the memories attached, just loose ends that felt real, that needed tying.

And the solution — the answers, lie *out there*. It couldn't be solved with a mother-daughter talk, not anymore, now that the bond of trust had been broken. A good night's sleep wouldn't solve the riddle, neither would ignoring the feelings, hoping they would go away. They were here to stay, at least until an explanation that included some type of closure could put them to rest.

A light was turned on, Rebecca had stepped forth from the shadows of doubt and uncertainty — into reality. And that was the only prescription she needed. A large dose of reality.

Laura watched in agonizing horror as Rebecca imploded before her eyes. It wasn't loud, or physical, it was an awakening. Powered by a force stronger than her, welling up and taking over. Her mind was downloading and processing information previously inaccessible, repressed and submerged, now bubbling to the surface. Rebecca was seeing the world for the first time as it actually was. And her place in it.

Laura wept at the sight, terrified for her, of the consequences. She cried, teeth bared, a contorted grimace of sorrow, helpless. "Becca, please…"

"Get away from me!" Rebecca cried out as she sidestepped Laura's attempt at embrace. It no longer offered comfort, only confinement. Rebecca's evasion provoked Laura and, in her exhausted state, sent her into a rage.

"Don't talk to me like that, I'm your mother! Now who the hell were you calling in the middle of the night?"

"You're not my mother," Rebecca said, straight as an arrow into Laura's heart. Laura dropped to her knees and grabbed Rebecca so tight, she'd have to leave her limbs behind to break free of Laura's grasp.

"You listen to me, you're not going anywhere but back to bed. And we're gonna see this thing through. You and me!"

"Why did you lie to me?"

"What did you want me to do? Tell you yes, your nightmares

are real?"

Laura held Rebecca till both of their eyes were overflowing with tears. Rebecca's emotions were a combination of fear and confusion; fear of the truth that awaited her, of seeing her mother as a stranger, of feeling lost - alone, and the confusion of the sudden rush of feelings for another family, emotions of painful loss - and reunion.

Rebecca stopped trying to wriggle away, giving in. She blew saliva bubbles as she cried. Laura drew a deep breath, calming herself.

"I'm sorry, baby. I know how hard this has all been for you; moving here, Daddy leaving, school, everything. I'm so sorry. It's all my fault." Laura pulled Rebecca to her breast, hugged her deeply, as if trying to draw her into her own body, shield her from the cruel world. "It's gonna be okay. You hear me? We're gonna get through this."

"We?" Rebecca said, her voice full of disillusion. Rebecca broke free of her embrace, leaving Laura on her knees. Rebecca moved towards the front door. Laura watched incredulously as Rebecca reached for her jacket. She turned the doorknob, opening it to depart into the cold night, come what may.

Laura saw red and leaped to her feet. Now it was a battle of wills. She stormed over and slammed the door shut so hard it shook the foundation of the rickety old house. "Stop it!" Laura shouted. The shock caused Rebecca to abruptly reverse course and head back towards the kitchen.

Rebecca reached for the phone again and began to dial. Laura chased after her, tearing the phone from her hands. "Enough!" Laura tossed the phone across the room.

Rebecca back peddled, turned, and fainted flat out onto the kitchen floor. Laura watched it happen in slow motion. She tried to lunge her arms out to catch her in time, but wasn't fast enough. She crumpled down beside Rebecca, whose face was pale and moist.

She cradled her small head. "Rebecca? Rebecca, please speak, open your eyes."

Laura could see Rebecca's eyes swim back and forth beneath

her thin, swollen eyelids. Slowly they fluttered and her eyes opened. Rebecca looked at her mother, this time with familiarity, as if waking from a terrible nightmare.

"My head hurts," Rebecca said softly.

Laura looked into her eyes and saw her little girl again. Her daughter was back, her spirit home from whatever dark place it had just journeyed. The universe had heard her cries and agreed to return Rebecca's soul to its rightful owner. Tears drained from Laura's very being and she let them release.

"Oh God," Laura said, her voice raspy, hollow. "Please…give me the strength." She hugged Rebecca tightly.

Upon hearing those words, Rebecca realized there was only one person that could help her; herself. She stared up at the ceiling, plotting her next move.

CHAPTER 43

The obstetrician glided the ultrasound across Patricia's petroleum slicked belly. At 34 weeks, the baby's features were clearly visible. Patricia looked at the monitor and swore her baby was waving back at her. "You see that, Bobby?"

"I see it," Robert said, squeezing his wife's hand, relishing a moment they had waited so long to enjoy. All the years of disappointment, the miscarriages, the hoping. There was no stopping this miracle. Just a few more weeks.

Martha, their obstetrician — who wore three pairs of glasses draped around her neck; one for reading, one for seeing, and one pair that darkened in sunlight — slid the sensor to the other side of Patricia's abdomen, who winced from the cold tickle.

"You sure you don't wanna know the sex?"

Patricia looked at her proud, wide-eyed husband, lost in the moment. "We've waited this long."

"We want it to be a surprise," Robert said, finishing her sentence.

"Like opening a present."

"Well, he...or she, is doing excellent. Size, weight look normal for 34 weeks. You wanna hear the heartbeat?"

They both nodded. The nurse turned a dial and the electronic squelch of the baby's heartbeat filled the room. Robert gently squeezed Patricia's hand in silent triumph.

Martha lifted the device off her stomach and draped a towel across. She winked at Robert, who took the hint and began gently wiping his wife clean. Martha wheeled the machine over to the wall and grabbed a paper towel to wipe her hands. "I recommend you stay close to home from here on in."

"Oh, we have our route mapped and everything," Patricia said. She pulled Robert close and planted a firm kiss on his lips, embarrassing him.

On the drive home, Patricia had an overwhelming feeling of optimism; she couldn't wipe the smile from her face. The world was perfect for a moment. She looked across at Robert, driving extra cautiously, which made her smile widen even more. She placed her hand on his leg and tapped it a few times.

Soon other thoughts began entering her mind, from baby proofing the furniture, to vacuuming the rug and other mundane everyday tasks. *And* they were having a baby shower in a few days. Then there was the packing for the move, calls to make, paperwork, mail forwarding. Slowly, reality started creeping back in.

"You know, my mom's so upset about the move, she's treating this get together like a damn funeral," Patricia said.

"She can always visit," Robert said, not really listening, deep in thoughts of his own.

"You know she won't get on a plane." Robert pumped his eyebrows, victoriously. Patricia frowned and looked out the window. The clouds passed in front of the sun, graying out the blue sky. "You go see Jack?" Robert's smile lost its luster. She knew what that look meant. "It doesn't matter."

Robert suddenly seemed preoccupied with driving, evasive. "This is a very positive moment in our lives. If your brother doesn't want to be a part of it, that's his loss. You tried."

CHAPTER 44

A string of bells hanging on the door rang out as Jack entered Rivera's Auto Repair Shop. It was lively inside, the busy sound of pneumatic tools and banging wrenches shouting back and forth. He leaned over the grimy counter to peer into the garage. A Hispanic man with thick salt and pepper hair, wearing faded red overalls, came in and placed a set of keys on a cork board hook. He swiped a customer's credit card through a reader and waited.

"I'm looking for a Mr. Rivera?" Jack said.

"I'm Rivera," he answered, not looking at Jack. The machine buzzed and spit out a receipt. He tore it off and stapled it to a form. When he turned to face Jack, Rivera could tell immediately he wasn't there to have his car repaired.

"I'm looking for *Victor* Rivera," Jack said, his voice implying this older gentleman could not be the man he was looking for. He placed the picture of Victor and Carmen on the counter to emphasize his point.

"Where you get this?"

"You know him?"

"He's my son."

"Is he here?"

"He's under the lift, he's working."

"What's your name?" Jack asked.

"Alfonse."

"Alfonse, I need to speak to Victor."

Alfonse wiped his mouth with his dirty hand, not moving. Jack couldn't tell if he was ignoring his request, or if he didn't understand. Jack flashed his detective's badge.

"Can you ask him to come out, or do I need to go in and get him."

Alfonse poked his head into the garage. "Victor!"

"Qué?" a voice called out.

"¡Vete aquí! Ahora!"

Another patron entered the waiting area; an old caucasian man with ghostly white hair and pale skin, visible blue veins on his hands and neck.

"Como esta, cabrón!" The man greeted Alfonse, clearly not his native tongue. Alfonse didn't return the greeting.

"Your car is ready," Alfonse said flatly, not taking his eyes off Jack. The old man leaned on the counter and looked Jack over.

"Ha, I told you if ya keep ripping people off you'd get busted. He uses gray market brake pads and tells you they're factory."

"Shut up," Alfonse said.

"You gonna run him in, copper?" the old man said, snickering.

Jack leaned in to Alfonse. "Have Victor meet me out front."

Jack stood outside in the cold. All the other storefronts were either auto repair or body work. A tiny boombox played merengue across the street at a car wash.

Victor pushed open the door and came out with his shoulders back and chest out. Upon seeing the serious look on Jack's face, he relaxed his muscles and put away the bravado.

"Victor?"

"Whatchu want?"

Jack flashed his badge, wasting no time with small talk. "Detective Jack Ridge, I'd like to ask you a few questions."

"What about?"

"Carmen Muniz."

Victor blinked, confused. He looked at the ground and nodded a few times. Jack could read a person from their first reaction to confrontation. Victor's body language said he wasn't hiding guilt. It was regret. Sorrow. No doubt he'd read the papers.

"You two knew each other."

"Yeah, a little."

"You were boyfriend and girlfriend."

"No. I wanted that. She didn't."

"She didn't want to be your boyfriend?"

"No - she wasn't… we only dated a few weeks. She was a little loco."

"How so?"

"Had a relationship with God. You know?"

"What do you remember about the night she disappeared?"

"I figure she just took off. Mother had a loose wire. Shit. Just fucked up."

"Were you with her the night she disappeared?"

Victor got defensive. "No. I broke it off a few weeks before."

"Why?"

"Long time ago, man. Had no patience back then."

"I don't understand," Jack said. Victor put his hands in his back pockets and twisted in place, trying to put it into words.

"…She was a delicate flower."

"How do you mean?"

Victor rolled his eyes. "An appetizer, no fun. A…prude?"

"Okay."

Another worker poked his head out of the garage. "Victor, what weight?"

"10 w 30."

"He's got 40 in there now."

"That's wrong. Too thick."

"What?"

"Gimme a minute!"

Jack held up his fingers signaling *two minutes*. The man mumbled something under his breath and went back inside.

"What else do you remember?"

"She used to paint… so beautiful. Damn, some fucked up shit, man."

"Yeah, fucked up. Where did she like to go, hang out? Do you remember?"

"Nowhere. School and back. I remember...she won some contest once, they hung her picture in the gallery at the Rec Center downtown. Dragged me there once."

"Can you tell me where it is?"

"Hamilton, next to the Library."

"Thank you Victor, I won't hold you up any longer." Jack turned to leave.

"Am I a suspect?" Victor called out to him. Jack looked him up and down.

"Of course you are."

CHAPTER 45

Teresa Mason's apartment was on the third floor of a six story apartment building. There were five other tenants on her floor. She checked her reflection in the bathroom mirror, pulling her hair back to swap her cheap everyday earrings for gold ones — a gift from her mother at Christmas. She'd never worn them before.

She checked her watch, Randall would be there any minute. She swished and spit her mouthwash, rubbing the static of her dress a few times, trying to straighten it out. No good, just made it worse.

The doorbell rang. "Shit." She shut off the bathroom light and went to the front door, checking her reflection as she passed the hallway mirror. She pulled at her dress, trying to flatten it one last time, wanting to make a good first impression. *Okay, ready or not.* She moved to the door, her feet throbbing already in her high heel shoes.

When she opened it, she saw nothing but flowers.

"Teresa?"

She craned her neck to see his face through the bouquet as he barged into her living room. "Randall?" The voice wasn't familiar.

He extended his hand and revealed himself. Her expression

turned to horror. He anticipated that, violently shoving the flowers into her face as he slammed the door closed, deftly covering her mouth as she attempted to scream. He smashed her atop the head with a closed fist.

The last thought that pulsed through her brain as she fell unconscious was *how could I have been so stupid?*

CHAPTER 46

Jack stalked through the halls of The Lansing Metropolitan Recreation Center, which was filled with inner city kids playing basketball in the gym and working with computers in the library, staying out of trouble. He approached a receptionist perched behind a tall gray counter, she was typing away at a computer.

Jack tapped on the counter with his fingernail to rouse her attention. She was engrossed in her work and didn't respond. He cleared his throat.

"Can I help you?" the receptionist asked, continuing to type at blazing speed.

"The art gallery, where is it?"

She spoke without taking her eyes off her screen. "You go down that corridor," pointing in the direction Jack had just come from. A woman stepped around Jack and handed the receptionist a cup of coffee.

"No sugar?" Still locked on the screen.

"In it," the woman said, moving past Jack and down the hallway.

The receptionist reached for her coffee and finally looked at Jack, curious why he was still standing there. "You go down the corridor, turn right, just up the stairs."

"Thank you." Jack turned and doubled back the way he came. He saw the mistake he made and wondered how he'd missed the bright green sign pointing the direction towards the Gallery. He shook his head and climbed the metal staircase.

The gallery was very simplistic, just a single corridor with a white divider down the middle. The partition created two long hallways of artwork on either side. Every few feet, there was a space in the partition that you could pass through to go from one side to the other. No one else there seemed to have an appreciation for fine art, so the area was very calm and quiet.

Jack admired each framed painting, searching. They were all good, but seemed pedestrian compared to Rebecca's work. *Or Carmen's.* He knew, if it was still there, it would stand out like a gold brick atop a pile of coal.

He didn't even bother to check the names, confident he would know it when he saw it. Finishing one full aisle of art, he turned around to come back up the other side. The third picture in caught his attention.

On second glance it nearly floored him.

It was a painting of a little girl holding her mother's hand. The little girl was wearing a bright yellow dress.

She was the spitting image of Rebecca.

Jack's eyes went wide, his lips curled into a tight seam. "It's not possible," he said softly. *But neither was the diary.* He reached out and touched the painting with his fingertip. He slid it down to the inscription on the bottom. *C.M.*

Under the frame was a bronze banner which read: *1st Prize Awarded to Carmen Muniz.* There was a small plaque alongside the portrait with a black & white photograph of Carmen. The plaque was titled: *Follow Your Dreams.*

Jack took a seat on a small two-sided white bench in the middle of the room. He couldn't take his eyes off the painting, off the image of Rebecca. He was shaken to his core, but excited at the same time. He felt privy to something extraordinary that most would dismiss as ridiculous fantasy. But here was more firsthand proof. His head spun with theories, attempts to inject some rationality into what he had experienced over the last few days.

He now fully comprehended Leonard's trepidations; this is why Leonard made him walk in his shoes first. It wasn't something he could describe — he had to see it for himself. It's very hard to dismiss something when you've seen it with your own eyes. *But had Leonard gotten this far? No, he hadn't dug this deep.*

Rebecca's clues had solved Carmen's disappearance and her story had opened his eyes to new possibilities about life. But was this exercise solely for his benefit? He bit down, grinding his teeth, angry and frustrated at himself. Jack hadn't been able to piece together the clues he'd been given and somehow solve the greater mystery. *Something is missing!* A clue he'd overlooked, an interpretation he'd gotten wrong. The answer was there, right in front of him, staring him in the face. *Dammit, Jack, think!*

Jack sat for a long while, feeling worthless. He'd begged for a chance to solve this case, to make good on his promise — and he'd been granted that opportunity in the most amazing of circumstances. He was getting closer, he could feel it. But his detective's acumen wasn't up to the task. He was blowing it.

He wanted to call Leonard, discuss it, get his thoughts, tell him maybe he would get a chance to re-write theology after all. But that conversation was miles long, and Jack didn't have the time. He had a murder investigation to solve, a killer to catch.

His cell phone rang, he let it buzz a few times. He was going to let it go to voicemail - *But what if it's Laura?* The guilt was still fresh from the other day.

"Hello?"

"Jack, it's Harrington. Get back to the station, quick."

"What's going on?"

"We got him."

CHAPTER 47

Laura paced in the kitchen, holding the phone to one ear and her other hand to her forehead. Her hair hadn't seen a shower in days. "I don't know what to tell you, Ted."

She listened to the answer.

"What about Val, can't she fill in?" Laura tensely twisted the cord with her fingers. "Well, I have a situation here, I just can't make it right now."

She looked out the window at a potted plant wilting in the cold, dry winter air. She had meant to bring it inside. It was all but dead now. Just another thing that had taken a back seat on her priorities list. *Can't even care for a potted plant. What am I doing in charge of a human being?*

"Fine, do what you have to. I'm sure I can get another job in a grocery, it's not like it's a fucking career. Yeah, fuck you too." She hung up and peeked over her shoulder, hoping Rebecca was not in earshot. Not that she hadn't heard her utter that phrase to her father a thousand times during their divorce.

Laura hung up the phone. She sighed weakly into her hands; no strength left, even for outbursts of frustration. She lit a cigarette, inhaling and exhaling angrily, falling deeper into depression.

She picked up the phone again and dialed, inputting the last known number of her nomadic ex-husband. The operator came on to tell her that *the number was no longer in service.*

She moved through the living room to the back door. She looked out into the yard, thinking Rebecca was on the swing, but the creaking metronome she'd heard was a persistent wind blowing it back and forth.

She headed upstairs to check on her. She entered her bedroom — empty — the grilled cheese sandwich and glass of milk she'd made her for lunch was still sitting on the table by her easel, untouched. "Rebecca?"

She checked every room upstairs. "Rebecca?" Her voice grew nervous.

She raced back downstairs and spun in place, not sure where to look next. She turned and went through the side door into the garage. The garage door was open, the cold blast of the outdoor air chilled her skin.

She saw Rebecca's bicycle was missing.

CHAPTER 48

Harrington briefed Jack as they walked through the precinct hallway towards the interrogation area. There was an electricity in the air, Jack could feel his hands trembling with adrenaline.

"Name's Teresa Mason, 26, she managed to give a description before she passed out," Harrington said.

"Mason? Doesn't sound like his M.O."

"HP cornered the bastard on the interstate, she gave a pretty solid ID to a neighbor who called it in. I think we got him, Jack."

"How is she?"

"Critical condition, suffered massive trauma to the head. Put up a good fight; they're not sure if she'll make it."

They entered the holding area adjacent to the interrogation room. Jennifer stood near the two-way glass, watching the suspect. He sat alone in a chair, light shining on him overhead, the rest of the room dim.

Jack stepped up to the glass, peering in. *Can it be this easy? My incompetence so immense that you had to hand deliver him to my doorstep?*

"Who is he?" Jack asked. Jennifer read from a printout:

"Edward Bishop, 42, plumber, has a prior record of sexual assault of a minor, served four years. Spent time at Northville Psychiatric Hospital on four separate occasions, self admitted."

Bishop sat slouched in his chair. He was boyish looking; wiry brown eyes so dark they were almost black. A thin, pointed nose. Scratches on his cheek. He looked disinterested. "He also works part time for Baxter Mills Inc. They contract out bonded cleaning services to offices, municipalities, schools. They're under contract to several universities in this area."

Jennifer handed the report to Jack.

"Someone should talk to Baxter about their employee vetting process. They search the vehicle?"

"We found a black duffel bag in his van," Harrington said, "gloves, rope, knives, and wire, along with these." Harrington placed a few professional looking laminated ID cards on a table, all different occupations, all had Bishop's photo. "We also found several stolen laptops."

"Forensics is running a trace on the vehicle for blood samples," Jennifer said.

"What about his residence?"

"They're tossing it as we speak," Harrington said.

Jack shot an anxious look towards Harrington. Harrington shook his head. "They didn't find anyone."

"How long has he been here?"

"I called you as soon as they brought him in, wanted you to be the first to speak to him." Jack turned to look in again at Bishop. He'd seen him before. His picture, his prior arrest. He was one of hundreds of potential suspects he had studied during the investigation.

Jack walked out and around to the interrogation room entrance, taking a moment to compose himself. He slowly turned the handle and entered.

Bishop stared at the floor as Jack approached. Harrington entered behind Jack and closed the door.

Jack bypassed his usual tactic of pushing the table across the room, leaving the suspect exposed. He had so many questions, he didn't want to start out confrontational. There was too much work to be processed between them. He took the seat across from Bishop. Harrington stood behind Bishop, his arms folded.

Bishop lazily tilted his head back to take a look at Jack. He observed Jack's labored movements, the pain he was trying to conceal. Jack placed the clipboard with Bishop's arrest report down on the table. Bishop lifted his handcuffed wrists and awkwardly scratched an itch on his cheek with the back of his knuckle. Jack felt a certain unease about him.

Bishop was unattractive, ugly, with thin hair combed forward to cover his receding hairline. He had a fresh bruise around his left eye. Jack sat perfectly still, staring at Bishop, hardly even taking a breath. He picked up the clipboard and read aloud:

"You live at 23 Washington?" Bishop remained silent, blank. "Is that your residence?"

Harrington stepped forward and grabbed Bishop's brittle hair, forcing him to look at Jack. Bishop grinned at Harrington's show of force, as if he expected it. Jack flitted his hand for Harrington to release him. Harrington obliged, letting go and taking a step back.

"Several messages sent to Teresa Mason were traced to an IP address registered to your computer," Jack said.

"I don't own one. But nice try," Bishop said, his voice effeminate, high pitched and nasal.

"Claims he was home all day," Harrington said. He looked down in Bishop's direction. "Lemme guess, didn't match your tall, dark, and handsome profile; things went downhill from there?"

"I have no idea what you're talking about."

"She's clinging to life in the ER. Claims you attacked her," Jack said.

"Who?"

"Two witnesses saw you exiting her apartment at the time of the attack," Harrington said. "They scraped your DNA from under her God damn fingernails. I'm sure that's not the only place they'll find it."

"You say you were home all day?"

"That's right."

"So what happened between 5 and 7 P.M. that caused you to race onto the expressway headed towards Ohio?"

"You guys are full of shit."

Jack tossed an ID card onto the table between them. Then

another, and another. "Forged plumber's license, telephone repair man." Jack turned over another one to read it. "I see you work for the US Post Office too?" Jack tossed it into the pile accumulating on the table. "You stay busy."

Bishop licked his lips and rolled his eyes, locking them in an odd angle, appearing quite deranged.

"Uniform's a good ruse to gain entry into a woman's home, isn't it?" Harrington said.

Bishop started to stand up; Harrington sat him down with one push from his powerful arm. Bishop shrank, sensing Harrington's immense strength.

"I read Teresa Mason holds a black belt in Karate. What happened, finally met your match?" Harrington said, a bullying grin, he wanted to hurt Bishop so desperately.

"Fuck yourself," Bishop muttered in a monotone grumble. Harrington cracked his knuckles in anticipation, but Jack's stare held him at bay.

Jack continued to read from the printout: "Attempted rape, attempted murder, resisting arrest." Jack raised his eyebrows at the next detail, then looked at Bishop, sizing up his thin, diminutive frame. "Attacking an officer? Resisting arrest? You're in a lot of trouble, Ed. But that's nothing new, you have a long track record of sexual offenses. Did time in jail for rape, paroled a little over 4 years ago."

"Would explain the gap in time between the murders," Harrington said.

"Yes it would," Jack said to himself.

Jack took a photo out of his inner jacket pocket. He placed it down in front of Bishop. It was a picture of Angelina.

"Recognize her?" Jack asked. Bishop looked away and spit on the floor. Harrington grabbed him again and twisted his head to look at the picture. "You look at it!" Harrington growled.

Bishop stared at the picture, breathing heavily through his teeth. "She's been missing three months now. Take a good look."

"Never seen her."

"If you don't help me, I can't help you," Jack said.

"You know what they do to sexual offenders in general

population, you've done some time," Harrington said.

"Take a good look," Jack said. "Do you know where she is?"

"After a while, they all start to look alike."

Jack stood up, frustrated.

"Give me a few minutes with him, alone," Harrington said.

The door opened and Jennifer entered. "Mr. Bishop's lawyer is outside."

Jack leaned over the table, placing both palms down, leaning right into Bishop's face. "Right now I've got you on aggravated assault, weapons possession. If Teresa dies, you're looking at murder."

"I want to speak to my lawyer, tell him how you physically mistreated me." Bishop flashed a big toothy grin. He looked back at Harrington, who remained stone faced, only the rule of law holding him back. Jennifer held the door open, Jack pulled on Harrington's shoulder to exit with him.

They retreated into the adjacent room. Jack looked in at Bishop, who was sitting up straight now, his hands on his lap, not a care in the world. Bishop turned towards the glass as if he could feel Jack's stare, sending the rare chill down Jack's spine.

"They found a tan Buick Skylark parked behind his house. It's registered in his name," Jennifer said.

"The Ann Arbor victim, Delgado, was last seen getting into a late model tan vehicle before she disappeared," Jack said.

"We have Teresa Mason's account, Bishop fits the profile," Harrington added.

"She doesn't," Jack said.

"Maybe he got tired of Latinos," Harrington said.

Jack watched as Bishop picked his nose, examining his fingertip for prizes. "I expected more intelligence from someone so meticulous and patient. Ten years is a long time to evade suspicion."

"Could be a ruse; they're master manipulators," Jennifer said. Jack watched Bishop's lawyer enter the room, taking the seat where Jack had been sitting.

Jack exited the holding area and walked down the hall. Carl Rosa entered his path from the other end, ambushing him head on. Carl was sweaty, on edge, ready to burst.

"Jack, I hear you're holding a suspect in custody?"

"That's right."

"Did he take my daughter?"

"I don't know Carl."

"What are you waiting for?"

"He's a suspect. If he knows anything, we'll get it from him."

Carl pushed past Jack. "I've waited long enough."

"Carl, you can't go back there," Jack's words prodded an officer nearby into action. He grabbed Carl, restraining him at the waist. Carl didn't resist.

As they walked him away, he paused and turned to Jack. "Do you have any idea what it's like to have the only thing you love in this world... ripped from your heart?"

Jack's lip quivered. He had no desire to bring Carl Rosa up to speed on his familiarity with grief and loss. And he understood, after years of hearing that question repeated in one form or another, that it was rhetorical.

Jennifer approached from behind to rescue him. "Jack, call for you."

"I'll take it in my office. Excuse me, Carl." Jack respectfully placed his hand on Carl's shoulder as he sidestepped him to get to his office.

He closed the door behind him and picked up the phone. "Hello?"

"Jack, she's gone."

"Laura?"

"I've searched everywhere. Her bike is missing-"

"Okay, okay, slow down. Where are you?"

CHAPTER 49

The rain pounded the pavement like buckets of water dumped all at once. Thunder cracked in the distance. Laura hopped in place, anxious, scanning the street.

Jack's car finally turned the corner and pulled up along the curb. Laura raced off her front porch and climbed in.

"What happened?" Jack asked, pulling away, not even asking which direction they should head.

"I don't know, I was on the phone - when I went to check on her, she was gone."

"Don't worry, we'll find her."

"I'm sorry, I didn't know who else to call."

"I'm glad you did."

"She's gotten worse, Jack. I don't know if I can handle it anymore. I haven't slept in days; I can barely see straight."

"What's the last thing she said to you?"

Laura paused a moment. "She keeps asking to go home." Jack looked at Laura. They both knew at that moment where she might be headed.

The rain streaked on Jack's dirty windshield, his wipers on the fastest setting, rocking back and forth as if they might fly off into the night. Jack had a swivel searchlight mounted on the side of his door. He rolled down the window and shined it along the dark side streets. He turned a corner and continued, twisting it back and forth, searching while trying to drive a straight line.

"This is my fault," Laura cried.

"No, it isn't. You've done everything right. If you want to blame anyone, blame me. I should never have brought her out there."

Jack turned another corner; they headed into the urban area of town. Laura looked up and recognized the street they were on. And where it led.

"I know this road," Laura said. Their eyes met for a moment, both thinking the same thing.

"This is crazy. She's so confused. All these thoughts have been put into her head, she's starting to believe it. It's all been twisted."

Jack held his tongue. He didn't want to upset Laura, add to her plate — it wasn't the time to bring up the painting he saw at the rec center gallery, inform her that Carmen somehow had a vision of her future incarnation and committed it to canvas. Maybe, when she was ready, he'd let Laura see it for herself. Dispel any doubt, like the kind that was beginning to creep into his own mind, the more he thought about Bishop.

Jack saw something reflect his light in the distance.

"Look," Jack pointed.

As he drove closer he could see the spokes of Rebecca's upended bicycle, the tire still spinning.

"How did she know to come this way? That Carmen lived over in this area?" Jack asked.

"Her address is written down in my phone book, Rebecca was looking through it last night."

Of course. Common sense versus the supernatural was waging war inside Jack's head. But...*there are no coincidences. Are there?*

"Is that her?" Jack pulled up along the shoulder.

"Oh my God!" Laura screamed. Jack climbed out of the car into the tall grass. He passed the bike, the chain had come undone again. Rebecca was lying face down in the mud, a few feet away.

"Is she alright?" Laura raced to join him.

They crouched beside her. Jack carefully turned her over onto her back. The heavy rain splashed onto Rebecca's face, rinsing off some of the mud. Her eyes fluttered. Jack crouched over her to shield her from the rain.

"Rebecca?" they both said at the same time. Laura brushed some of the dirt away from Rebecca's cheeks and nose. Rebecca opened her eyes and looked up at Jack.

"It broke again," she said, her voice shallow and weak.

"You had us worried sick!" Laura said, trying to calm down.

Us? It sounded strange to Jack, to hear a woman say *us*, referring to *him*.

"Let's get her in the car," Jack said. Using all the strength he had left, Jack hoisted her up and carried her. Laura opened the door and Jack slid Rebecca into the back seat.

Laura climbed in next to her, to hold and comfort Rebecca on the ride home. Jack quickly retrieved Rebecca's bicycle and placed it in the trunk, then got back in the car.

He leaned over the seat to make sure everyone was okay. Rebecca was sitting up, breathing loudly through her nose as Laura wiped mud from her cheeks and hair. Jack spun around to grab the wheel and put the car in drive. He hung a U-turn and sped off.

"Why did you run away?" Laura asked.

"I just...wanted to see..." Rebecca trailed off. Jack's eyes found her in his rearview mirror.

"What brought you all the way out here, Rebecca?" Jack asked.

Rebecca hesitated, "Just a feeling."

"Like a gut feeling?" Jack asked. She dropped her head onto Laura's shoulder. Her hair dripped small round droplets onto Laura's hand.

"You don't understand. No one understands."

"We *do* understand," Laura said.

"Everyone thinks I'm crazy." A drop of rain dripped from the tip of Rebecca's nose. She blew it off defiantly.

"No one thinks you're crazy," Laura said.

"I just don't want to be scared anymore."

"Me neither," Laura said, pulling her close.

Rebecca's eyes closed from exhaustion. Jack watched the two of them in the mirror. Laura returned his gaze, her expression said *"thank you."*

No thanks necessary...

CHAPTER 50

Laura entered the kitchen. "She's asleep, finally." Jack sat at the kitchen table, a half empty coffee cup in front of him. She poured herself a cup and sat down in the seat across from him, wiping her hands down her face, emotionally spent. They sat in silence for a few moments.

"Sounds like the rain is letting up," Jack said, just trying to make conversation. The clock above the sink ticked loudly in the quiet.

"I'm sorry for the other day."

Jack shook his head. "It was my mistake to bring her there."

"Thanks for helping me tonight. I just don't know what to do anymore." Laura cupped both hands around her coffee mug. She slowly lifted it to her lips and took a short sip. Jack noticed her hands were trembling.

He turned away and looked over at some of Rebecca's artwork displayed on the fridge. Jack grinned, even her doodles were fantastic. He wondered if Laura ever knew what it was like to have a child, a real child. Rebecca seemed so old in her skin. Was she ever just simple, innocent?

There was a small photo of Rebecca as a baby sitting on Santa's lap, one of those expensive photos people stood in line at the mall for hours to get. Her smile was big and bright.

Next to the photo was a drawing of a dog. Jack squinted to focus. It bore a striking resemblance to the dog that licked his face at Hester's home. A Collie, same markings around the eyes. Jack marveled at how Rebecca's renderings were so accurate; even when she doodled a sketch of a dog, you could not only clearly tell it was a dog, but what damn breed it was.

Laura looked at Jack and followed his line of vision.

"She's always been drawing. Since she could hold a crayon. When she was five years old, she drew a picture of the baby sitter. It was so lifelike. When I arrived home she up and quit, said Becca was possessed. I reported her. What happens when you hire out of the Penny-saver. Not sure what I was thinking." Laura took a sip of her coffee, then rubbed her arms briskly, a shiver. "The doctor, Hellerman, he tried to tell me. I didn't want to listen."

"What were you afraid of?"

"I don't know. The more I think about it, the more things I remember her doing or saying that just don't make sense. Things she knew that she shouldn't have known. Things about me. When she started drawing, it frightened me. Her talent, it wasn't natural. I just wanted my little girl. I don't know. So much shit in my life... I guess, I was afraid somehow of losing her too. If she started believing all this craziness, what then? I needed to be the voice of reason for her." Laura rubbed her hands together, scratching at her knuckles nervously. "You knew where she was going tonight."

"I suspected," Jack said.

"I want to help her. But how?"

Jack looked across at the drawings on the fridge again. "Maybe it's like when a child finds out they're adopted. Suddenly they have to go back, re-imagine their entire life as it might have been. Their first instinct is to try and find out who they really are, where they come from."

"I'm her mother. She came from me," Laura said sharply. Jack finished off the last of his coffee. He pushed out his chair a little, ready to get going.

"You want some more coffee?" Laura asked, rising to grab the pot.

Jack shook his head. "I really should get back. We're holding a suspect in custody." Laura refilled his cup anyway.

"Can I ask you a question?" Jack shrugged and waited. "How long have you had it?" Jack played dumb. She sat back down, not taking her eyes off him. "I know what cancer looks like."

Jack's eyes slowly drifted from hers down to his coffee. "My father had it," Laura continued, "thin as his sheets when he died."

"They didn't tell me how long I've had it, just how long I will have it."

"I'm sorry," Laura said. Jack shrugged indifferently.

"When did your father pass away?" Jack asked.

"Last June. It took him getting sick for us to finally reconcile." Laura let out a long sigh. "He had scotch for breakfast. I left home to escape the abuse, then married into it. When my father got sick, I refused to visit. Until he was admitted to the hospital. I figured...I could keep my distance there."

Laura sniffled, containing it. She saw Jack was still listening so she continued, "I saw that big, frightening force reduced to a helpless pile of bones. I almost felt sorry for him. And for the first time, we actually had a normal conversation, father-daughter." Laura remembered something and smiled. "He commented on how nice my hair looked." She puffed air at the thought, drifting back. "He never paid me a compliment my whole life. It was such a simple gesture..."

Jack watched her fingers as they nervously traced the handle on her coffee cup over and over. Clearly, he was the first person she had opened up to about this.

"I realized, all this time...he was just a prisoner in a bottle. I know it's not an excuse to justify what he did — how he treated us — but that's how I was able to forgive him. The day they prepped him for surgery, I had to work late. I arrived just as they were wheeling him into the operating room. He smiled, *'See ya soon.'* I wanted to say I love you so badly, but all that came out was 'good luck.'"

Jack nodded, knowing how the story will end.

"When the doctor came out, I just knew. My father was a very bitter man. Looking back, he wasn't blessed with much luck in his life. Just one disappointment after another. I think, in the end, that bitterness ate him up inside."

Jack's face was still as he listened.

Laura exhaled; telling that story took a lot out of her, but sharing it also seemed to lift a weight from her shoulders. "How's your family taking it?" she asked. Jack simply shrugged. "Don't you have any family?"

"…I have a brother."

"Does he help out?"

"We don't speak."

"Why?"

Jack rolled his tongue over his front teeth. "Long story."

"Sometimes it's easier to talk to a stranger." Laura leaned forward and gently placed her soft hand atop his. It was warm.

He looked into her eyes. "I don't consider you a stranger." Laura smiled a satisfied smile. Jack scratched at his 5 o'clock shadow and pursed his lips, hesitating, searching for the words.

"About 12 years ago, we were at a restaurant, it was my birthday. Me, him, his wife Trish, and my wife…Sarah." It pained Jack just to speak her name. "We were all pretty liquored up. I got called in to the station. I should have never answered the page. My brother said he'd drive Sarah home. I was so wrapped up in my case, I didn't—" Jack beat himself up emotionally, clenching his fist and lifting it to his forehead, tapping it. "They stayed late. He dropped Trish off, then drove Sarah home. Trish asked her to just stay the night, but she had to get up for work in the morning. My brother was in no shape to drive."

Jack rubbed his nose and cleared his throat, which was getting dry. "I got a call at the station. Their car had veered into oncoming traffic."

Laura covered her mouth with her fingertips. "Oh God," she whispered.

"When I arrived at the hospital, Sarah was in surgery." Jack's face hardened, recounting this caused him physical pain. "Standing next to me in the lobby were two sisters discussing their father. He'd been shot during a holdup at his jewelry store. The bullet miraculously missed his heart. They praised God for watching over him. At that same moment, the surgeon came out and told me they had done all they could…but my wife was gone."

Jack looked at Laura. "All I can remember thinking was…does that mean God wasn't watching over Sarah? Didn't God love my wife too?"

The emotion hung thick in the air. Jack's head bobbed a little, the memory coursing sorrow through his veins. "My brother and I never spoke again. I wouldn't even let him attend her funeral."

"You haven't spoken in 12 years?"

"Actually, I'm going to be an uncle."

"Then now's your chance."

"For what?"

"To make things right."

Jack shook his head. "Never thought I'd be afraid."

"Of what?"

"Dying."

Laura got up and moved to the chair beside him. She held his hand again. Her touch eased Jack's blood pressure, his tight shoulders relaxed. "Don't carry that anger with you," she said with the softest of voices. It was like silk to Jack's ears; angelic, like the voice from his dream. "Get rid of it, while there's still time."

Jack gazed into Laura's eyes. No one had listened to him in a long while. Laura was thinking the same thing. There was a feeling of mutual respect and empathy, they had connected on a deep level. Jack contemplated kissing her; he felt his body leaning forward.

Just then his phone rang, shattering the moment. He answered it.

"Ridge."

"*Jack, where are you?*" Harrington said.

"What is it?" Jack asked. Laura sensed the urgency in his voice and stood up to give him some space.

"*Teresa Mason is dead.*"

Jack nodded solemnly. "I'm on my way."

Jack pushed out his chair and stood up wincing, his legs had fallen asleep. "I have to go."

"Are you gonna be okay?"

Jack nodded. "Laura, if you need anything..." This time he touched her arm.

"I was going to say the same to you."

He grimaced and exited the kitchen. As he passed through the living room, he spotted Rebecca curled up asleep on the couch. He slipped past her quietly.

He took Carmen's gold necklace out from his coat pocket and placed it on the table beside her. As he closed the front door, Rebecca opened her eyes.

CHAPTER 51

Jennifer greeted Jack at the front entrance of the precinct to walk him in. He sensed an urgency at her presence.

"About time," Jennifer said, "after Harrington confronted him with news of Teresa's death, he started babbling about how lucky we were."

"Lucky?"

"Said he was ready to confess. Harrington's in with him right now."

"To killing Teresa Mason?"

"All of them. Where've you been?" They turned a corner and headed for the interrogation room, Jennifer had to keep slowing down to not leave Jack in the dust. Her last comment sucked the spring out of his step.

They entered the holding area, Jack peered in at Bishop through the two-way mirror. Harrington was inside, standing over him menacingly, shouting.

Jennifer stood beside Jack and spoke softly, "He knew that Ketamine was the drug used to incapacitate several of the victims - I checked the prior toxicology reports. Traces were found in his van."

Jack nodded. "It's a common rape drug."

"He also knew where the bodies were found, post-mortem specifics."

"Those details have been published in every newspaper."

"We checked into his work history at Baxter Mills, one of their contracts is with Monroe College for the Arts. Bishop was employed there during the time Carmen Muniz was a student. It links him with proximity."

Jack's expression clouded, "What about Angelina?" Jennifer reluctantly switched on the speaker so they could listen in on Harrington's interrogation.

"I want to hear it again," Harrington said, his voice on the speaker sounding condensed and small, as if transmitting from a CB radio miles away. Bishop, exhausted, mumbled something incoherent. Jack leaned his ear towards the speaker.

"Speak up!" Harrington shouted, kicking a leg of Bishop's chair, jolting him upright.

"The sedation began to wear off," Bishop began, "I knew she would scream... I choked her until she went unconscious again. But she wouldn't stay out, so I grabbed a rock...hit her in the head. She started bleeding from everywhere, wouldn't stop screaming, so I kept hitting her."

Jack listened, his eyes tightened to narrow slits, still skeptical. He folded his arms and stood with legs shoulder width apart, his head tilted to one side.

Harrington put his hands on the table and leaned into Bishop's face. "You used a rock to crush her skull."

"No choice," Bishop said, avoiding eye contact. Harrington sat down.

"Where is she now?"

Bishop mumbled again, "You won't have to dig to find her."

Harrington slammed his fist on the table. "Speak up!"

"The reservoir."

"State for the record, Mr. Edward Bishop has just confessed to the abduction and murder of Angelina Rosa," Harrington enunciated for clarity.

Jack winced, the small candle of hope that fueled his purpose flickered and was extinguished. Jennifer could almost smell the smoke. She backed away and gave the man space, a man she respected, who never had an ill word for anyone. The man that inspired others to work harder, stay up longer, honor the badge.

"I'm sorry Jack," was all she could offer. Jack shook his head, not accepting it.

"No, but she, she looked right at him." Jack mumbled.

"What?"

"I need to speak to him."

Jack burst into the interrogation room, startling both Harrington and Bishop. Harrington spotted the purpose in Jack's step and quickly vacated the chair. Jack sat down and placed a picture of Carmen Muniz on the table under Bishop's nose.

"Tell me about her," Jack said, like a cynic about to ruin a magician's trick. Harrington watched with intrigue.

Bishop's eyes crisscrossed the photo. "I already told them everything."

"I want you to tell me."

Bishop looked down at the picture again, picking at his teeth with a dirty fingernail.

"Did you know her?" Jack asked. A tiny jagged smile crept across Bishop's face. Jack fought back the urge to take out his .38 and cut him down right there. He composed himself. "Did you rape her?"

Bishop grinned an ugly grin. He picked up the picture, leaned back as if reminiscing with it, expanding his chest, proud of his accomplishment. He turned the picture so Jack could see. "Look at that mouth."

Bishop flipped the picture back onto the table. Harrington flexed, anticipating Jack's reaction to be violent. Surprisingly, Jack remained calm and dignified; he merely clenched his jaw and proceeded.

"How did you kill her?" Jack asked. Bishop gazed up at the ceiling as if he were a clerk and Jack had asked him in what aisle could he find the tool section.

"Strangled her?" Bishop said playfully. Jack wasn't amused. Harrington stepped forward, ready to pounce some discipline into the back of Bishop's skull, but Jack shook his head *no* to ward off the attack.

"Are you asking me, can't you remember?" Jack asked, his patience on slow boil.

Bishop's shoulders swelled with arrogance. "I remember she smelled sweet like an avocado, ripe and fresh. Pretty for a spic whore." Bishop smiled, showing teeth, his eyes twinkling with a macabre delight.

Jack saw red. He leaped from his chair, clawing at Bishop's throat. Harrington grabbed Jack, restraining him, prying Jack's fingers from around Bishop's neck. Jack finally saw reason and released him. Bishop coughed, making the most of it, dramatically rubbing his throat as if he had glimpsed the grim reaper.

"You can't fucking do that! You can't fucking touch me!" Bishop coughed, his eyes watery and red.

Harrington walked Jack calmly towards the door. Bishop sat hunched over, still clutching his neck, breathing heavily.

"I told them at the clinic I had problems. They wouldn't listen. Maybe now you'll listen to me."

CHAPTER 52

Jennifer, Harrington, and Jack stood huddled in the adjacent holding area. Jack seemed listless and distant as he studied Bishop through the glass. Bishop's eyes seemed like black sockets in the overhead fluorescents, a frightening expression of emptiness on his face.

"We'll need to get a dive team over to the reservoir tomorrow morning," Harrington said.

"You did everything you could Jack," Jennifer said.

"No, I missed something..." Jack checked his watch for no reason, not sure what to do next, dazed.

"Thanks to you he's off the streets," Harrington said. "He finally made a mistake and we got him."

Jack turned, his eyes ablaze. "We didn't do shit! He's been coming and going as he pleases, getting away with murder for over 10 years. And the only reason we have a suspect in custody is because some brave young girl defended herself long enough to hand him to us!"

Jack ended his rant with a loud cough that multiplied. He doubled over, red in the face. Jennifer put her hand on his back to steady him.

"Jack, are you okay?" Jack stepped away from her.

"Do you need your pills?" Harrington asked.

Jack scowled at Harrington with embarrassment. He wiped his mouth, the fit subsiding.

"I just need to catch my breath, can I do that? Move back so I can catch my breath." Jack leaned up against the wall and took out his pills. There was no use hiding his condition any longer, his tenure was over — what more was there to stay for? And his condition was no secret to anyone, no matter how noble his efforts to shun sympathy had been.

"I'll get you a glass of water," Jennifer said, leaving the room. Jack's taut breathing slowed, returning to normal. Despite his hardened shell, he was appreciative of their concern. They were good, caring friends. Denying his suffering was just his way of denying the inevitable, denying death.

Harrington leaned in close to Jack, capitalizing on their time alone. "Jack, we knew the odds she'd be found alive were a million to one. Carl knew it, or should have." Jack fumbled to get his pills in his mouth, his hand shaking. "I know how much you wanted to believe that little girl's story. But don't do this to yourself. Good detective work solves crimes. You're one of the best. He'll never hurt another child, thanks to you."

Harrington placed his hand on Jack's shoulder and squeezed it. Jack appreciated the gesture, and what he said. Whatever bitterness he had just been feeling seemed to morph into self-loathing and depression.

Jennifer re-entered holding a styrofoam cup filled with water. She held it out for Jack. "Thank you." He took a sip and placed it down on a table. "Jennifer, can you get Carl Rosa on the phone for me?"

"No need. He hasn't left."

Jack exited the room and moved somberly down the hall. He wasn't looking for Carl, he'd run into him eventually. He simply ambled forward, his mind dark, devoid of any coherent thought. He passed his office and paused to glare at his name on the frosted glass door. He suppressed an urge to drive his fist through it.

He entered the main hallway, spotting Carl asleep on a bench. Someone thoughtful had brought him coffee, the half empty cup balanced treacherously on the arm of the bench.

Jack slowed, thinking he might let Carl sleep a little longer, have one more dream with a happy ending. He would have the rest of his life to relive this crushing moment, what's the rush?

Just then, Carl's eyes fluttered. He spotted Jack down the hall and sat up straight. *No turning back now.*

Jack came to understand the best way was to just look them straight in the eye, tell the truth, then shut up. Nothing else you say will matter, unless you know of a way you can bring their loved one back from the dead. Just shut your mouth and let them grieve, however they choose.

Jack thought about what that poor doctor must have felt, having to tell him he'd tried and failed to save Sarah's life. *I'm sorry, Mr. Ridge, she didn't pull through. She didn't pull through...* He remembered how the doctor didn't waiver and looked him in the eye bravely. How difficult that must have been.

Carl shifted in his seat as Jack stepped closer. *She didn't pull through, Carl.*

Carl stood up and Jack motioned for him to sit back down, which made Carl want to stand up all the more. Sitting down meant dreadful news. He stayed on his feet.

Jennifer entered the hallway from the far end and spotted Jack talking to Carl. She couldn't hear what he was saying. She watched as Carl went limp and collapsed into Jack's arms. Jack helped him to the bench and eased him down.

Jack sat motionless beside Carl, who wept into his hands. They sat that way for a long time.

CHAPTER 53

Jack closed his office door and slumped down into his chair, emotionally drained. The cassette player still sat on his desk. He reached over and pressed play. Rebecca's voice came to life on the tape again. *"Trusted him...lied to me."*

Jack pressed fast forward at random. *"Rebecca?"* Leonard's voice spoke.

"I hear church bells. Santa Maria, Madre de Dios-" Jack forwarded again. *"The fruits of our labors... find Jesus on the hill. Find Jesus..."* Jack stopped the tape. What had he overlooked? Misinterpreted?

There was a photograph of Angelina on his desk, a large 8x10. He picked it up and studied it one last time, then tossed it into the pile of victim's photographs.

He walked over to his file cabinet. A small bend in the metal made it difficult to open. He tugged it hard and it slid all the way out with a metallic screech. He removed the large scrapbook of mugshots Rebecca had examined the other day.

He flattened the book out on his desk and flipped through. As Bishop's mug shot came into view, the thing that stood out the most about him was his very unique face — ugly, memorable — not ordinary at all. Not a face you'd forget, or confuse with someone else's.

Rebecca had stared at this picture, he was certain. *But she said nothing.* For someone who had dreamed of this face for so long, woke up screaming from it, supposedly carried it with her across lifetimes, you would think seeing it up close would illicit a very powerful reaction. But *she said nothing.* Which meant she had never seen him before.

He thought about what Laura had said, that they'd all taken what Rebecca had conjured up in those therapy sessions and applied whatever explanation they saw fit, never fully realizing the obvious. However all of those coincidences had transpired, it was certain that they were just that, *coincidences.* Dumb luck, as Harrington called it.

Jack felt consumed by regret — and guilt. He had been a party to this, he contributed to her confusion as much as Leonard. Laura was the only one who had remained lucid and sane. They'd taken a few startling occurrences, some ramblings, and conjured a fantasy. One he was more than willing to subscribe to. Facing death, desperate, knowing that his cherished memories of Sarah would be lost to oblivion forever, memories that kept her spirit alive. *All those moments.*

The hope that perhaps there was a reason to life, fate, karma, another chance to learn, reconnect, live again. He bought it. All of it.

But Rebecca's clues didn't find the killer, did they?

In the end, it was Teresa Mason's bravery that collared their man. Not the supernatural. Laura, Harrington, they had tried to talk some sense into him. How easily we're misled when we want to believe something for our own personal motivations. How had he let his normally conservative judgment become so clouded? That lapse in reason took his investigation off on a tangent and, because of that, Angelina was dead now.

The phone on his desk rang. He watched the little yellow button blink off and on. He pressed it.

"Ridge."

"I hear you arrested Edward Bishop," Leonard said.

"That's right." Jack could hear Leonard sigh on the other end.

"Bishop is a former patient of mine. I evaluated him during his rape trial. He's been in and out of the psych ward for years."

"What's your point?"

"Carmen knew her killer, she trusted him, went with him willingly."

"He already confessed."

"He's lying."

"Leonard, I've played along long enough."

"Jack, listen to me, the answer is there, we just haven't figured it out yet."

"I have to go."

"Edward Bishop doesn't have the ability to facilitate friendships, even temporary. Speak to him."

"I have."

"He doesn't fit the description."

"Description? Right now I have a description from a girl who died trying to defend herself, his DNA was scraped from her fingernail bed. I got a car that matches a vehicle description from a witness in Ann Arbor. I have verification that he was working at Monroe College while Carmen was a student."

"I'm not denying he attacked the Mason girl, but he's not the one who killed Carmen, he's probably not the one who took Angelina."

"Hard evidence and solid police work solved this case."

There was a long pause. "10 years of solid police work didn't find Carmen's body," Leonard said.

"Dumb luck."

"Bullshit. Angelina still hasn't been found."

"He named the location."

"Where?"

"The reservoir."

"You won't find anything. I guarantee it." Jack gave Leonard's words some consideration, but only out of respect for their friendship.

"I don't have time to debate this with you, Leonard."

"I stopped by to visit Carmen's mother, Jack. Don't worry, I didn't tell her why I was there. I simply said I was from the police department and offered counseling. She refused, but she did say that you were there again recently. You didn't explain to her exactly why, either. What were you looking for in the girl's bedroom?"

Jack was silent.

"The diary... You were looking for the diary-"

"Goodbye, Leonard-"

"I want to come in and question him! You can arrange that!"

"Leonard, this is a murder investigation, I don't have time to help you conduct research for your God damn book!"

Jack slammed down the phone. The image of Rebecca from Carmen's painting kept surfacing in his thoughts. *Must remain rational. Coincidence. Mere coincidence.*

Harrington opened the door and entered. Jack hadn't heard the knob click, *was he outside the whole time, listening?*

"Jack, you never gave up. Everyone knows that. Carl Rosa knows that. You're a good man."

"Not good enough." Jack stood up and reached for his jacket. He looked out the window and caught a glimpse of Carl walking towards his car, his head down, reporters smothering him, shoving microphones under his chin in desperation to squeeze a sound bite of grief out of him for the 6 o'clock news.

"Don't beat yourself up, Jack. It's not worth it."

"Worth it? I'd rather work 25 hours a day than face those few seconds right before you give someone news that's going to destroy the rest of their lives."

"That's our job."

"No. Our job is to try and prevent those moments from ever happening."

Harrington conceded, never intending to have a long conversation, already wearing his coat.

"Well, I gotta go, gotta explain to the wife why there was 1,300 dollars stuffed in my sock drawer. One of my kids told her I won it on the Denver game. Believe that? These kids and their crazy imaginations."

Harrington exited. Jack looked down at the cassette player.

"Yeah..."

Jack reached down and placed his finger on the eject button.

He tapped it and Rebecca's tape spit out. He held it up for a few seconds, frowned, then tossed it across his desk, scattering a few papers. One of them, the invitation his brother had left, fluttered to the floor by his feet.

He reached down to pick it up. He slid his finger under the lip of the envelope and opened it.

CHAPTER 54

Laura turned down Hastings Boulevard and noticed how much things had changed since she last traveled these parts as a teenager over a decade ago. It was much dirtier now, several stores she used to frequent had been shuttered. The corner drug store where she once stole cigarettes was still open.

"Where are we going?" Rebecca asked from the back seat.

"To see an old friend." Laura had decided to just put it all out on the table for Rebecca. Whatever the consequences. She knew this was all inevitable. It was time.

Laura exchanged glances between Rebecca and the road, watching her expression for any changes, looks of recognition, any reaction at all. But Rebecca just sat quietly.

She turned down Woods Avenue, Hester's apartment complex came into view. It was all coming back to her now. Carmen had always seemed embarrassed by her family, especially her mother. Hester was very religious and often said or did things to make it seem like Carmen was being raised in the middle ages. She came across as a fanatic to the uninitiated. But Laura never thought anything less of her, or considered her weird. Compared to her own upbringing, most other families seemed normal.

As she pulled up to the curb, she gazed at the iron railing along the steps that led to a small balcony by the apartment entrance. On days with nothing to do, she and Carmen had stood up there and watched the traffic go by.

On one occasion, a blue and white-striped butterfly with an enormous wingspan fluttered past them and landed on Laura's shoulder. Laura remembered screaming with excitement. The noise brought Carmen's mother, Hester, to the front door to see what all the fuss was about. Carmen reached out to touch the butterfly and Hester yelled at her to leave it alone. She remembered Hester saying if a butterfly lands on your shoulder, it means that you have a good aura and a kind spirit. And that other spirits would want to remain close to you, love you. *How's that working out, Laura?*

Carmen commented on how beautiful the butterfly was. Hester then asked Carmen if she had thanked God for showing her such beauty. She then made Carmen say it out loud. *"Thank you Lord, for revealing to me your beauty in the world."* Carmen was so embarrassed, she didn't speak the rest of the afternoon. That was the only really odd moment that stood out in Laura's mind.

Laura put the car in park and walked around to let Rebecca out. Rebecca didn't act unusual, she didn't show any emotion at all. Laura was surprised. Blank wasn't the reaction she was expecting.

She took Rebecca's hand and walked her towards the building. As they got closer, Laura noticed Rebecca was squeezing her hand.

Laura climbed the steps, but Rebecca hung back, frozen.

"Come on," Laura insisted. Rebecca slowly shook her head.

"I'm going in without you then," Laura said, insincerely. Laura released her hand and climbed the steps.

She knocked and waited. Francisco opened the door, wearing his military uniform. He pushed open the screen door. "Yes?"

Laura looked him up and down, recognizing him. "Francisco?"

"…Yes?"

"You don't remember me."

He stared blankly. "I'm sorry, should I?"

Laura grinned. "Laura Lowell. I was a friend of your sister,

Carmen." Francisco tried to retrieve the data from his memory banks. All he could do was smile back and repeat her name vacantly.

"Laura Lowell... Laura Lowell..."

"¿Quién es, Francis?" Hester asked from inside. She gently pushed past him, revealing herself at the door. She looked exactly the same as Laura remembered, only heavier.

"Yes?" Hester said, but instantly there was a recognition in her eyes.

"I don't know if you remember me?" Laura said. Hester's smile got broader. "I'm Laura? I was a friend of Carmen's."

Hester reached out and took Laura's hands. "Laura, yes."

"It's been a long time."

"Yes, it has."

Laura stepped aside, revealing Rebecca, still cowering at the bottom of the steps.

"Your daughter?"

"Yes, her name's Rebecca." Laura turned to Rebecca. "Come on, sweetie." Rebecca put a hand on the railing and took a slow step. Then another, like a child afraid of being punished.

"Don't worry, I don't bite," Hester said.

"It's okay, Rebecca," Laura said. Rebecca took a few more steps. Hester bent over to her. "Oh, so pretty. Come in, come in." Hester backed up, letting them both enter. As Rebecca passed, she looked up at Hester with dread.

They entered the kitchen. On the table were multiple arrangements of flowers, sent from friends and family members. One large bouquet had a framed picture of Carmen in the middle.

Francisco stepped back towards the corner of the room. Laura turned to him. "The last time I saw you, you were this high," she said, holding her hand just above her waist.

"My big man now," Hester said, "he take two week leave when we get the news about Carmen. Today is his last day, he report back tomorrow." There was a packed rucksack near the front door, a camouflage jacket draped over it, ready to go.

Rebecca looked around the room, pausing at every distinctive item — a framed painting of Jesus on the wall, a man's hat hung on a hook, an old worn out dog's bowl on the floor. Each elicited a unique reaction on her face.

There was a collage of snapshots of Carmen and family on the refrigerator. Rebecca turned and looked up at Francisco. He gave her a curious smile.

Hester pulled out a chair at the kitchen table for Laura to sit down. The table had a floral pattern of yellow and pink under an outdated laminate, scratched and stained from years of use. Laura remembered it.

"Would you like something to drink, Laura? Some tea?"

"Yes, please." Hester put the kettle on the stove.

"How about you, Rebecca?" Hester opened the fridge and bent to search inside, moving a few items. "I have some juice..." Rebecca was silent. "No?"

"Rebecca? Manners?" Laura said, sticking her neck out and opening her eyes wide to emphasize her point.

Hester closed the fridge and walked over to Rebecca, who was fascinated by an oil painting hanging in the hallway. Hester stood behind Rebecca, joining her in admiration.

"My daughter paint this. You like?"

"The color's faded," Rebecca said flatly. Hester didn't quite hear.

"It's my favorite. That is Saint Peter."

"Saint Joseph," Rebecca corrected. Hester's eyes swiveled down to Rebecca. A sudden, odd tension filled the room.

"What?" Hester said, very interested in what Rebecca had to say now. But the moment was interrupted as the family dog somehow managed to escape from the room he'd been quarantined in. He raced across the floor and dove right for Rebecca. Rebecca's eyes burst with a sudden joy, she knelt down to embrace the slobbering animal.

"Faucet!" she cried out. Hester turned to Laura, somewhat stunned.

"You told her about the dog?" Hester asked. Laura slowly put her hand to her mouth, touching her lips with her fingers.

"No."

Rebecca and the dog were like old friends, a bond reunited. The dog licked her face like she was made of sugar, slobbering all over her, much to Rebecca's infinite delight. She laughed with squeals of joy.

"He really likes you," Hester said as Laura's eyes shifted back and forth. "That dog won't die. Just sleeps and eats. So old."

The dog jumped up, knocking Rebecca over playfully. "Okay, Faucet, okay!" Rebecca laughed.

"Okay is right; Francis, put him outside." Francisco leapt into action and grabbed the dog by the collar. "Vete aquí, let's go." He pulled the dog to the front door and pushed him outside. The dog tried to nose his way back in, so Francisco used his knee to corral him and closed the door.

Hester sat down at the kitchen table. Rebecca got back up on her feet and brushed herself off, her dress damp from the dogs saliva. Laura stared at her.

"Come here," Hester said to Rebecca. Rebecca didn't budge.

"Rebecca-" Laura insisted she listen. Rebecca slowly obeyed and drifted towards the table.

"Rebecca, how did you know my dog's name?" Rebecca blinked but didn't answer. "I don't bite, come here." Rebecca took another step forward. Hester reached out to tickle Rebecca under her chin. "Well?"

"Because I named him," Rebecca said. The room fell silent. Hester's eyes opened wide — but not from Rebecca's outlandish remark — something *else* had caught her attention.

"Where...where did she get that?" Hester said, almost stuttering.

Laura stood up and lifted Rebecca's chin. She saw the gold cross around her neck. Laura frowned, not at Rebecca, but at Jack for giving it to her. "Where she get it?" Hester repeated.

"A friend gave it to her," Laura said apologetically.

"The detective?"

"Yes."

Hester stood slowly. "That belong to Carmen." Rebecca took a step back, holding the cross with her fingers, protectively.

"I'm sorry," Laura said, reaching for the necklace. Rebecca

dodged her defiantly.

"Why she wearing it?"

"Rebecca, give her back the necklace."

"But it's mine."

"Rebecca, now." Laura grabbed her arm to pull her close but she resisted, twisting and squirming away. "I'm sorry, we've been having some problems. Rebecca, now!"

"No!" Rebecca shouted. She looked at Hester. "You gave it to me, for my first communion."

Hester's face went pale. She turned to Laura. "What does she mean?"

Rebecca broke free and held up the cross. There was a tiny inscription on it. Laura reached again and Rebecca slapped her hands away. She read the inscription aloud — not looking at it — *from memory*:

"El te bendice con su amor. Dios te bendinga, hoy Y siempre."

As Rebecca recited those words, Hester mouthed the same, simultaneously.

Laura stood dumbstruck.

"Why? Why are you?" Hester's mouth was quivering.

"I know it sounds crazy," Laura said, "but...Rebecca thinks she remembers this place. Remembers you. She has these dreams, that she and Carmen...are the same person."

Rebecca caught a closer look at the framed photo of Carmen amongst the flowers. A yellow flag in the center read: *In loving memory.* "Please don't be angry," Rebecca whispered softly to Hester.

Hester turned to look at the photo, sorrow welling up in her eyes. "The night she disappear, we had a fight. I said things. Terrible things. I tell her, Jesus will never take you now, you have shamed him, shamed yourself. She rip her cross from her neck and throw it at me. She never come home—" Hester's words got caught in her throat from the emotion. It spilled out, tears flowing.

Francisco stepped towards her, reaching out. "Mama?"

"I pray and pray; please, Jesus, I honor you every day of my life. I ask, please, give me another chance. Please, let me speak to my daughter one last time...tell her how much I love her." Hester's eyes closed with grief.

Laura got caught up in the emotion too. "These last few months have been so hard... I didn't know what to do. I thought if I brought her here, it would satisfy something, but... Oh God, Rebecca."

Hester turned to Laura, gulping air, her eyes draining tears. "How...?"

Laura smiled. "I don't know-"

"How dare you?"

"What?"

"Get out!" Hester shouted, her face red. Her words were like a slap across Laura's cheek. Laura looked back with absolute confusion, nearly losing her balance as the rage in Hester's voice grew with intensity. "Get out of my home!" Her voice echoed loudly in the tiny kitchen, the air in the room grew hot.

Rebecca reached for Hester, but Hester slapped her hand away like it was diseased. Hester's cheeks hardened with anger and resentment. Rebecca recoiled at the fierceness of Hester's disgust. Laura hugged Rebecca close.

"How dare you come here and tell me that my Carmen is anywhere but by the side of Jesus!" Hester nearly fell over with rage. Francisco reached for her. "Cuidado, Mama!" As he comforted her, he looked over at Laura. "I think you should go. I'm sorry." His sorry was genuine and heartfelt, as if a part of him believed.

Hester wailed, collapsing into her chair in a pile of grief, head down. Francisco rubbed her shoulders. She came up for air, face wet and contorted from crying. "My Carmen sits beside Jesus in Heaven!"

Rebecca pushed out her bottom lip as her face went red. She too started to cry. Laura pulled her towards the door.

"I'm so sorry, for everything," Laura said. Francisco gave her a nod of understanding. Satisfied with that, Laura exited with Rebecca.

She held her hand as they descended the steps in retreat. She could still hear Hester crying out, "Jesus cradles her in his arms!

Jesus cradles her in his arms!"

As they reached the ground, Rebecca pulled away from Laura and raced back up the steps. "Rebecca!"

Laura watched her go back inside, but didn't follow.

Rebecca approached Hester, whose head was still down, sobbing. She fiddled with the clasp on the gold cross necklace. She opened the latch and unwrapped it from around her neck.

She draped it onto the table next to Hester's hand and gave one more look to Francisco. He stepped forward and knelt down to her, gently embracing her.

"Thank you," he said, staring into her eyes, spotting something familiar. It made him smile.

His acceptance brought no smile to her face, just wonderment. Rebecca wasn't sure what she was feeling, but the sense of urgency she had been experiencing for so long seemed strangely absent at the moment. She went to breathe in and her heart skipped a beat, which made her gasp mid breath. She turned and ran out the door, so hard and fast the screen door slapped the metal guardrail outside with a thwack.

She flew down the steps to where her mother was waiting. Laura didn't ask why she went back, but noticed the gold cross was no longer around her neck. She put her hand on her shoulder and they walked back to the car.

Laura wiped one errant tear from her cheek and started the engine. Rebecca turned and looked out the back window, Francisco was watching from the balcony. She waved to him.

He lifted his hand to acknowledge her. As Laura pulled away, Rebecca kept staring at Francisco until he was no longer in sight. She kept looking back until the building disappeared around a bend.

Finally, she turned and sat down. She faced front the entire way home, not looking out the side window, not looking at her mother in the rearview mirror. Just looking straight ahead.

CHAPTER 55

The large wooden doors of the detention center swung open. Reporters and curious onlookers battled to get a glimpse of the killer. Bishop was led out wearing a white coverall jumpsuit, his hands zip tied behind his back. Two burly officers escorted him forcefully through the crowd to a waiting police van. He appeared meek and frail next to them; his cheekbones flush and protruding, as if he was sucking in, clenching his jaw.

Bishop played to the cameras, not talking, but not shying away from their lenses either. He appeared calm, almost serene in the chaos, the attention not disagreeing with him. From the look on his face, it was clear that this was the moment he had been working towards. This lonely drifter was now in the spotlight, people were shouting his name. So what if it was because they hated or feared him. So what if he would be infamous for such violent, nefarious deeds. He was *somebody* now. He stuck his chest out, almost strutting, but remained silent. They would have to wait and wonder what went on in the mind of this *mindless* killer.

"Did you murder those girls?" one reporter shouted.

Another, the same woman that had interviewed Jack on the 6 o'clock news, stuck her large rounded microphone under Bishop's nose. "Can you tell us why you did it?" One of the officers swatted her microphone away with the back of his arm.

Reporters started to overlap each other, screaming questions at the same time, louder and louder, trying to drown each other out, hoping their voice would be the one that solicited a reaction from the monster.

Bishop was hustled into the back of the van. An officer climbed in and closed the door, nearly taking the arm off another reporter for The Detroit Free Press.

The officer sat beside Bishop as they rode through the city to the courthouse. Bishop's air of indifference — the look on his face, the lingering smile — irritated the officer more as each second passed.

"Wipe that shit grin off your face," the officer said. Bishop widened his smile to show teeth. "You're the flavor of the hour. Tomorrow you'll be locked away, left to rot in a cage. And no one's gonna give a shit."

Bishop continued to smile, infuriating the officer, who kept making fists inside his leather gloves, anxious to vent his disgust. Then bishop's face abruptly grew solemn and straight. He looked at the officer with a sort of pity.

"My place in history is secure."

"As a fucking nut job."

"Exactly." Bishop ate back a smile. "It's you who'll be forgotten. I've left my mark on society. They'll spend years agonizing over clues they missed, how I could have been stopped, studying me in order to prevent the next one." Bishop couldn't contain his grin, perhaps trying to goad the officer into a physical altercation.

"I know all about you," the officer said, looking away, not giving him the courtesy of eye contact as he spoke. "Let's see; loner, parents were assholes, no friends at school, probably bullied because you were such a witless pile of shit. No girl will have anything to do with you, so you sit home alone, pity yourself, and you get angry. You want what you can't have, what no woman will give you. You got tired of paying for it, so you decided to just take it, take out your frustration on a poor defenseless girl. And it made you feel like a man. But that's all you can do, because you're not a real man, you're a rat. A worthless piece of trash no one gives two shits about. And now, for the first time, people are saying your name, talking to you, and you feel important. You're even grinning like some fucking retard. But by tomorrow you'll realize what your mother must have realized long ago — what a total failed experiment giving birth to a fuck up like you was. As you stare at those same four cement walls for eternity, you'll have forever to think about what a complete fucking loser you turned out to be. I give you three weeks before you hang yourself with your bedsheets."

Bishop stopped smiling. He rode the rest of the trip to the courthouse in silence.

CHAPTER 56

The sun broke through the clouds. Jack lifted his face, inhaling the cold November air. He gazed out at the reservoir as divers went under and resurfaced, searching.

Harrington was leaning on the hood of Jack's car, overseeing the investigation. There were officers and forensic personnel standing by the shoreline, awaiting the gruesome task of retrieving and bagging any evidence that might be discovered at the bottom. Harrington twisted to see if Jack was still behind him, he was being so quiet — had been all day.

Jack didn't answer his phone that morning, Harrington feared something might have happened to him overnight. A macabre thought, but Jack had seemed inordinately down and depressed the night before. And you never know how people might respond to that depth of despair. Some might put a gun in their mouth.

But a few minutes later, Jack had pulled up. Any small talk Harrington had offered up was met with silence.

The hours of watching and waiting were starting to get tedious. Harrington tried again to start a conversation.

"So…Carl's not coming?"

Jack inhaled the cool dry air. "Refuses to believe she's down there."

"Where's he now?"

"At the arraignment."

Harrington nodded. "I'll be real happy when this one's over. I spend any more time at work, I'm gonna come home and find the wife with the mailman."

Jack looked up at the sun. "Forecast said rain."

"What do they know? Good thing, wouldn't that have sucked. I hate standing around like this. So do you, you get all jittery when things take too long."

"I'm in no rush to see it."

Harrington turned to look out at the divers. "Yeah…who knows, maybe Carl is right. Maybe Bishop's pulling our chain." Jack ran his tongue over his teeth.

"Maybe."

"All that hard work, and it's dumb luck that cracks it," Harrington said, looking back at Jack. Jack's face was expressionless.

"That's usually the case. They make a mistake, you catch a lucky break. It's never what you expect."

"What *were* you expecting?"

Jack looked out at the water. He tucked his cold hands in his jacket pockets. "I don't know. You stare at something long enough, your mind starts to play tricks on you."

Harrington began to say something, but held it. Then said, "I know what you mean, I keep trying to put together that winning parlay. Lions were getting 7, I thought they were a lock at plus 17. I had it, but shit never works out the way you plan it. I guess if it did, I wouldn't be doing this. I'd be playing left tackle. Fuckin' hamstring." Harrington stretched and scratched at the sky with a loud moan. He took a few steps towards the water. "They must be freezing down there. Shit, it's cold. This is taking too long, maybe we should just drain it."

Jack walked over to the driver's side of his car. "Call me when they find something. You're in charge now." Jack climbed in and closed the door. Harrington hardly had time to process what Jack had just said when Jack started the engine and threw it in reverse.

Harrington threw his hands up. "Where are you going?

Whaddya mean I'm in charge now? You make it sound like you're not coming back." Jack reached the road and stopped, eyeballed Harrington over the steering wheel. Their gaze locked for a brief moment, Harrington sensed Jack was saying goodbye. Jack straightened out onto the road and drove off, kicking up a cloud of brown dust.

"Jack?" Harrington jogged up to the road, watching Jack leave. He meandered back down to the water's edge, his makeshift seat now driven away.

He spotted a ripple in the water. A diver emerged, his head popping up with a loud burst of air. The diver spun around, disorientated. He found Harrington on the shore. Harrington held his palms up, *anything?* The diver shook his head, *no.*

CHAPTER 57

Robert's home was a small three bedroom colonial with beige siding and a chain-link fence. There was a gate in the center, the hinge broken. He stood on the front steps, greeting two more guests at the door. A man and a woman handed him a wrapped gift with a card taped on top.

"Thanks guys, come on in." Robert lodged the gift under his arm and waved them across the threshold. Patricia gave them a second greeting from the living room, which was overflowing with guests now.

"Oh my gosh, you're ready to burst!" the woman said, extending her hands out to touch Patricia's very pregnant middle, bulging under her sweater. Trish smiled and allowed the guest to rub her stomach, beginning to feel more like a sideshow attraction than a party host. She wiped her sweaty forehead and smiled, initiating small talk, even though she felt a little nauseous and tired.

Robert noticed, but didn't pay it too much mind. She'd been feeling off for a few days — she'd just gotten over a cold — probably just remnants of it lingering.

Robert stepped outside and watched the street, scanning the passing traffic expectantly. Cars were parked all along the curb in both directions. One was partially blocking his neighbor's driveway. He would tell them to move it, anticipating the obligatory complaint. Not that he really cared; they were moving soon, he'd never see most of these people again.

His manufactured grin cued up as another late guest folded back the broken gate and walked up the path to greet him with a handshake. He ushered him inside.

His expression dimmed as he took one last look. He stepped back inside and closed the door. Patricia could see the disappointment in his face. She walked over and took his hand. "We're what's important today; us, the baby, nothing else." His eyes greeted hers and she pulled him close with an affectionate one armed hug. They rejoined the party as the happy couple.

CHAPTER 58

Jack stood in front of the bathroom mirror. He ran a comb through his hair and splashed a little water on his face. He gently patted the water off his cheeks, staring at his reflection. He wondered, how much longer would he be Jack Ridge? Would he ever look through someone else's eyes? Or was this it — a few months of agonizing pain, then oblivion. No absolution, no summation of his journey.

Judgment? God? He wanted to believe, but doubt and disappointment clung tight. He recalled a case he'd worked on years ago, when he first started. A boy, about 15, had been hailed as a hero for battling — and finally beating - cancer. Surviving a long, arduous battle that many local people donated money to support. There were plastic buckets with his picture beside every cash register in town.

A week after being released from the hospital, he was killed while walking to school, hit by a sanitation truck that had turned a corner too quickly and skidded. It was an accident. Jack was assigned to the case as a patrol officer, this was long before he'd made detective.

It was a gruesome task, the boy's body was mangled beyond recognition. Jack remembered someone making an off-hand comment about the irony of it all. He labeled that particular moment as the moment he stopped believing in God. By the time Sarah met with her fate, he was already a full blown cynic.

Sarah's accident, however, was the pivot that could have turned him in either direction. Had she recovered miraculously, perhaps if God had answered his prayers and pulled her through, his faith might have been challenged and restored. But it just didn't happen that way. The penny landed heads down.

Jack had met many individuals who'd lost their religion upon coming home and finding their loved ones murdered, countless stories of undeserved sorrow that led to an unraveling of faith. But then there were others who'd *found* religion as they watched their six year old daughter dance in her first ballet recital. A roll of the dice. *And only a few chips left to squander, Jack.*

He grabbed the card Robert had given him off his dresser and re-read it. Still the same address. Robert's home wasn't far from where Laura lived, a few miles or so.

He returned to the bedroom and opened the closet. He spotted the navy blue suit he'd bought to be buried in. He removed it from its cover for only the second time, the unraveling of the plastic felt like a second chance at a new beginning.

He put it on and shrugged the shoulders, the give was comfortable. It was a good match with his tie, dark blue stripes. He slapped his hands at his sides. "Okay."

Jack got into his car and drove to the end of his street when he realized he was heading to a party without a present.

He pulled into a strip of stores. He entered a small antique place and picked out a very nice centerpiece for a dining room table. It was expensive, but he'd saved a lot of money over the years. Many nights home alone, cooking for himself. He could afford it. He certainly didn't need to hoard for retirement.

It felt good to buy something for someone, especially something expensive. It was a strange time to think about it, but as he factored in his head just how much money he probably did have saved in the bank, he realized he didn't have a will.

The cashier asked him if he wanted it wrapped, snapping him

back to attention.

"Yes, please."

He placed the box, wrapped in pink and teal paper with a beautiful ribbon that curled at the ends, in his car. He could have never done that himself; he was glad he spent the extra five bucks.

He closed the trunk and spotted a department store anchored at the end of the strip mall.

He walked the aisles of the large store, searching. He stopped a clerk to ask a question. The clerk held up his hand and told him to wait a minute, then disappeared. Jack decided not to wait. He turned down another aisle, *what do you get for a new baby?* He found the children's toys, spotted a stuffed teddy bear and tucked it under his arm. He continued walking, passing the large screen TVs, the appliances. He reached the sporting goods aisle and found the other thing he was looking for.

CHAPTER 59

The tiny brown and white rabbit cowered behind the bush. Rebecca strained with a whine as she stretched her arm out to reach him, flicking her fingers to try and coax him out. The rabbit hopped in place, terrified.

"I won't hurt you," she promised. She reached in again and the rabbit bolted over her forearm, leaving scratch marks on her skin.

"Ow! Wait!" She scampered after the rabbit around the back of the house when she heard a car pull up. She turned and saw Jack climb out, immediately noticing his nice suit. As he got closer, she saw his face looked different - he'd shaved.

"Hi," Rebecca said.

"Hi. How are you?"

"Good." Jack noticed her eyes weren't as swollen as he remembered. She seemed spry and colorful, her skin not as pale. Like a child after a fever breaks, pink again. Even her "Hi" wasn't weighed down with anxiety and angst like before. Something had happened.

"Your mom around?"

"She's inside."

"I got something for you." Jack returned to his car and popped the trunk, disappearing underneath. Rebecca watched with anticipation, stretching on her tippy toes to try and get a look.

Jack closed the trunk and came back around the car holding a shiny new bike, pink with white trim and streamers on the handlebars. Rebecca's face lit up.

"I was gonna fix your old one, but I figured it was ready to be put out of its misery. Hopefully this one will be a little safer, do you like it? They had other colors…" Rebecca climbed onto the retro, banana shaped seat and squeezed the brakes, elated. "Its got 21 speeds. And a chain guard. You like pink? Cause I wasn't sure-"

"You look nice," Rebecca said, catching him off guard.

"Thanks."

Laura exited the house and approached them.

"Give it a spin," Jack urged. Rebecca stood all of her weight on one pedal and put the wheels in motion. Soon she was speeding down the sidewalk.

Laura got a look at Jack in his suit.

"A little loose," she said. Jack looked himself over.

"I'm half the man I used to be." Laura gave a melancholy smile, not allowing the reality of the statement to dampen their spirits. She lifted her hand to block the sun, watching Rebecca go up and down the street, jumping curbs and dodging parked cars.

"They said it was supposed to rain today," Laura said.

"I heard."

They stared at one another. Jack couldn't help but notice that a layer of anxiety and worry seemed to have been peeled away from Laura too, revealing a fresher, healthier person underneath.

"I was watching the news," Laura said, "they won't leave that poor father alone." Jack nodded bitterly.

"Tragedy is entertainment when it's someone else's."

"You did all you could, Jack." Jack nodded, poking his tongue into his lower lip, making it protrude.

Laura saw Rebecca speeding in their direction, her face flush and excited. "You didn't have to do that," Laura said. Jack shrugged.

Rebecca sped by in a blur. "Hi, mom!" Laura looked at Jack and raised her eyebrows victoriously. *Mom.*

"How is she?"

"Better. We had a little…breakthrough. Slept all night. First time that's happened in I don't know when."

"I'll keep my fingers crossed."

Laura looked him over, his tie didn't match his suit at all. But she didn't have the heart to tell him. "Where you off to?"

"I've decided to give peace a chance."

"Good for you." Laura smiled as Jack adjusted his collar and fiddled with a button on his shirt.

"Go with me," Jack said finally.

"Why?"

"This way, if I decide to leave, it'll give me an excuse, I can say you're-"

"No, Jack. This is something you need to do on your own. Besides, those art professors you showed Rebecca's work to at the university called, they wanna stop by and meet her."

"Might be good for her self esteem."

"Yeah. They said some people will pay a fortune for unique artwork like hers." Laura laughed. "Maybe I'll retire."

Rebecca rode up on the bike, a little too fast. She slammed on the brakes at the last minute, making a screeching sound as the tires skidded to a halt just in front of them.

"Whoa! Take it easy," Laura said, holding up both hands.

"I love it!"

Jack turned to Laura again. "Sure you won't change your mind?"

"Just make sure you don't."

Jack winked at Rebecca, then turned to leave.

"Well, take care," Jack said. He got a few feet away when Laura called out to him.

"Jack?" He turned around. "Don't be a stranger."

"No chance." He continued slowly back to his car. Rebecca rode her bike up next to him.

"Jack?"

Laura watched as Jack leaned down at Rebecca's behest. She whispered something into Jack's ear. Jack listened, looking back at Laura. He smiled at Rebecca's comment, *ridiculous,* then climbed into his car.

As Jack drove away, he watched them shrink in his rearview mirror. He saw Laura embrace Rebecca, placing a kiss on her forehead. Jack's heart swelled at the sight, pleased he'd decided to stop along the way, even if she did turn him down.

CHAPTER 60

Harrington still stood where Jack left him. He took a bite of an apple, watching divers surface and descend over and over.

He checked his watch.

At that same moment, Jack was sitting in his car, parked down the block from his brother's soon to be former home. Twice he reached for the door handle and stopped. A drop of rain splashed on his windshield, followed by another and another.

"Come on."

He took a deep cleansing breath and climbed out of the car, taking three brave steps towards the house before realizing his arms were empty.

He popped the trunk, grabbed the nicely wrapped gift, and closed it.

He headed for the front door, skidding a bit when his foot slid on the mat before the steps. He made it safely to the top and hesitated, listening. Behind the door was nervous chatter, one person was shouting. It didn't sound like the noise of laughter and partying. It sounded more like the aftermath of an event - something had happened.

He knocked. Patricia's mother, Edith, answered the door.

"Oh my God," Edith said, her mouth left open.

"Hello, Edith."

"Jack. I can't believe my eyes."

"Am I too late?" Jack hunched his back as the rain started to get heavy.

Edith's expression grew serious. "I'm afraid so."

Jack frowned, aware he might not be welcome after all this time. "I see…"

Edith quickly put her hand on his arm. "No, Robert took Trish to the hospital."

"Hospital?"

"Her water broke. Guess the baby got tired of waiting. Must be all this excitement."

"Is that Jack?" a deep male voice said from inside. It might have been Patricia's father, Jack couldn't quite tell.

"He was hoping you'd come, he'll be sorry he missed you."

"Which hospital did they go to?" Jack asked, walking backwards.

"St. Charles."

Jack turned and headed back to his car. He tossed the gift on the passenger seat and sped away.

He had a pretty good idea which was the shortest way to the hospital, but the rain had slowed traffic to a crawl. He shifted in his seat; anxious, frustrated.

"Shit!" He slammed his fist on the steering wheel and reached into his inside pocket to pull out a piece of paper with a number written on it. He opened his cell phone and dialed, exchanging glances with the stop and go traffic, trying not to crash into the car in front of him.

Robert stood beside Patricia's hospital bed, patting her forehead with a damp cloth. The hospital was teaming with people. Robert frantically searched the faces of doctors and nurses, coming and going, hopeful that one of them would finally be Martha, their obstetrician.

Patricia winced in pain. "Where is she?" Robert squeezed her hand.

"She'll be here, any second now. Just stay calm. Breathe." Robert stepped forward into the stream of traffic and grabbed the arm of one of the passing nurses.

He recognized her, she helped admit them when they arrived. "Is our doctor here yet?"

"She called, she's on her way." Robert nodded. He dragged his hand across his face, squeezing his mouth, exhaling hard and loud.

His cell phone rang. "Hello?"

Before Robert could hear who was on the line, a threatening look from a passing nurse made him pull the phone away from his ear.

"You can't use cell phones in here," she said.

"Robert? Robert?" Jack yelled Robert's name into the phone, but he never heard it. Robert gave the nurse a *whatever* nod and turned off his phone.

Jack heard the line go dead. "Robert? Robert? Shit."

The traffic snarled, a total log jam. *Fuck it.* He switched on his spinning blue police light and pulled out onto the shoulder. His tires kicked up mud and rocks as he sped past two jammed lanes of cars, taking the exit ramp.

"Where the hell..." He didn't know if he should turn right or left, so he took a chance, turning right and tearing down a side street.

He looked at his watch, Bishop would be going in front of the judge right about now.

CHAPTER 61

Down at the courthouse, spectators were packed in thick, waiting for the entrance of the accused killer. The main hallway, an expansive area with 30 foot ceilings and handcrafted marble pillars, was filled to capacity with onlookers.

One of them was Carl Rosa, who clenched every muscle in his small frame when he spotted officers leading Bishop in. Carl stood up, regretting his decision not to bring a gun once he realized they were going to walk the bastard right past him.

Bishop kept his face hidden as they approached, denying Carl the opportunity to stare his daughter's murderer in the eyes. Bishop seemed limp, almost as if the guards were dragging him. Suddenly, Bishop looked up — right at Carl. Carl caught a glimpse of the killer's surprisingly meek and timid face, so thin and ugly. He shuddered at the thought that this hideous psychopath was the last thing his beloved daughter saw. It took every ounce of strength to restrain himself from leaping through the entourage of officers and squeezing Bishop's neck until he was dead. The moment Bishop passed and disappeared through the courtroom doors, he regretted it. Any punishment would have been worth the retribution.

* * *

Laura was at home on the couch, watching the arraignment on TV. A reporter was at the scene. She grabbed the remote to raise the volume.

"Edward Bishop has confessed to killing at least four women, including the rape and murder of Angelina Rosa, whose remains have still not been recovered, and most recently, the abduction and murder of Teresa Mason, who managed to give police a positive ID of her attacker before she died. Bishop's arraignment is scheduled for 1:30 - Oh, wait, I think they're bringing him in now-" The reporter spun around as the camera tracked Bishop's entrance. It followed as they marched him in front of the judge, the entire affair now deteriorating into a circus, flashes going off on all sides.

Laura poked her head up and caught a glimpse of Rebecca riding her bike past the house. She wasn't thrilled about letting her ride around in the rain, but her daughter seemed so happy, she didn't want to spoil it. *Long may it last.* She turned her attention back to the TV when the doorbell rang. Laura shot up expectantly.

She peeked through the front curtain and saw a man holding a briefcase, getting soaking wet. She opened the door as fast as she could.

"Hi!" Laura said with a smile, pushing out the screen door politely.

"Hello. Ms. Lowell? Michael Ketcher, from the University? We spoke on the phone…about Rebecca?"

"Yes, of course, won't you come in?"

"Thanks." Michael stomped the mud and rain off his boots and stepped inside.

"Can I take your coat?"

"Thanks." He turned as she helped him off with it. "My colleague, Helen, apologizes for not being able to make it, but she'd like to stop by tomorrow if that's okay with you?"

"Yeah, sure."

Michael found a painting of Rebecca's leaning up against the wall, several more stacked behind it.

"May I?"

"Yes, I put them out for you to take a look at. There's more inside on the table."

Michael flipped through them, his eyes danced with excitement. He paused to admire a portrait of a woman holding a baby. "Oh jeez, remarkable, just incredible. Is she here?"

"She's out riding. A friend bought her a new bike. She should have come in by now." Laura turned to look out the front door impatiently.

Michael caught a glimpse of Rebecca in a school photo, hanging in a frame on the wall.

"Well, I can't wait to meet her. I've been a teacher in the arts for over 20 years, I've never seen talent like hers at such a young age. How old is she now?"

"She just turned nine."

"Unbelievable. I'll be honest, I'm a little skeptical."

"Some of her other work is in here. Would you like to have a look while we wait?"

"Sure." Laura guided him into the living room. She'd laid out more of Rebecca's artwork across a fine red linen tablecloth on the dining room table.

"Tell me again about the kind of money people will pay for artwork like hers?"

Michael emptied his lungs with passion. "Oh jeez...sky's the limit."

CHAPTER 62

The rain continued to pour, Jack swerved to avoid an oncoming car that had drifted into his lane. His right tire dipped into a deep puddle, splashing a wave of water a good 10 feet in the air. He fought the wheel, turning into the skid to regain control.

"Come on!"

The road he was expecting wasn't there, he must have made a wrong turn. It didn't matter too much, all the roads in this area terminated along the same main stretch a few miles up. He'd just have to double back. But any time he might have saved going this way was now lost.

Jack's phone rang, he fumbled along the seat for it, refusing to take his eyes off the road again, even for a second. It was Harrington.

"Yeah?"

"Jack, we found something. They're bringing it up now."

Jack swallowed, his emotions conflicting between closure and bitter failure.

"Where are you?" Harrington asked. Jack strained to see the name of a street sign through the rain.

"Lost..." Jack hung up and took the turn, hoping he could double back quicker than he thought. His car swiveled on the slippery surface, he slowed down a bit to correct it. He passed a few rural homes, small two and three bedroom colonials, each separated by an acre of property. One house had several junked cars parked on the lawn. He made his way towards the main road again; another 2 miles, he figured.

A sign pointing to highway 406 confirmed it and he accelerated. He looked out over an expansive patch of grassy field. It was brown from the onset of winter, large patches of earth where flood water was collecting in thick pools from all the heavy rain. Adjacent to the field was a steep hill where power lines stretched to infinity. Something caught his attention along the top.

High up at the apex of the hill was a large, rusted water tower. Jack squinted to read something on its side, a worn slogan:

Find Jesus.

Jack slowed to a stop. He rolled down the window to get a better look, rain splashing off the door into his face. He put the car in reverse and turned down an adjacent road. He wanted to get closer.

The road was narrow, uneven, the ups and downs of the terrain were a little much on the shocks of his old car. He felt each bump in his spine, ignoring the pain.

He passed a few more houses, one was in great disrepair, its windows and doors boarded up while the walls themselves crumbled down. On his left, he passed a small church whose facade had seen better days. Scattered shingles from the roof littered the grass from a recent storm.

He spotted something in the distance, a small long abandoned fruit stand.

JACK SLAMMED ON THE BRAKES.

He pulled over and stepped out of the car. The sign on the fruit stand read:

The Fruits of Our Labors.

Jack stood stunned. He read it, then re-read it, wiping his rain-soaked face to make sure his eyes weren't playing tricks on him.

He took a step to his right and could see the water tower - its slogan, *Find Jesus* — clearly visible behind it.

Jack turned in place. Behind him was a small white house, a

light on inside.

He looked back at the church down the road. Then at the fruit stand. Then the water tower.

"*There are no coincidences,*" Leonard's voice repeated in his head.

Jack turned back towards the tiny house and reached inside his jacket for his gun. His hand was shaking uncontrollably. Maybe it was from the freezing rain. Maybe.

As Jack slowly approached the house, he noticed a basement window facing the road with protective metal bars on it, the kind normally used in the inner city. He stepped quietly across the grass and up the two broken steps to the front door.

He knocked. No answer. He knocked again and the door swayed open loosely. Jack looked over his shoulder, his car parked in the middle of the street. He turned and took a cautious step inside the house.

He found himself in a small kitchen. There were dirty dishes piled ten high, a month's worth, empty glasses filled with liquids, flies swarming loudly.

"Hello?" Jack called out. He could hear a TV, someone was watching a game show in the living room.

"Lansing Police Department. Is anyone home?"

He passed through an open doorway into the living room, his gun leading the way. There was a TV on, but no one was watching it. The floor was littered with dirty food trays, dozens of upended pill bottles, and crumpled tissues. A dust covered wheelchair parked in the corner. The rancid smell was nauseating.

A toilet flushed - Jack spun in the direction of the noise. A bathroom door opened and an elderly woman, holding her robe together with both hands, stepped slowly into view. She reached for her walker. Jack holstered his gun.

She looked terribly malnourished and disheveled. Her skin hung from her bones, covered with liver spots and small cuts and welts. Her tattered robe was full of stains. Her face looked like it hadn't touched water in months. She made her way back to her La-Z-Boy.

"Ma'am?" Jack finally said, but she didn't even turn to acknowledge him. She sat down and resumed her program as if no one else was in the room.

Jack took a step closer.

"Turn up the heat, will you?" the old woman said finally, her voice hoarse and scratchy, like the witch from the Grimm's fairy tale. "It's cold in here. Aren't you cold?"

She spoke to Jack as if she'd known him all her life. He stood there, confounded.

"I'm sorry ma'am. The door was open. My name's Jack Ridge. I'm a police detective."

"So cold in here," she said, pulling her robe tighter, "is it cold?" She kept her eyes glued to the TV set.

"Ma'am, is there anyone else here?" Jack wasn't expecting a coherent answer.

"Where's that damn remote?" She fished around the seat of her chair unsuccessfully. "Damn it. What time is it? I'll miss it."

"Do you mind if I look around?" The woman finally turned to Jack. Her ghostly, lifeless eyes looked right through him.

"Hand me that water will you dear?" Jack spotted a glass of water on a nearby table. He reached out and handed it to her.

"Ma'am?" Jack hoped she might pop into lucidity, even just for a moment. He had questions.

The woman took a shallow sip of her water and turned back to her program. Jack gave up trying. He turned around, stepping cautiously, navigating his way out of the maze of china dishes and glasses strewn across the floor, wondering how the old woman had not tripped and killed herself long ago.

Jack spotted another stack of food trays left beside a door that he guessed led to the basement. He tried the handle — it was old, rusted, and hard to turn. He gave it a strong twist and it popped open. There was a staircase leading down into darkness. He felt for a light switch, but it had been removed, covered over with black duct tape.

Jack had none of his normal equipment with him, but he kept a small novelty flashlight on his keychain, a cheap piece of shit from the dollar store. He switched it on, its pinhole light was just enough to navigate the darkness.

Each step was creaky, the flimsy wood straining under his

weight. There was another door at the bottom, which was locked. Jack figured he'd been patient enough. He gave it a strong kick, immediately realizing from the searing pain and the deep muffled thud that it must be made of steel. Jack examined the door frame and noticed it was also reinforced. Someone wanted whatever was behind that door kept a secret. The bars on the basement windows now made sense.

There were two locks, one on the handle and a secondary bolt. Jack thought about shooting off the lock, but a metal door like that — it could ricochet and hit him. He had a small kit in the car, he could pick the lock. He climbed back up the staircase.

He passed through the living room, the woman didn't even look up.

Jack reached his car, leaned in and opened the glove compartment. He tossed the contents and grabbed a few long pieces of metal with different points on each end.

His cell phone rang, it was Harrington again.

"Yeah."

"Hey, Jack, false alarm; it was only animal bones."

Thunder rang out as Harrington's words buzzed in Jack's ear. "Call Central, have a car sent over to 8 Cobbler Road." Jack dropped the phone, not giving Harrington a chance to ask why.

CHAPTER 63

Michael sat at Laura's dining room table, examining several of Rebecca's paintings, spread out. There was one of a man and woman locked in an embrace, done in oil colors.

"How long did you say?" Michael asked.

"A few hours," Laura guessed. "Sometimes I watch her, and it's like she's not painting, more like she's waving a brush and simply revealing the picture beneath, as if it had always been there on the paper."

Michael put his palm to his forehead. "She doodles with the talent and maturity it takes most artists a lifetime to achieve. If one of my students did this, I'd probably keel over."

Laura watched over his shoulder, concealing a proud ear-to-ear grin with her fingertips. Michael stood up and, with meticulous care, lifted the painting and placed it with the others he'd already examined.

The next one caught him by surprise. It was of a girl holding her mother's hand. The girl looked like Rebecca, her face seemed desperately sad. It's why it stayed so permanently in his memory. The expression on the little girl's face had a quality that was surreal, haunting. Michael gripped the painting on the sides, unable to place it down.

"That's one of my favorites," Laura said.
"I feel like I've seen this painting before…"
"What?"
"But it can't be. That's your daughter's face in the portrait. Just seems so familiar. I know I've seen it before."
"That's impossible, I've never shown it to anyone. She only did it a few months ago."
The front screen door opened. Laura exited the room. "Rebecca?"
Michael set the painting in question aside. Underneath was a disturbing, graphic rendering of a girl with long black hair, smeared in pink and red, lying next to a river. Floating above the girl was an angel, just above the trees. The drawing was very simplistic, more typical of a child's scribbles than her other works. As if she purposely drew it poorly, trying to avoid the meticulous detail, avoid facing whatever thoughts in her head prompted her to put it on paper.

CHAPTER 64

Jack held the tiny flashlight in his teeth as he attacked the lock from multiple angles, manipulating the keypins with the metal pick back and forth. He dropped his arms a second, his shoulders giving out from fatigue. He took a few short breaths, which triggered a cough that spit the flashlight from his lips. It went out, leaving him in darkness. He fished around for it on the floor, hitting it with the tip of his finger, pushing it under the door.

"Shit…"

He reached up to have one more go at the lock. He inserted the two pieces of metal. One piece broke off, getting jammed.

"Fuck!"

Jack stood up and pulled out his gun. He shielded his face, and fired. The lock blasted open with one shot, splintering the frame into pieces. Jack kicked open what was left and entered, wafting away the smoke from the barrel. He reached down and found his small keychain flashlight that had slid under the door. He clicked it on and aimed it around.

He had to cover his nose to reduce the putrid odor. It wasn't decaying flesh, he knew that awfulness. This was more like feces, filth, mold, a ghastly combination of foulness that literally choked him.

Transience

There were three rooms. It looked like the basement had been modified into an apartment at one time; crude, unmeasured sheetrock, exposed wires hanging down through torn ceiling tiles, old brown paneling peeling off the glue from moisture and mildew. There were cardboard boxes lining the floor. Jack didn't bother to check their contents.

He moved into one room, it was a makeshift studio. He felt around the walls, found a switch, flipped it. A dim red bulb flickered and lit. Not bright, but enough to look around.

There were several cameras on tripods, a few lights on stands. Computers were stacked on top of one another. There was a painting on an easel of a young girl.

Jack turned to a shelf filled with several boxes, each stuffed to overflowing with photographs of young girls in various states of undress. Jack grabbed a stack and flipped through. Beneath the dozens of posing innocents was a batch of much more vile images, dozens of photographs of young girls tied up and gagged. He didn't recognize any of them until he came across a few of Lisa Delgado, they were the same pictures he'd held in Sheriff Miller's office.

He tossed them back in the box and sifted through a few more. One of a half naked girl stood out. Something familiar about her. He examined it closely, holding it under the light.

It was Angelina! Her face was bruised and battered, barely recognizable. He noticed a few scattered business cards on the dusty table. He turned one over, a card for a modeling representative. It had a professional sheen, *a clever ruse. Was this the job Angelina was heading to? Deceived by vanity and false promise?* Jack's mind raced.

CHAPTER 65

Laura found Rebecca in the kitchen, she was on her tippy toes reaching into the freezer, her hair and clothes soaking wet from the rain.

"What are you doing?" Laura asked.

"Gettin' some ice cream."

"I thought I told you just a few minutes? Where were you?"

"Just outside riding." Rebecca pulled a tub of chocolate chip out and dropped it on the counter next to a waiting bowl and spoon. Laura touched Rebecca's still dripping hair.

"You're soaked."

Rebecca scooped some ice cream into the bowl. "Whose car is that outside?"

"Someone I'd like you to meet."

"Now?" Rebecca said, her mouth full of chocolate. Laura took Rebecca by the arm, her hands cradling the bowl of ice cream. She walked Rebecca into the dining room, where Michael was still hunched over the table, preoccupied with Rebecca's disturbing picture.

"Rebecca, I'd like you to meet Michael Ketcher, he's an art professor."

Michael turned to Rebecca. "Hey darlin', whatcha got there,

ice cream?"

Rebecca lost all sensation in her body. The bowl slipped through her fingers, shattering on the hardwood floor, sending ceramic pieces and chocolate in every direction.

Her face contorted as she let out an ear-splitting scream. Laura watched with utter confusion as Rebecca backed away, shivering and shrieking in terror.

But what was worse-

The look of surprised fear on Michael's face. A strange, guilty desperation, as if he had something to hide. And suddenly it all somehow came together for Laura, as it must have instantly for Rebecca. And all three knew that something terrible was about to happen. Laura blinked first, grabbing Rebecca's hand and sprinting for the front door, but Michael gave chase and struck her down to the floor like a bolt of lightning.

CHAPTER 66

A rustling noise spun Jack around. He took a step towards the sound, holding his breath, silent. He aimed his gun at the dark corners of the room, his heart racing.

He navigated his way through the darkness into an adjacent room, gun barrel leading the way. He stepped around stacks of boxes piled five high, nearly taller than him. There was a hanging chain attached to a lightbulb in the center of the room. He cautiously tugged it, turning it on. A wall of slat board shelving held all types of old camera equipment. A workbench was buried beneath dirty plates, used cups, cruddy silverware, and meals half finished. And more boxes, everywhere.

Jack flipped open the top of one, dispersing years of dust into the air. Inside were expensive looking art supplies and paints. Jack turned and spotted several pictures on the wall; the same man in each, posing with various people. He stepped closer, focusing. The man in the pictures was Michael Ketcher. *Son of a bitch — she did know him!*

Had he and Leonard misconstrued what Rebecca was saying when she blurted out *"catch her"*? Had she named her killer after all? One picture showed Michael smiling, standing next to several Black and Latino youths in front of the Community Center.

Behind them a banner read:
Pursue Your Dreams.
Another sign read:
Sponsored by Monroe College for the Arts.

He moved to the last room, there was daylight coming through a window. He looked out and spotted the patrol car he'd ordered pulling up.

He could see the fruit stand from here. "The fruits of our labors," he whispered. He could also see the water tower far in the distance on the hill, the words *Find Jesus* clearly legible.

"Find Jesus..."

Then a strange rattling noise spun him around again. *Mice? Rats?*

The light from outside reflected off a large metal cage, the kind very big dogs are kept in. Jack inched closer, there was something *moving* inside. He could hear whatever it was...*breathing.* Jack shined his tiny flashlight.

It was a young girl! Naked, hunched over, the cage not much bigger than her body. Her hair was black, her skin bruised, bloody. Underneath the elevated cage was a bucket for human waste.

"My name's Detective Jack Ridge, can you speak?" The girl turned her bruised and battered face towards him. It was the face he'd been agonizing over for months. It was Angelina. She was alive!

"Christ." Jack searched for a way to pry her cage open, something to smash the lock. He could hear the officer walking across the ceiling upstairs.

"Detective Ridge?" the officer called out.

"Down here! Call an ambulance!"

CHAPTER 67

The top of Laura's head had struck the sharp corner of the kitchen counter before smashing onto the linoleum floor. She was out cold, a small puddle of blood pooled under her hair.

Rebecca collapsed beside her mother. "Mommy! Wake up!" Rebecca shook Laura, trying to rouse her. Michael kicked Rebecca onto her backside. He reached for her, but she pushed off with her legs, sliding across the floor until her back was up against the wall. Michael stepped forward, bent over, and callously slapped her hard across the face.

Rebecca's cheek stung, the shock of the blow left a loud ringing in her ears, making her dizzy. She'd never been struck by an adult before. Her entire life, her mother had never once laid a hand on her. Laura had made a vow never to strike her children during a particularly vicious beating doled out by her father when she was 15. One night he'd come home drunk after losing big at a poker game. She was in view and he needed to vent. Laura lost a tooth in the attack, and kept it as a reminder. She would never hurt her own child. Ever.

Rebecca clutched the side of her face, but fear overshadowed the pain. The man from her nightmares was standing over her, his breath real, as was the back of his hand.

Michael kicked open the side door and went outside. Rebecca felt a huge wave of relief — the evil was gone. But in the time it took her to slowly roll onto her side and wipe her eyes, he was back. Kicking the screen door open again, nearly taking it off its hinges, he stomped into the kitchen carrying a duffel bag.

"Do you love your mother?" he asked. Rebecca squirmed. He grabbed her by the hair viciously. "Sweet girl, why do you look so confused? You seemed so certain just a few moments ago."

Rebecca blinked, she felt her insides knotting up in fear. "Okay, I'll ask again, do you love your mother?" Rebecca shook. He tugged at her hair like reigns on a horse, but spoke calmly. "Answer me."

"Yes."

"Of course you do. Now, tell me, and don't lie, because if you do you won't like the bad things I do to Mommy. Understand?"

She nodded hard and fast.

"Good." He opened his fist, releasing his grip on her hair. It fell back onto her head and spread across her face. He gently brushed it from her eyes and lifted her chin. Tiny tears rolled down onto his fingertips.

"Tell me, who else lives here?" Rebecca's eyes darted back and forth.

"Just us."

"Who's us?"

"My mother and me."

Michael leaned in close to her face. "What did I tell you about lying to me?" The calmness in his voice stood her hair on end with terror. "We're both artists. We both pay very close attention to detail, don't we? When I arrived, I noticed a photo — of you, Mommy, and I'm guessing... Daddy? Where is Daddy?"

"I...I don't know," Rebecca cried, closing her eyes, awaiting the worst.

"You don't know?"

"He left, moved away. I don't know where he went. We don't know, I swear."

Michael released her chin, letting her head droop. Her body shivered like she was naked in snow. He sat back and stared at her with pity.

"Jeez, I think that's the saddest thing I've ever heard. I believe you, darling." Rebecca exhaled, she had been holding her breath the entire conversation. "Now, I'm going to make sure Mommy doesn't do anything stupid."

He reached for her again. She turned her face inward, tucking it into her shoulder like a bird cleaning its feathers. "The only danger would be if you tried to run while I'm making sure Mommy is secure. Do I have your word? Because it sounds like Daddy was a real jerk — he'd have to be to leave two beautiful ladies like you behind. And I don't want to have to do anything that would leave you all alone to fend for yourself in this cruel world."

He waited. Rebecca didn't look, but she nodded into her shoulder, whimpering.

"Good girl."

CHAPTER 68

Several EMT's wheeled Angelina on a stretcher to the back of a waiting ambulance. The elderly woman stood in the doorway on her walker, looking confused as all hell. An officer spoke with her, making about as much progress as Jack had earlier. The EMT's carefully collapsed Angelina's stretcher and guided it in. One man sat beside her, holding up an IV.

Jack was on his cell phone, listening to the dial tone for the fifth time. "Shit. Pick up Laura..." Jack hung up and looked into the back of the ambulance.

"Is she going to be alright?"

"She's dehydrated, her pulse is weak but her vitals are stable. She's gonna be fine, we'll take care of her."

Jack saluted the man and rushed to his car, still running. He threw it into gear and sped off, racing back to the main road, taking the turns way too fast.

He slalomed around other cars as if they were standing still. His car drifted up onto the shoulder doing 90mph, his tires churning mud and rocks into the air.

Maybe Laura took Rebecca out somewhere. Maybe the meeting was cancelled. An overwhelming feeling of dread washed over him.

His cell phone rang. *Please, please...*

"Laura?"

"Jack, it's Jennifer. I just got off the phone with Northville Psychiatric Hospital. They're claiming Bishop was a patient there from June to October of 2009."

"Yes, I know-"

"Well, according to the report you brought back from Ann Arbor, Lisa Delgado was murdered in August 2009. So there's no way Bishop could have committed that crime."

"I know he couldn't."

"How?"

"Because I found her."

"Who?"

"Angelina. She's alive."

"Oh my God. How did you-"

"No time to explain- tell Harrington to call off the search."

Jack checked oncoming traffic, accelerated around a large truck in his way, then swerved back into the lane.

"I don't get it, why would Bishop lie?"

"Linking himself to a pattern of homicides makes it easier for him to plead insanity."

"Where are you?"

"I know who he is, his name is Michael Ketcher, he's a professor at Monroe College for the Arts. Carmen was his student! That's why he was so careful to bury the body. It was too close to home."

"Jesus."

"Send whoever's available to 31 Cedar Road. I'm on my way there now."

"Okay, but-"

"Just get everyone there as fast as you can. And call Carl, he's at the arraignment. Tell him the good news; they're bringing her in right now. Tell him... she's gonna be okay."

"Be careful, Jack. Wait for backup."

Jack hung up and pushed the accelerator to the floor. He dialed Laura's number again.

"Please, Laura, pick up..."

CHAPTER 69

Michael reached across the countertop and grabbed the ringing phone, ripping the cord from the wall. He smashed the receiver on the ground and kicked it across the floor.

It had taken him less than a minute to bind and gag Laura where she lay. He used the same framing wire he'd taken from the art classroom. It hurt, and it didn't give. Laura's eyes remained closed, her breathing was short and slow.

Rebecca hadn't moved the entire time, she sat wedged in the corner, her hands over her ears. She hoped this was just another nightmare, that any minute she'd wake up in her bedroom. The dream started off wonderful, especially the bike. But now she wanted it to end, this was the worst one ever.

He stared down at Laura, satisfied with the job he'd done. She rolled onto her back, her eyes flickered.

Laura moaned through her gag, then suddenly — as if the blow to the head had merely hit the pause button — she came to with a jolt, picking up right where she'd left off. Her head lurched forward and snapped back. She quickly realized she was immobile; she screamed through her gag with an awful, muffled cry that vibrated the walls. Rebecca covered her face and wept.

Laura saw Rebecca coiled up in the corner and her eyes went

wide. She lost all sense of self and started rolling back and forth, squealing, desperate. She pulled with all her strength, but Michael had wrapped her bindings too tight to even wriggle. She could feel blood running down her hair and into her ear. She fought, like a weightlifter who had reached fatigue, trying to summon that last ounce of strength for one more rep. She lurched and spasmed several times, much to Michael's amusement.

"Go ahead, I could teach a class on that. You're not going anywhere."

Laura stopped, exhausted. She struggled to get air through her clogged nose, her nostrils puffed in and out like gills on a fish. Blood started to seep into her eyes, it stung.

Michael heard a voice coming from the den. He entered the room, the TV was still on, a reporter at Bishop's arraignment was speaking:

"With the apprehension of Edward Bishop, the public can finally exhale, knowing a killer who has had this community on edge is no longer roaming the streets."

Michael watched with a smug expression.

CHAPTER 70

Carl sat at the back of the courtroom as Bishop stood before the judge. The room was wall to wall with onlookers, many of them recognized Carl from interviews he'd done on TV. And as the charges were read aloud to the judge, everyone turned to gawk at Carl's reaction.

"Of the rape and murder of Teresa Mason, how do you plead?"

Bishop's lawyer held up his hand to keep his client from answering, but there wasn't much chance Bishop would break his silence. His lawyer's theatrics were all for the cameras, he'd hit the 15 minute celebrity jackpot and would be checking his reflection for hairs out of place for the next two years.

"My client pleads not guilty by reason of insanity."

"And of the charge of rape and murder of Angelina Rosa, how do you plead?"

"My client pleads not guilty by reason of insanity, your honor."

The judge continued to read down the laundry list of charges against Bishop. Carl was a burning cauldron of seething rage, his lips started to quiver as raw hate boiled to the surface.

But outside, a situation was brewing. There was a murmur building, growing stronger and louder by the second. As if perhaps someone important had arrived, a celebrity maybe?

Curiosity built to a fever pitch, until everyone was standing to get a better look at what was going on.

It got so out of control that the judge had to bang his gavel. "Bailiff? What's going on out there?"

One of the large courtroom doors slowly opened, reporters and bystanders nearly fell over each other following an officer, who signaled for someone inside the courtroom to get Carl's attention.

Carl slowly stood, as people pressed him to move forward. Others got out of his way so he could exit the row of seats to follow the officer who had an odd grin on his face. The whole slew of onlookers that had filtered in bristled like they had a secret they were bursting to tell. People flooded in behind Carl with anticipation.

Carl was led into the main hallway as the curious crowded around. Cameras and microphones fought to get close.

"Please, what is going on?" Carl asked, his legs growing unsteady.

"There's a call for you, Mr. Rosa," the officer said, handing him a cell phone. Carl slowly brought it up to his ear.

"Hello?"

"Mr. Rosa, this is Officer Jennifer Brown, I'm calling to inform you that your daughter, Angelina, was found alive. She's being rushed to Liberty Medical Center as we speak."

Carl felt his heart stop and start.

"Is this some kind of joke?"

"No sir, Detective Jack Ridge asked me to call you personally and relay the news. I'm sending a car that will escort you to the hospital."

Carl's head grew heavy, he collapsed to his knees. It was the same reaction he'd had when he'd been told his daughter was dead. This time it was joy, not pain, that overwhelmed him. He shook with rapture and elation.

"Oh my God, Oh thank God..."

The crowd erupted in cheers and applause. The entire courtroom was now in chaos, everyone wanted to get close to Carl to congratulate him, share in his happiness.

Carl clasped his hands in thankful prayer. "Thank you, Jack...

Transience

Bless you."

CHAPTER 71

Jack's car screamed into Laura's front yard. He opened the door and nearly fell out, scrambling towards the house, his adrenaline pumping furiously.

He spotted Ketcher's tan car parked in the street, it matched the description given. Jack drew his gun and checked the chamber, creeping up to a window. He peered inside to the den, the room empty. He stayed low and made his way to the side door.

He crouched with his back against the wall, clutching his gun with both hands prayer-like, panting for breath. The screen door had been knocked from its hinges, just hanging by a thread. He placed his hand on the peeling paint of the old wooden inside door. Pressing gently, it opened with a creak. He entered, gun ready.

He checked behind the door and moved through the living room, past Rebecca's artwork still laid out on the table. He stepped over the broken bowl of melted ice cream and entered the kitchen. It was tossed — broken glass, chairs and table upended. There was blood on the floor, the phone ripped from the wall, smashed into pieces.

His expression grew desperate, intense. He glanced at a picture of Laura and Rebecca up on the refrigerator, afraid his victory would be counterbalanced by failure and misery. Once again, his job had taken precedence over protecting those he loved.

Yes, he loved them. And for a moment he regretted ever taking that file from Leonard, involving Laura and Rebecca in his investigation. He'd led the killer right to their door.

Angelina was saved, thanks to Rebecca. There was zero doubt about that now. But at what price? What sacrifice? Jack felt the oppressive force of evil working its malevolence on his small section of the universe. What horror lied in wait? *Please, not them, please don't save one and sacrifice the other.*

The thoughts caused Jack to stagger, he had to brace himself along the wall. He made a fist and threw a shadow punch at it in slow motion, wanting so much to hit it hard — holding back, grinding his teeth in bitterness. He made a promise to himself, right then and there, that before he shuffled off this confusing mortal coil, he'd spend the remainder of his days making peace with Robert. He would leave the past behind, empty himself of all the anger and pain, like a wounded airplane dumps fuel when it knows it's going down.

He inhaled after a long silence, his lungs wheezed. Then he heard a soft moan, a woman's voice. His entire being perked up. *Laura?* He stepped silently around the corner, the kitchen emptied into a laundry area.

He found Laura on her side, her limbs still bound tightly. Jack knelt down and peeled the blood soaked hair from her eyes, making sure she saw him, his look warning her to stay quiet and remain calm.

Her eyes opened wide upon recognizing him. He made a shush gesture with his finger, waiting until she nodded in understanding. She did, and he removed the gag.

"Where?" Jack whispered.

"Upstairs."

Jack nodded. He felt around the wire bindings that held her wrists together. He found the notch that looped around but couldn't get it to twist loose. He motioned to Laura that he was going to lean her forward. She complied, and he went to work, prying her bindings apart with the adrenaline of three men, nearly cutting through his own fingers in the process.

Laura wriggled and pulled her hands free.

"Can you move?"

Laura said nothing — she shot to her feet, pushing past him, pure maternal instinct. Jack chased her down and gripped her mid torso just as she reached the bottom of the staircase. He held her firmly in place. He looked into her eyes again, focusing her.

"Let me."

"He's going to kill her-"

"I won't let that happen. Is he armed?"

"My kitchen knife." Laura's eyes crossed, the pain in her head making her woozy. Jack touched her cheek.

"Okay, I need you to stay here. Police are on their way right now, just get safe, let me handle this."

Laura again tried to claw her way past him, but he held her back. "Laura, please. Do as I say."

Laura stopped fighting him. Jack held her a second longer. *You're alive!* He wanted to kiss her right there. Never again would he bottle up every emotion. He was going to let it all out from now on, consequences be damned. He was going to live.

Just before he could kiss her, she kissed him, right on the lips, no pretense. It was quick, it was emotional, and it empowered him with courage and strength. He felt invincible. He didn't have to say the words. She knew.

Jack headed up the staircase, gun barrel pointed up in the air. He didn't want to be startled and shoot out of reflex and risk hitting Rebecca.

He reached the top and craned his neck to peer around the corner, checking the upstairs hallway. Empty.

His adrenaline-fueled, nervous mind observed every detail of the hallway. The red thick-threaded carpet, the light fixture in the ceiling, the alignment of the three doors, the window at the end, the rain outside still hammering away relentlessly, the musty aroma of old wood, the pronounced smell of Rebecca's paint supplies — every one of his senses on high alert. He took a few steps before he heard the sweetest sound in the world.

Rebecca's whimpering. *She's alive.*

He maneuvered himself next to Rebecca's door, which was open just a sliver. He was able to peer inside, but couldn't determine their whereabouts. He listened, careful to silence his own breathing. Michael was speaking, but Jack couldn't make out what he was saying. He prepared himself, took a breath, and opened the door.

Michael sat on the bed, Rebecca on his lap, as if reading her a bedtime story. Jack looked closely and spotted the blade just below Rebecca's chin, resting on her pulsing artery. One false move and he could slit her throat faster than Jack could even pull the trigger.

Rebecca seemed dazed, she looked up at Jack as if paralyzed, her face red. He noticed smears of blood on her cheek and around her mouth, which seemed swollen. *He'd struck her!*

Michael's eyes found Jack in the doorway. He grinned. Jack took him in head to toe. He was a good looking man. *Of course he is. How easily he could have lured these young girls to their doom unwittingly.* Only by slicing open his handsome head and examining his brain could you have spotted the defects in workmanship. A perfect front.

"You're right," Michael said, "there he is. How did you know he'd come? You're just full of surprises."

"Let her go," Jack's voice was calm, controlled. Michael responded by tightening the blade under her chin threateningly.

"I don't like guns." Michael pressed the blade even more, drawing a small amount of blood. He pumped his eyebrows, impatiently eyeing Jack's gun. "Now."

"Don't be afraid, Rebecca," Jack said with certainty. He complied and tossed his gun across the floor. Rebecca stared back, immobile, helpless.

Michael leaned around to get a look at Rebecca's face. "We're old friends, Rebecca and I, she told me." Michael stood up as he spoke, keeping Rebecca in front of him. "Isn't that right, Rebecca? Or whoever you think you are..." Michael circled the blade by his ear, implying to Jack that *she must be crazy.* He lodged the blade back under her chin and tightened his grip on her hair.

"Don't do this," Jack pleaded.

"Why not? You already caught the killer." He was holding the sharp edge of the knife very tight, Rebecca had to go up onto her toes to relieve some of the pressure of the blade.

"Jack..." Rebecca said in a sad whisper, as if it was already too late, resigned to her fate. Jack stared into her teary eyes, keeping her focused on him.

"Rebecca, look at me, keep your eyes on me."

Rebecca began to squirm, making it hard for Michael to keep his grip.

"Don't," Michael warned.

"Let her go, Michael."

"She said you'd come. You knew I'd be here today. This was inevitable."

Jack knew Michael's next move was to slit her throat, then shoot him dead. He had to think fast. He spotted Laura in his peripheral vision at the top of the stairs.

"Stay there Laura!" Jack shouted. Jack took a step into the room towards Michael.

"Back!" Michael shouted.

Jack held up his empty hands. "It's over, just let the girl go." Michael's face became an odd rotation of emotions, disturbing and twisted.

"...Carmen, she was my best student. So brilliant. So shy. She never screamed once, the whole time I had her." Michael looked down admiringly at Rebecca. "All she would do is pray. And when I hurt her, she would just pray louder. What a prize."

As Michael got caught up in his own monologue, Jack plotted, studying him for a weakness, waiting for a lapse in defense so he could strike.

"Even as I choked the life out of her body, she just kept looking me right in the eye, almost as if she wanted to... remember my face." Michael's grip on Rebecca started to loosen, distracted by his own story. He started gesturing with the knife, slipping it in and out of place under her chin.

"But the one thing that sticks with me the most, was begging me to let her die a virgin. For God. I'm not religious, but I gotta tell you, when I finally tore that white dress off and penetrated her, it was as if I was hurting God himself." Michael's lips curled into a sinister grin. "That was the only time she screamed…"

Jack waited as Michael got enveloped in his confession, timing his attack. Michael's grip loosened on the knife. "That was my property you stole by the river."

Jack got Rebecca's attention. "Rebecca, remember what we said about bullies?" Rebecca locked-on instantly to Jack's line of thinking.

"Remember option number two?"

Rebecca nodded. Michael caught on to their little back and forth just as Rebecca *elbowed* him in the groin.

As Rebecca tumbled away, Jack leaped at Michael, grabbing his knife hand.

"Run, Rebecca, run!"

Michael, still stunned by Rebecca's sharp blow, easily overpowered Jack, but he'd bought her enough time to get clear.

Rebecca dashed out the door, right into her mother's waiting arms in the hall, pulled to safety.

Jack and Michael traded blows, gasping and spitting through bared teeth as they wrestled for control of the knife. Michael ripped free of Jack's weak grasp and plunged the blade deep into Jack's stomach.

Jack crumpled and fell backwards, knocking over Rebecca's easel, scattering paint jars and brushes all over the floor.

"Jack!" Laura shrieked, watching from the door, Rebecca shielded behind her.

Michael remained standing, gripping his blade victoriously, drenched with Jack's blood.

"Get down!" a voice screamed from behind. Harrington pushed Laura and Rebecca out of the way, clearing his shot.

Michael barely had time to look up to see who it was taking aim at him when the shot rang out. The bullet clipped his shoulder, piercing right through the muscle and embedding in the wall behind him.

Michael flew backwards but remained upright, his eyes wide with shock. Harrington deftly took aim again. Before Michael could even clutch his bleeding shoulder, Harrington fired a second time, hitting Michael in the leg, shattering his knee. He crashed backwards onto the bed in a heap of blood and agony.

"Move, move!" Harrington shouted. Two waiting officers rushed by him to subdue Michael, cuffing his wrists behind him as he flailed and screamed.

Harrington dropped to Jack's side, whose stomach was spilling blood like an overflowing toilet. "We need an ambulance!" Blood oozed from Jack's mouth as he tried to say something. "Hang in there, Jack."

Rebecca broke free of Laura's grasp and knelt at Jack's side.

"Jack!" she cried out. She saw the blood and began to weep openly. She reached out to touch his bloody hand, but was afraid. Jack's blurry eyes swiveled and found her. He grasped loosely for her small hand and held it.

Laura pushed past an officer and joined Rebecca. She saw the blood. "Oh no. Jack…"

Jack coughed, blood spattering onto his chin. He mouthed something a few times, breathless, then finally got enough air in his lungs to get it out.

"Robert… Robert, I'm sorry." Jack's eyes began to glaze over.

CHAPTER 72

At that very same moment, Patricia screamed out in pain. Their obstetrician had finally arrived - two hours late, finding her ready to burst.

Patricia cursed and wailed, regretting not taking the epidural. Robert gripped her sweaty hand, kissing it every time she cried out in agony. He noticed a concerned look on Martha's face. "Is something wrong?" he asked.

"She still hasn't fully dilated," Martha said without looking up from between Patricia's legs. "Just breathe Patricia, breathe." Robert squeezed her hand tightly as she bared down. "That's it. Good. Good."

Back in Rebecca's bedroom, EMT's were attending to Jack, who still gripped Rebecca's hand, holding tight as if it was the only thing anchoring him to this world.

"Everyone back away!" Harrington shouted as the medical team got to work. Laura moved aside as they checked Jack's vitals.

One EMT called out, "Where's that stretcher?"

Jack's body was trembling and cold.

"Don't be afraid," Rebecca said. Jack looked into her eyes. He squeezed her hand, letting her know he wasn't. But it told her more. There was friendship, love, in his squeeze.

"...Jack," Laura cried, unable to contain her emotions. Jack's eyes found her. He held her gaze as long as he could.

The paramedics worked furiously to stem the bleeding.

"We need to prep him to be moved now!" an EMT shouted.

"Just a little more time," Jack whispered breathlessly, no air behind his words. "Robert. Robert..." Jack's eyes closed, the oxygen leaving his brain. His face fell to the side.

"Oh God no!" Laura cried.

"Fight it, Jack!" Harrington shouted.

"Pulse rate?" an EMT called out. Jack began to spasm, his hands and legs shook violently, his nervous system shutting down.

"We're losing him," another replied.

Rebecca lost her grip as Jack's body began to convulse. The sight of it frightened her. Laura reached over to pull her away as the paramedics fought desperately to save him, pumping his chest, performing CPR.

"One, one thousand, two, one thousand. Breathe!"

Rebecca pressed her face into Laura's breast as she watched Jack die, her eyes not crying, just sad.

"Blood pressure's dropping."

"We're losing him!"

"Don't be afraid Jack," Rebecca said.

A single tear slipped from Jack's closed eyelid. He could still hear what was happening around him, but it was growing more and more faint with each passing second. Soon there was only silence. The paramedics continued to battle, but it was too little, too late. There was a synchronicity to birth and death, and it was his time. Nothing was going to bring Jack Ridge back.

Jack found the silence almost pleasurable. Welcoming. The darkness didn't frighten him.

A sweet voice whispered in his ear, "There's a reason..." The velvet sound of her words warmed his soul, erasing any fear. He didn't reflect on anything, not on the dream, not on his life, not on his death, he was perfectly in the moment, not an errant thought in his mind. Just a feeling. A gut feeling, that everything was as it should be.

And then, a tiny circle of white light appeared. It danced back and forth as it grew larger. Jack couldn't tell if it was moving closer towards him, or if he was floating towards it.

It grew bigger, brighter. Jack could feel warmth emanating from it, he wanted to touch it, embrace it. But it remained just out of reach. It reminded him of when he was a boy, he would chase the moon, trying to catch it. He followed, not moving his body, just moving, as if being towed weightless on a string.

Then it was as if a sheet was lifted, and he found himself in a grassy field. He felt a cool breeze, it made a soothing whisper as it caressed the grass. It was just like the dream, only real. He was there.

He turned to his right, before him was the giant oak tree, more beautiful than ever. He watched as the branches swayed in the wind, moving in slow motion. He looked to the sky, which was bluer than he'd ever experienced before.

Soaring high above was the yellow kite. It swirled in the breeze and then plummeted, crashing into the ground. Jack followed the thin white string to its owner, a small boy, about 6 years old, with soft pale features, bright blue eyes, and white blonde hair. The boy started to wind the string up when he turned and saw Jack standing there.

They stared at each other, motionless for a moment. Then the boy smiled at Jack, as if he'd been expecting him, a warm, welcoming expression. Jack smiled back.

The boy approached him with no fear, reaching out and taking Jack by the hand, pulling him with him. Jack followed effortlessly.

The boy led him towards the tree. Jack could see two people sitting beneath it, sharing lunch beside a small pond. The perfect day.

Jack looked closer at the two people. It was Robert and Patricia, slightly older. They called to the boy to join them. The boy turned to Jack and smiled one last time. He darted off into the arms of his parents, they scooped him up lovingly, exchanging hugs and small kisses.

Jack watched, filled with desire and relief. Filled with joy at the happiness in their eyes. He wanted so much to join them. His heart and soul rejoiced, an indescribable feeling of peace. He was so grateful for his life, and for this moment.

Then all at once, everything around him went dark again. All except for the glowing circle of light that had led him there. It emitted a soothing emotion to him, like the embrace of an old friend. It began to drift towards him, this time getting much closer. The ball of energy made a silent outreach into his mind, proposing a question to him in thought only. The language was a feeling, transmitted the way a hug communicated love. Jack internalized the question.

It was asking him if he was ready. Jack did not resist.

The light drifted down, illuminating only him. It was brighter than anything he'd ever seen before, but there was no need to shield his eyes. He stood receptive, open, willing.

The light began to spin, forming a tunnel that drew him inside. It spiraled as it enveloped him, surrounding him with color and warmth. Whatever this experience was, he didn't want it to end. He wanted to remain here, in this moment, forever. Peaceful, safe, loved. But something powerful beckoned. It pushed him through this tunnel of soft warmth. Jack could see an opening, an even brighter light in the distance. A passage to another world. It grew wider, brighter. He felt compelled to obey, to pass through, embrace the source of this love and peace.

He could hear voices, muffled. Distant.

"There we go. One more," a calm voice said. Then a painful scream, followed by the calm voice again, "Push. That's it. One more. Almost there. Push!"

Jack felt a powerful force thrust him through — into the bright light. It was blinding. The luxurious warmth fell away, leaving him cold, wet, and disoriented.

"It's a boy."

Martha wrapped Patricia and Robert's new baby in a white and purple hospital blanket. Patricia, recovering from all the pain and exhaustion, managed a grin as Martha handed her the crying boy. Robert leaned over to get a closer look and kissed Patricia's cheek.

"He's beautiful," Patricia said. They each stared lovingly into their newborn's bright blue eyes.